Ransom

at the

Opera

Ransom
at the
Opera

A Ransom/Charters Mystery

Fred Hunter

St. Martin's Minotaur
New York

www.minotaurbooks.com

Library of Congress Cataloging-in-Publication Data

Hunter, Fred.
    Ransom at the opera : a Ransom/Charters mystery /
Fred Hunter.—1st ed.
        p.   cm.
    ISBN 0-312-26257-4
    1. Ransom, Jeremy (Fictitious character)—Fiction.
2. Charters, Emily (Fictitious character)—Fiction.
3. Women detectives—Illinois—Chicago—Fiction.
4. Police—Illinois—Chicago—Fiction.   5. Chicago
(Ill.)—Fiction.   6. Opera—Fiction.   I. Title.

PS3558.U476 R27 2000
813'.54—dc21   00-040242

First Edition: November 2000

10 9 8 7 6 5 4 3 2 1

For George Harvey and Florence Winters

Acknowledgments

I would like to express my appreciation to Ann Whitney for her invaluable "backstage" assistance; Florence Winters and George Harvey for their tireless help in all matters of the opera; Martin McClendon and Karin Kopischke for their technical assistance; and, of course, Lucy Zahray, the poison lady.

L'amour est enfant de Bohême,
Il n'a jamais, jamais connu de loi
Si tu ne m'aimes pas, je t'aime;
Mais si je t'aime, prends garde à toi!

Ransom

at the

Opera

Prologue

I have a friend who plays the French horn," said Lynn Francis as she breezed into the kitchen, her arms wrapped around two large bags of groceries.

"What a startling announcement," Emily Charters replied. She was the elderly woman for whom Lynn cleaned house twice a week.

The young woman stopped short. "Emily, what are you doing?"

"The breakfast dishes."

Lynn placed the bags on the table. "I can see that. I meant *why* are you doing them?"

Emily glanced at her with a twinkle in her eye. "Because they were dirty."

Lynn laughed despite herself. "We've had this conversation before. You know you don't have to do anything on the days I'm here to clean. That's what I'm getting paid for."

"Yes, I know," Emily replied with a sigh. "And I do appreciate it. And I appreciate Jeremy having hired you. But I think it's important to keep oneself occupied. I feel like I've been sitting around the house and growing older." She dried her hands on the blue striped towel that was kept looped through the handle of the top drawer to the left of the sink. Although Emily liked to keep herself busy, she was fond enough of the young woman to allow her to do the work.

"I have the perfect remedy for that, which brings me back to my friend with the French horn."

"Yes?"

As Lynn explained, she filled the kettle with water and put it on the front burner of the stove. "Her name is Roberta Jackson, and she's fairly well known among the musicians in the city. She's the first one called whenever an orchestra is being put together—you know, when a touring company is coming to town, or when one of the local theaters decides to do a musical."

"She must be very good," Emily said as she took a seat at the table.

"She is. Good enough that she's been hired to play at the Sheridan Center."

Emily's eyebrows inched upward. "Really?"

Lynn nodded, then reached into her fanny pack and pulled out a small envelope. "Guess what I've got? Two tickets, one for you and one for me, to opening night of *Carmen*."

"I thought that was already sold out!"

"It is. But everybody connected with the center was allowed to buy two tickets to opening night ahead of time, and Roberta let me buy hers. I thought you might like to go. You like the opera, don't you?"

"Very much," the old woman said eagerly, though if the truth be known she was more excited at the prospect of a night on the town than at the actual destination. "Thank you so much for thinking of me. I'm sure it will be most enjoyable!"

Lynn smiled as she started to unpack the groceries. "The opening of this new theater is really big news, Emily. This isn't just going to be a night at the opera, it's going to be an event!"

1

There had been five years of planning and discussion, two years of architects with sample sketches that were scrutinized by a newly selected board of directors, and a full year and a half of bidding wars between a variety of contractors before the ground was broken for the Sheridan Center for the Performing Arts. But as is the case with most construction in Chicago, once the first shovelful of dirt had been limply tossed by the mayor in a ceremony widely covered by the media, the building seemed to erect itself overnight.

The site chosen for the new center was the slightly shabby stretch of Kingsbury Street, approximately half a mile north of the centermost armpit of the Chicago River, where Wacker Drive turns south and the river turns north. With primary funding coming from the wealthy and prestigious Sheridan family, who were endowing the center in memory of Edwin Sheridan, their late, great patriarch, it was not difficult for the already occupied land to be bought and cleared of buildings that would've deterred the march of progress. The faceless warehouses that had once stood on the bank of the river were replaced by a giant stone edifice fronted by a soaring colonnade. A broad staircase, bordered by twin ramps for easy wheelchair accessibility, led to a wide entryway and massive glass doors. The foot of the staircase was flanked by a pair of large stone lions resting on their haunches and brandishing shields carved with the family crest of the Sheridans.

Along the riverside of the building was a tree-lined promenade spotted with cement benches where early theatergoers could enjoy a quiet liaison during warmer weather. And the perennial parking problem was resolved by the addition of a sprawling, multilevel lot at the rear of the building, exclusive to the use of the center's patrons.

Edward Carnegie stopped at the foot of the stairs as he did every morning on his way into his office. He drew a deep, satisfied breath and exhaled with pride. It had been six months since he'd officially assumed his duties as director of the Sheridan Center, before construction on the interior had been completed, but still he could barely believe his good fortune. Of course, he never would have openly admitted that fortune had played any part in his capturing this important position, but he couldn't deny that at the age of thirty-three he might be considered a bit young to be appointed head of a venue that many in the city hoped would gain national recognition. But Carnegie had presented the board a comprehensive plan for the Center's future, and the board was forced to believe that what he lacked in practical experience was more than made up for in energy, enthusiasm, and direction. Carnegie's detractors maintained that it hadn't hurt that he had the full backing of the Sheridan family.

However, even his detractors couldn't deny that Carnegie had delivered on his promise. In a move that stunned the arts community, he announced upon taking office that he'd secured the Santa Marta Opera Company for the Center's opening to perform their *Carmen,* a production that had appalled classical critics, thrilled popular ones, and dazzled audiences on the West Coast, garnering headlines in national trade and arts publications. Even one of the local Chicago papers had done an article on the "upstart opera company." Nobody would dare question Carnegie's abilities after that.

He closed his eyes and inhaled deeply again. The air was

scented with grass, water, and a tinge of dead fish, but there was something clean and real about it. He let his eyes open, adjusted his tie, and mounted the steps.

"This place is a disaster! It's a sty!" Maria Cortez said as she threw her oversized leather shoulder bag onto the counter.

"What's wrong with it?" David Cunningham asked with no inflection. He was the manager of the Santa Marta Opera Company and had dealt with Maria long enough to know the importance of responding to her without any implied partisanship.

"Just look at it!" She gesticulated broadly.

The dressing room was not large but was pleasant and serviceable. The requisite makeup table and light-encircled mirror were offset by deep carpeting, creamy white walls, and a pair of round easy chairs that were more comfortable than they looked. The wall directly opposite the door was covered floor to ceiling with mirrors that added depth to the room, as well as hiding the closets. To their left was a private bathroom, which might not have been very big but made up for it in convenience.

"It's a sty!" Maria repeated.

"Hardly that," David replied affably. "This place is brand new."

"Brand new." Her lips were so full that when she tried to pout they wrinkled like a circular accordion. "I know it's brand new! It smells of carpet and paint! It's revolting!"

"I don't smell anything."

"Of course you don't! You have no nose! You have no eyes, either! You can't see how small this room is! I don't know how I'll be able to dress in here."

"There are no hoop skirts in *Carmen*," David said somewhat wearily. "You'll be able to slip into your dresses without banging into the walls."

Maria threw herself onto the chair at the table. She leaned her right elbow on top of it and rested the side of her face against her hand. "I suppose I'll have to manage, won't I?"

David studied her in the glass. Despite her frequent, childish outbursts, Maria Cortez was almost hypnotically exotic: a perfectly oval face, skin the color of suede, and large, hooded eyes. Her hair was long and dark red, and the haphazard way she kept it pinned up made her look like a high-class slattern. The only thing lacking to complete the picture was a rose in the décolletage of her rust-colored dress.

"Why did you bring us to this place?" Maria said to his reflection.

"You know why. All of the critical acclaim in the world isn't going to make up for what it cost us to mount this thing to begin with. We're played out in California. This offer was a godsend. Bill and I can use the two months you're here to prepare the next production. Look, when we were offered this engagement during our 'hiatus,' I couldn't refuse."

"I was supposed to have a vacation." She ran her slender fingers along her throat. "The instrument needs to be rested."

"The instrument needs to be used or you'll lose it!"

"I need to rest!"

He placed his hands on her shoulders and looked at her in the mirror. "Maria, you have a beautiful voice, but you don't understand the economics of this business."

"Business!" she hissed.

"We've had one hit, which didn't even pay off the original investment. And like most new companies, we are one miss away from disaster. If our next production isn't as big a hit as *Carmen,* there's every chance that the company will be no more."

She narrowed her eyes. "That would be terrible, wouldn't it?"

His hands seemed to rise from her. "I wouldn't set too much store in the press. They can be very forgetful . . . and very unforgiving."

"And insightful. Evidently, they can recognize where the real talent lies."

"You've been lucky so far in the amount of press you've

gotten, and that this has turned out so well for you. You have the Santa Marta Opera Company to thank for that."

She glared at his image in the glass. "I have nobody but myself to thank for my success. All you did was provide the package!"

David was on the verge of injudiciously losing his temper when they were interrupted.

"Did I hear the tender tones of our diva lodging a complaint?"

Riccardo Nuevo appeared in the doorway, leaned against the jamb, and folded his arms across his broad chest. He was clad in a white shirt and white pants, a combination that made his olive skin and black hair look even darker.

"Riccardo!" Maria exclaimed, the right corner of her mouth crooking upward. "I didn't know you were here."

"I didn't have to wonder about you, though," he said. "I could hear you through the wall. I'm right next door."

"You see?" Maria said, turning to David's reflection. "The walls are paper thin!"

Riccardo laughed. "They don't have to be thin to hear you, my darling. Your voice could pierce concrete. What are you complaining about now?"

"Riccardo, you're a bad boy," she said lushly. "You shouldn't take that tone with me. You make it sound as if I'm a small girl who never has her way."

"Not at all. You complain like it's been your way of life for a very long time. Now what's wrong?"

Maria looked away from him and didn't answer.

"Maria just thinks the dressing rooms are a bit small," David explained.

"Small? Really?" Riccardo said with a faint smile. "The dressing rooms are much smaller at the Met."

David braced himself for the coming explosion and looked at Maria. She let her hand drop to the tabletop and her eyes glared upward at Riccardo from beneath half-closed lids.

"Are they really smaller there, Ricky?" she said in a measured sneer, placing special emphasis on the corruptive of his name.

Riccardo's naturally dark complexion was marred by an ugly red flush. He turned to David with elaborate refinement and said, "The dressing rooms are perfectly acceptable to any rational person. You have no need to apologize."

With this he pushed off from the jamb and disappeared down the hallway.

David looked at his own confused reflection. "I wasn't apologizing for anything."

Maria erupted into unrestrained laughter.

The Sheridans lived on Astor Street in a mansion that had been built in the 1930s by the late Edwin Sheridan's father, Jeremiah, a self-made millionaire whose fortune had come from the manufacture of machine parts. Like many of the homes built by the nouveau riche, Sheridan House was designed with more money than taste. It was an oblong, dusty-bricked, three-story cracker box with small, evenly spaced windows that gave it the appearance of a railroad mausoleum.

The interior of the house was a study in musty opulence: heavy furniture and hardwood floors, both thick with layer upon layer of varnish, walls covered with endless coats of paint, and stagnant air. These things all conspired to make the infrequent guests feel as if the house was closing in on them. The small rooms with their rectangular portholes, coupled with the fact that the house had long since been hemmed in by other homes, left the interior in a perpetual dusk, so that even on the brightest days lamps had to be lit.

Steven Sheridan, Edwin's only son, stood in front of the full-length mirror on the door of his wardrobe, his chin raised as he knotted his pin-striped tie. He was about as comfortable in business attire as he was in the family home, both of which had been forced on him by the misfortune of birth. Even his own bedroom felt to him more like a museum than a refuge from the rest of the world.

He tucked the thin end of the tie through the label loop, then smoothed the tie against his chest. He paused to check his general appearance in the mirror.

He didn't consider himself bad looking: His dark hair could've been straighter and he wished that the tone of his skin had been either ashen or olive, rather than falling into the murky area in between. And there was a sadness about his eyes that had settled in at childhood and deepened with age. But he mitigated any minor flaws by carrying himself with a confidence that he didn't necessarily feel. He slipped into his suitcoat, straightened the lapels, and gave a single tug to the hem, then left his room and went down the narrow, curved staircase to the first floor. He found his mother seated at the head of the long mahogany table in the dining room.

"Good morning, Steven," said Margaret Sheridan as she spooned some of the contents of her fruit cup into her mouth.

"Morning, Mother." He pulled out the chair to her right where his breakfast had already been laid out, unfolded the cloth napkin, and placed it in his lap.

"You're a little late this morning," his mother said in a toneless way that implied disapproval.

He sighed inwardly. "The foundation can operate on its own for a little while without crumbling."

Mrs. Sheridan gently ran a hand along the side of her head, careful not to dent her coiffure. Her hair was lacquered to the consistency of cotton candy, and was far too golden for her age. "It's important to set a good example. If you're lax, the employees will believe that the only reason you have your position is that you're family. It's up to you to prove to them that you're not only capable, you're the best man for the job."

"It's father's foundation," Steven replied as he poured himself a cup of coffee. "No matter how well I administer it, everyone will believe that the only reason I'm in charge is because I am his son." Mentally he added, *So why bother?*

She laid down her spoon and looked at him pointedly. "People may believe anything they like. It's up to you to prove them incorrect."

Steven smiled. "Are they, Mother? Do you think I'd have this position in any other foundation?"

His mother continued to stare at him, unblinking. "The money should be administered by a member of the family. I wouldn't trust a stranger with it."

"You could've done it yourself," he said, taking a sip of coffee.

She sighed and absently fiddled with the double row of gold buttons that made her black dress look like a uniform. "And what would you have done? Sat at home and dissipated? It's important that you make your way in the world, like your father did."

"My father inherited the family business."

She smacked her lips. "You're trying my patience. You know what I'm saying. It's important that you work. That you keep yourself busy. That you do something with your life."

"Yes, Mother."

Mrs. Sheridan was about to continue when the phone rang, cutting through the cold tension in the air. Steven rose and dropped his napkin on the table.

"Let Dorothy get it," his mother said. "It's her job."

"I can answer the phone." He picked up the receiver from the phone on the small corner table. He stood with his back to his mother.

"Hello."

"Is that you?" said a familiar voice.

"Uh-huh?"

"Are you alone?"

"No."

"Okay. I just wanted you to know that they're here."

"Good. Thanks."

He replaced the receiver and returned to the table.

"Who was that?" Mrs. Sheridan asked, her frown showing that she disliked being disobeyed even on minor matters.

"Wrong number." He took another sip of coffee.

"The reason for the success of my production of *Carmen*," said Marc Berger, "is that I approached it as a piece of musical theater rather than as an opera."

"Our production," David Cunningham said under his breath.

They were at a table in the center of the room at the Winterset Café, in the heart of River North.

Across from them sat Heidi West, the arts-and-entertainment reporter who had been given the plum job of writing an article about the Sheridan Center's premier production. A combination of stature and girth meant that she could choose her assignments without being challenged. She nursed a tall glass of iced tea that had a slice of lemon firmly embedded on its edge. Her leather-cased tape recorder whirred steadily at the center of the table.

As she asked her questions, Marc Berger, the man who had directed the production, carelessly munched a cobb salad while Cunningham lightly tapped his thumb against the white tablecloth.

"Marc is one of the hottest directors of musicals on the West Coast," Cunningham explained.

West looked at him with raised eyebrows. "Oh. Was it you who decided to approach the opera this way?"

"Well . . . yes. At first. I wanted the staging to be theatrical. Marc took that a bit further than I expected." He tried to sound enthusiastic, but West noted the undertone of embarrassment.

Marc adjusted the black plastic frame of his glasses and speared a mound of crab meat with his fork. "Opera seems really stodgy to the masses, for good reason. It is." The reporter's face hardened slightly as she turned her attention back to him. "But that's only because of the way it's staged. Usually it's really boring.

They throw a bunch of singers up on stage, and they just stand there like a bunch of posts and sing. People can move while they sing, for Christ's sake! They do it all the time in musicals!"

"Of course, the approach we used with this production wouldn't work with every opera," Cunningham said quickly. "I don't want you to think we've completely tossed convention out the window."

"Yes . . . I can't really imagine people bouncing all over the stage during *Aida*," West said with a smile.

"Ah, so you've heard that that will be our next opera."

"Yes, I've read about it. I must say I was a little surprised at the choice. It's very ambitious for a new troupe."

"Exactly why we chose it."

"And it doesn't have nearly as good a role for a mezzo."

Cunningham hesitated. "I'm not sure I understand."

"I would think on the heels of all the publicity Maria Cortez has received, you'd want to feature her again."

"Not right away," he replied slowly. "We're dedicated to featuring a variety of singers that are new to the public."

"So why did you decide to start with *Carmen*?"

Berger smacked his lips around the crab meat. "Because it's just so damned musical!"

"Mm-hmm." She had directed her question to Cunningham. When Berger answered instead, she turned the tape recorder slightly.

"Nobody wants to see opera the way it's been done over and over again, with no theatrical sense and these big, hefty women playing these great beauties. Who would want to see that?" He lifted the edge of a spinach leaf with his fork, peered under it, then let it fall back into place.

West watched him with a frown for a moment, then turned to Cunningham. "I understand that the way you went about forming your company was fairly unconventional as well."

"Yes, it was," he replied, sitting up straighter. "We decided that instead of courting stars, who we wouldn't get anyway, we would scour the operatic world for the best unknown talents in the business. Up-and-coming singers who would flourish in the limelight. It was . . ." he paused self-effacingly, as he had in every one of the dozens of interviews in which he related this story. ". . . maybe not a stroke of genius, but it certainly turned out to be a good move on our part. We got some fresh, exciting new blood, and the singers got a leg up, so to speak."

"How do you mean?"

"Just that our leads are getting an opportunity that . . . perhaps they couldn't have gotten elsewhere, at least at this stage in their careers."

Berger emitted a derisive "humph" as he shovelled some dressing-soaked spinach into his mouth.

West shot him a glance, then said to Cunningham, "The two stars certainly have gotten a lot of press, particularly Maria Cortez."

"She's a very dynamic performer," Cunningham replied colorlessly.

"Where did you end up finding Miss Cortez and Mr. Nuevo?"

"Maria Cortez is from Cuba. She came up here to study at the L.A. Conservatory of Music. She did some work with a light-opera company out there, which is where she first came to the notice of Bill Stauffer—my partner—and myself."

"She's become a major asset, hasn't she?" West asked as she took a sip of her tea.

There was a slight beat before he replied. "Our entire company is, I think, an excellent mix."

"Yes, of course. What about Mr. Nuevo? Where did you find him?"

"He's from Spain. Like many singers, he felt underappreciated in his own country and came to America. When we discovered him, he was doing a small role in the Seattle Opera."

West eyed him for a second, then said, "I see. I've heard that Maria Cortez has been receiving offers from some established opera companies around the country."

He cleared his throat and flushed slightly. "Yes, well, I've heard that too, but . . . I think I should say this off the record." West hesitated for a second before reaching over and shutting off her recorder. "She wouldn't be a star. None of the established companies would give her the roles she can have with us. At least, not yet." He glanced at the tape recorder and she switched it back on. He continued. "So, Maria has no plans to leave our company. And we're awfully glad to have her. She's an amazing performer. Very original."

"And she has a two-year contract with your company."

"That's true," he replied, obviously surprised that she knew this.

"Isn't that kind of arrangement a bit unusual?"

"Perhaps. But I think it hedges everyone's bets."

"In what way?"

David sighed inwardly. He hadn't really meant to go into all this. "Any new venture like this is very risky. If it's a success, then we end up repaying each other. We took a risk just by trying to start the company, and by using unknowns—not that we had a terribly big choice in the matter; we couldn't exactly get Domingo in. If we were successful, then the singers under contract would have two years' worth of work. Not bad. If one of the singers was particularly successful, then they would spend a couple of years paying us back for having given them their chance. Still not bad."

"Ms. Cortez has made quite a name for herself."

"Yes. So we're all happy."

West mulled this over. She was dying to press the point further, because the scuttlebutt was that Cortez was very anxious to leave the company. But West decided to let it go. *After all,* she told herself, *I'm supposed to be writing a puff piece, not an exposé.*

"So, I understand that the Sheridan Center has brought in your entire company."

Cunningham nodded. "Except for the children and the supernumeraries. We're using local talent for the children and the "spear carriers." That's why Marc is in town—to rehearse them. But the rest of the company will be here."

"How did that come about? You've been running this opera for an incredibly long time now. I mean, for an opera."

"That's mostly thanks to the press. Santa Marta is driving distance from Los Angeles, and once the *Times* did a story on us things started happening. We were asked to bring the production to San Diego, then San Francisco. We did two months in each place. We just finished in San Francisco last week. Edward Carnegie read about the production while we were still in Santa Marta and came out to see us. The rest is history."

"Hm. I have to say, it seems to me that both your company and the Sheridan Center are going out of your way to tempt fate."

"I . . . don't understand."

"Historically, isn't it considered bad luck to open your season with *Carmen,* let alone opening a new theater with it?"

"You mean like *The Pajama Game*?" Berger chimed in, wide-eyed.

They both shot him an irritated glance.

"Oh, that," Cunningham said, turning back to West. "The Met has done it without the house falling in, so I think it'll be all right here. *Carmen* has already been very lucky for us."

"Well, why don't you tell me about your production? What makes it so different? Even the critics on the West Coast who disparaged it had to admit that it was exciting."

"I'll leave that one to the director." Cunningham felt relatively safe in doing this because it was the one area in which Berger could usually shine without getting into trouble.

Once Berger had the floor, he went on at length about his innovative staging, the great performances he'd elicited from the principals, and how he'd transformed the stiff, wooden chorus into a spectacle of movement. He remained relatively inoffensive until the end. "I've done everything I can to drag the opera kicking and screaming into the twenty-first century. People who *hate* the opera will love this production."

"And what about people who love the opera?" West asked coolly.

"They're dinosaurs!" Berger replied as he stuffed a forkful of spinach into his mouth.

Heidi West completed the interview, collected her tape recorder, paid the check, and bid the company manager a cordial farewell as they all left the café. The look of distaste she displayed when she said a terse goodbye to the director spoke volumes.

"You've got to stop doing that!" Cunningham exclaimed angrily as he strode up the street.

"What?" Berger said, scrambling to keep up.

"Talking about the opera like that!"

"Like what? I built us up!"

"You built us up by tearing everyone else down, you idiot! I've talked to you about that before!"

"Don't call me an idiot!" Berger shot back petulantly. "And slow down! I'm not your goddamn dog!"

Cunningham complied and measured his pace, though not by much.

"I thought you liked my interpretation of this opera! It's sure as hell been profitable enough for you!"

Cunningham came to an abrupt stop and wheeled around. Berger barely escaped colliding with him. "If it had been all *that* profitable, we wouldn't have needed to accept this engagement! We'd be in California right now doing exactly what we should be doing, preparing our next production. And you know that I *love* what you did with *Carmen*! It's new, it's fresh . . . it's everything you say it is!"

"Then what's the problem?"

Cunningham took a deep breath and sighed. "All that showy staging of yours is no substitute for hundreds of years of tradition! Don't you get that?"

From the puzzled look on the director's face, it was evident he didn't. "What are you talking about?"

Cunningham sighed more heavily. "Our *Carmen* is a *stunt*! A stunt to get people into the theater, not to breathe life into the opera! That's the only way you can launch a new company, by making waves! That's why we brought you in to begin with, as a stunt! And it worked! That's why the Sheridan Center wanted this production for their opening . . ." He found himself at a loss for the right word. He didn't want to say *act*.

"Well, so what?" Berger said after a beat. "So what's wrong with what I said? If you feel that way about it, you should be happy if you think I'm making people mad."

Cunningham made a hissing noise through his teeth, turned on his heel, and marched off. Berger followed. "I don't get it! Why are you so upset?"

He raised an index finger. "First of all, there are traditions to be upheld . . . or at least, respected. *Respected*. A word that you don't even have a nodding acquaintance with!"

"Yeah? So?"

"Secondly, Chicago is the home of one of the best opera companies in the world!"

"So what! My *Carmen* will blow them away!"

Cunningham stopped again and turned to face him. "Not if they don't come to see it, which very well may happen if you refer to our target audience as a bunch of dinosaurs! It was bad enough when you pulled crap like that in California, but if you don't keep your mouth shut, you're going to ruin us here!" He let out another truncated hiss through his clenched teeth. "I never should've brought you out here. I should've had John rehearse the locals."

"My assistant?" Berger's mouth dropped open and his lower jaw jutted to one side. "He's an idiot!"

"He's smart enough to know when to keep his mouth shut!"

Cunningham turned and walked away.

"Why do you insist on embarrassing me?" said Riccardo, stifling the imminent cough he felt due to the thick perfumed air. Maria's hotel room was awash in flowers, for which the management had had to provide additional vases.

"Do I embarrass you, Ricky?"

"Don't call me that. You know I don't like it."

"Sorry . . . *Riccardo*," she replied, emphasizing his name. She took a deep drag from her cigarette, then tapped the dangling ash into the small metal ashtray on the table. Her eyes traveled lazily around the room, which was not up to the standard to which she wanted to become accustomed: The drapes were tan, as was the carpet, the chairs, the lamp shades, and the bedspread. Everything else was white, including the sliding doors that covered the pullman kitchen. It was, thought Maria, a study in mediocrity. It didn't matter to her that the Dover Hotel was considered one of the little-known treasures of Chicago, or that it was clean, serviceable, and relatively upscale. It still wasn't as elegant as she believed befitted a diva. She would've loved to complain about the accommodations, but without David Cunningham there to needle about it, there was no point. And Riccardo wouldn't care.

"So how did I embarrass you this time?"

"In front of David," he said. "In your dressing room."

"I didn't mean to."

"Of course you did. You have no respect for me at all, calling me by that name and treating me as if I were a little boy. And laughing at me." He hesitated, knowing that he shouldn't say what he was thinking. But he couldn't help himself. "I don't know how you can treat me that way when you know how much I love you."

She laughed. "You're a child! You mistake our publicity for the real thing."

"How can you say that?" he said earnestly as he sat down next to her. "I told you the second week of rehearsals that I was in love with you. You gave me every reason to believe that you felt the same way. You acted as if it were true."

"You don't love me!" she spat back. "You lie when you say that! If you loved me you would've backed me up!"

"In what?" His brown eyes were wide with surprise and hurt. "In saying that your dressing room was not adequate?"

"No, you fool!" She tamped out her cigarette angrily. "In not coming here! When I said I didn't want to come here you should've backed me up, but what did you do? Instead, you said, 'Oh, sure, let's do it, of course!' Like Cunningham's little puppy dog!"

He shrugged helplessly. "We're singers. It's what we do. I'm surprised you would even consider passing up the opportunity to expand your audience."

Maria sliced the air with her hand dismissively as she rose from her chair. "I wanted my vacation! I wanted a rest! I wanted to go away!"

"Come now, Maria. I know how much you love being in the limelight. You wouldn't have passed up this engagement . . . unless there was something special about the vacation you had planned."

She stopped in the midst of her pacing, caught by the level of suspicion in his tone. She looked at him coldly and folded her arms beneath her breasts. "I needed to rest my voice before we begin work on *Aida*."

"In which you do not have a starring role," he said.

She chose to ignore him. "Instead I'm forced to overwork my voice as if I'm pushing a plow!"

Riccardo smiled knowingly. "So all of this temper is because you won't be having your little vacation? Or is it because you didn't get your way?"

She crossed behind him and placed her hands on the back of his chair. "I didn't get my way because you didn't back me up. If we both had refused, they wouldn't have had a choice!"

"We're both under contract. David had the right to extend our engagement. It's our own fault that we didn't realize he could extend it to another city."

"Ha!" she said bitterly as she stepped away from him. "If you really loved me you would've defied your contract! This is the third city to which we've moved!"

He rose and faced her. "Defied my contract? Why would I want to do that? What is this all about, Maria?"

"I've told you."

"I don't believe you. I know how badly you want to spread your fame. What's really the matter?"

She put her hands lightly on her hips, and for the first time looked uncertain. After a beat she said, "I don't want to be introduced to a new audience in a peasant company like this!"

Riccardo's complexion turned deep red. "So you thought maybe you'd come to Chicago as a star at the Lyric? You are many, many years away from anything like that happening, no matter how talented you are."

"After the notices I've gotten for this? I wouldn't be too sure."

"You haven't really proven yourself yet. Neither of us has. You know the opera world better than that. And why are you talking about this as if it only affects you? I thought we were planning to remain together. Were you planning to run away from me?"

Again Maria hesitated. She was furious that her plans had been ruined, and even more furious that she had ever been in a position where the best thing she could do for her career was to sign a contract that would allow her little freedom over the next two years. But what was done was done. It was all a loss. And the vacation was gone. But she was here, and Riccardo was here, and she had no intention of throwing away a bird in the hand.

She allowed some of the hardness to melt away from her countenance and produced a coquettish smile. "I was not going to move on without you."

"Do you mean that?"

"Of course I do."

She went to him, wrapped her wrists around his neck, and pulled him forward. Their lips met, and for a few moments nothing seemed to matter.

Riccardo gently pulled back and looked down into her eyes. She smiled up at him.

"Tell me," he said softly, "who were you going away with on that little vacation of yours?"

Her eyes narrowed. For a second she was frozen in place, then suddenly she reared back and slapped him hard across the cheek.

"Get out!" she yelled.

Franco Giannini reluctantly climbed out of bed in answer to a knock at the door.

"Just a minute!" He grabbed the white terry-cloth robe provided by the hotel, slipped it on, and paused in front of the dresser mirror long enough to smooth his hair into place. The equal amounts of black and premature gray gave the thirty-year-old man an air of distinction that, augmented by his confident bearing, made him the perfect choice for the role of Escamillo, the toreador.

"Franco, it's me," the muted voice said through the door, followed by a second knock.

He looked back to the bed and said, "You'd better make yourself scarce."

The request was complied with reluctantly.

Franco went to the door and opened it wide enough to be cordial but not enough to imply an invitation.

"Gabrielle," he said in his pleasing baritone, "You made it."

"Uh-huh," she replied with an anxious smile. She couldn't keep her eyes from doing a quick survey of his frame. "I just got checked in. I asked at the desk what room you were in. I just wanted to stop by and . . . let you know I'd gotten here. Are you all settled in?"

"Oh, yes. I got in a couple of hours ago."

Gabrielle glanced past him at the rumpled bed. "Oh! You were sleeping! I'm sorry!"

He shook his head apologetically. "I was just lying down. I had a long and tiring trip."

"I didn't mean to disturb you."

"It's no problem. I'm glad you let me know you were here."

"Has . . . everyone else arrived?" she said after a beat, searching for a way to prolong the conversation.

He smiled warmly. Gabrielle was painfully transparent, which was oddly endearing. "The principal players have all arrived."

"Franco and Maria? They're here?"

"They're here, all right. Maria has already had her first tantrum, from what I understand."

She clucked her tongue. "I can't believe it! What about this time?"

"I don't know." He actually did know, but he didn't really want to go into it.

"I suppose she'll always find something to bitch about. But you would think . . . I mean she has so much talent, you'd think she could be a little . . ."

"Nicer?" Franco offered.

Gabrielle nodded. "You know how she acts toward me."

"That's just jealousy," he replied with a quick glance over his shoulder. "She knows how good you are. She'll never be happy having another talented woman around."

Gabrielle's pale, round face glowed at this. "You're so sweet."

He smiled back, but said nothing more. There was an embarrassed pause during which Gabrielle tried hard to think of something else to say, but couldn't. Her smile faded. "Well . . . I guess I should let you get back to bed."

"Yes. I don't mean to rush you off, but I really would like to get some rest."

"Okay. Well, I'll see you at the rehearsal, day after tomorrow, if not before. . . ."

"Mm-hmm."

Gabrielle slowly walked away, and Franco closed the door.

"Well, Frank! That was amusing," his companion said, coming into the bathroom doorway.

"It was sad. Poor thing. But I don't do anything to lead her on."

"I know."

"And that's nothing compared to the way she moons over Riccardo."

"I know."

Franco smiled broadly and undid the sash of his robe as he crossed to the bed. "But she's in danger of turning our relationship into a bedroom farce."

2

The auditorium of the Sheridan Center was designed to imitate the city's older, more classical theaters. The predominant colors were deep red and gold. Filigreed cherubs hovered above both sides of the proscenium, smiling down on the stage. The walls were a series of rectangular frames filled with velvet, and central to each was a sconce consisting of very bright, three-tiered electrical candles that were repeated along the front of the two balconies. The carpeting on the aisles was so untrodden that anyone walking from the back of the house to the stage was apt to find the prints of their shoes left behind as clearly as footprints in the sand.

The stage was vast and deep, with high flies and wings that were more spacious than the norm. The plan had been to build the stage so that it could accommodate every conceivable type of theatrical event, from opera to ballet to touring companies of Broadway shows. In fact, the latter would find the Sheridan Center a particularly enticing home since it had been built with an eye toward the demands of modern theater. Shows might still have to be scaled down somewhat in order to appear at the Center, but not nearly so much as they would for the old war-horse theaters in the Loop.

Currently the auditorium was alive with activity. Crews were noisily hammering together pieces of the first-act set, an intricate and evocative representation of a square in a Spanish town, incorporating the cigarette factory in which Carmen works and the guard room for the dragoons, as well as a pair of archways, the tops of which were used as bridges. A staircase curved down to stage left from the far end of one of the arches.

Over the sounds of the crew was a chorus of not-very-angelic voices accompanied by the rehearsal pianist who sat alone in the orchestra pit. The pianist directed sporadically with one hand, trying to keep the music going with the other as the boys sang:

> *Avec la garde montante,*
> *Nous arrivons, nous voilà!*
> *Sonne, trompette éclatante!*
> *Ta ra ta ta, ta ra ta ta.*
> *Nous marchons la tête haute . . .*

"No, no, no, no!" Marc Berger exclaimed, jumping up from his third-row seat. He punctuated each repetition with a loud clap of his hands. "Jesus Christ! Haven't any of you little urchins ever played soldier before?"

The pianist let his accompaniment trail off, and the boys did likewise with their voices. They turned puzzled stares at the director. The uncertainty on their faces meant they didn't know whether or not they were supposed to answer the question. None of them had played soldiers outside of a video-game setting, and certainly none of them could have been expected to have pretended to be Spanish dragoons, let alone know what a dragoon was.

After a pause during which the construction noise continued, Berger rolled his eyes and huffed testily. "You're *supposed* to be serious. You are *supposed* to look very, very fierce! You want to be soldiers when you grow up! You're doing this in front of the soldiers! You want them to think you're serious about it! And instead you're all standing there like a bunch of little . . . kids in a sandbox! You're not playing with dolls now, you're playing with guns! You're fierce! You're mean! Now for Christ's sake, act like it!"

He stamped back to the third row and stood in front of his seat.

"Where from?" the accompanist called from the pit.

"The beginning of the scene. I want them to go all the way through the entrance business." He turned to the children. "And let's try to do it with a little more élan this time, huh?"

The boys didn't move. They stared at the director in total befuddlement.

"Marc . . ." David Cunningham said wearily. He sat on the armrest of the aisle seat two rows back.

Marc glanced over his shoulder, huffed again, then turned back to the boys. "With a little more energy. *Excitement.* Now get going!"

The children scattered to opposite sides of the stage and the pianist began to play. The boys raced on stage and went through a pantomime fight, trying to make it look realistic while carefully avoiding being hurt.

Cunningham rose and came up to Berger. "You might want to remember that most of those urchins' mothers are seated behind you."

The director wrinkled his nose. "If they want them treated like princes, they should keep their little darlings out of the theater."

They watched the boys for several seconds, then Cunningham said, "They look like they're doing fine to me."

Berger grimaced. "I want the production to be alive from beginning to end. I don't want it to grind to a halt when these brats run onto the stage."

The boys reached the point where they broke into song:

> *Avec la garde montante,*
> *Nous arrivons, nous voilà!*
> *Sonne, trompette éclatante!*

"Is it really as bad as all that?"

Berger sighed dramatically. "I suppose not. I'll whip them into shape. It would've been nice if I had more than a few days to rehearse them."

"It would've been nice if *we* had the money to do something like that."

The boys continued:

> *Et la poitrine en dehors,*
> *Les bras de cette manière,*
> *Tombant tout le long du corps . . .*

Berger's gaze went back to the stage, and he raised his eyes to heaven at what he saw. "No, no, no, you little—"

"Marc!" Cunningham cut him off warningly.

The director checked himself. "Like soldiers! Like soldiers! I told you, I want you pointed out front, stamping forward like you're stalking the audience! Wait a minute, I'll come up there and run through it with you again!"

The executive offices for the Sheridan Center were located on the third floor, across the hall from the entryways to the second balcony, discreetly hidden behind a door that was identical to the rest of the wall panels, save for the addition of a handle.

Behind the door, the studied elegance of the Center ended and modern efficiency took over. The large outer room had flat, eggshell walls and a row of six-foot windows covered with white sheers. Several cubicles, only half of which were occupied, were scattered around the room, far enough apart to give the illusion of privacy.

A large area had been set aside at the far left end of the room for Bonnie Payton's work space. She was a twenty-three-year-old woman whose overly developed professional demeanor guarded the door of Edward Carnegie's private office. Her long auburn hair was kept pinned at the back of her head with an ornamental clip that resembled an antique brooch, not unlike the faux scarab she wore on the lapels of her various business suits. To the uninitiated, Bonnie Payton might appear to be a society matron in waiting, but nobody who had ever tried to gain admittance to Carnegie's office would ever mistake her for anything so ineffectual.

Steven Sheridan was perhaps the only person who could pass her desk unchallenged, at least in the usual sense.

"Good morning, Miss Payton," he said.

She tilted her head slightly. "Good morning, Mr. Sheridan."

Only four words, practically an echo of his own, yet she managed to make Steven feel like a complete fool. Although he couldn't put his finger on it exactly, there was something in her tone that implied that the largesse she granted him was due to his name rather than any personal merit. He was left with the abject feeling that Miss Payton felt she was better than he was.

Of course she does, he said to himself as he opened the door to the office. *She came by her job honestly.*

He closed the door before speaking to make sure they wouldn't be heard by anyone in the outer office.

"Steven!" said Carnegie with a broad smile. He rose from the chair behind the desk.

"Hi, Eddie." Steven crossed the mint-green carpet and laid his briefcase on the desk. Carnegie came around to the front of the desk and the two of them embraced affectionately. "I'm sorry I couldn't see you last night. I had to escort my mother to another one of those damn stinking charity dinners."

"Isn't that part of your job?" said Carnegie, releasing him.

"As what? Head of Daddy's foundation or head of the household, as if I'm really either? She just expects me to take my father's place on her arm at those things."

Carnegie clucked his tongue sympathetically as he went back behind the desk and sat down. "What's she going to do when you're gone?"

"Find someone else. Or maybe she'll finally realize that a steamroller doesn't need any help." He sat in one of the chairs facing the desk.

Carnegie laughed and put his hands behind his neck, intertwining his fingers. Steven took in the room, not for the first time. The decor of the outer office was continued there, with the windows covering the north and west walls of the corner office. The only furniture beside the desk and chairs was a credenza, that set far enough away from the wall to allow the sheers to move. The room was lighted by a pair of white halogen floor lamps and a solitary desk lamp.

"How is everything going?" Steven asked.

"Very well. As I told you on the phone, the company has arrived. They're going to be rehearsing on the stage for the next couple of days. Everything is proceeding right on schedule."

"It looks like you were right about the company. They were the right thing to bring in."

Carnegie nodded. "I knew it when I saw the production in Santa Marta. I've met the leads. Both of them are fairly young, but their voices are surprisingly mature, which really seems right for this opera."

"Are they as volatile as you'd heard?"

Carnegie produced a wry smile and shrugged. "You'll also be glad to know that publicity is going very well, thanks, no doubt, to your mother's influence. No less than Heidi West herself is coming in this afternoon to interview the stars. She's already done their manager and the director. There's going to be a full-page article about the opening this Sunday in the entertainment section of both papers, all about the center, and that 'upstart company from the West Coast.' From the tone of the questions we've been getting from the media, I get the feeling that expectations are very, very high . . . but at the same time, everyone seems confident that they'll be met. And of course, ticket sales are speeding along."

"That's great!"

Carnegie lowered his head for a second, then looked back up. "Has your mother been . . . at all . . . upset about the expense?"

"She fully expected to lose money on the opening production. It's all deductible."

"It's an awful lot of money."

Steven laughed bitterly. "It doesn't matter. Anything to bury the family skeletons."

"She hasn't said anything at all about it? The foundation has had to put out a lot to subsidize this production."

Steven leaned forward. "I told you at the outset that mother didn't really know how much this would cost. Even if she had any qualms about it, she would never admit it. Not even to me. And why would she? Hell, she has more millions than she knows what to do with."

"I don't think that makes me feel any better," said Carnegie, sitting up straight. "Will she be paying us a visit this week?"

Steven laughed again. "Good God, no! She won't enter the theater until opening night, and then she'll look like she's attending a coronation."

Carnegie shook his head. "It's really hard for me to imagine anyone who doesn't have to keep track of every penny."

"I don't have to imagine it. I've lived with it all my life."

"You'll excuse me if I don't feel sorry for you. I've had to work for everything."

"I'm not asking you to," said Steven as he leaned back in his chair. "I just want you to understand that everyone has his own private hell."

"Riccardo!" Gabrielle exclaimed as she stopped in his dressing room doorway. The children could be heard still running through their chorus on the stage.

"Gabby! I'm glad to see you!" He waved her into the room. When they embraced, Gabrielle made an attempt to place a kiss on his lips, but he turned suddenly as if distracted and she had to settle for his cheek. When he let go of her, her face was red and she was having a difficult time looking him in the eye.

"Please, please, sit down," he said, indicating the loveseat. "Are you here for the interview?"

"Of course not," she replied resignedly. "The only ones of interest to the press are you and Maria."

"Now, now." He was about to sit beside her on the loveseat, but stopped himself. He decided it would be better to resume his seat at the makeup table. "You have a major role in this opera. And you sing it beautifully."

"I'm the wallflower. It's a role I'm familiar with."

He ignored this. "When you sing your aria, there isn't a dry eye in the house."

She laughed. "I'm forgotten the minute Maria steps back on stage. Everyone remembers Don José, and Carmen, and Escamillo. Who remembers poor little Micaela?"

"Carmen is a flashy role," Riccardo replied kindly. "Like all villains, it stands out. But you have a beautiful voice. A soprano has many, many more roles to play than . . . some people. And you will be wonderful in them all."

"Maria can sing soprano roles."

"But not as well as you."

There was a pause, then Gabrielle smiled. "Thank you."

"I was about to make some coffee. Would you like some?"

"No, thanks."

From a large sports bag on the counter he pulled a bundle wrapped in paper and tied with string.

Gabrielle laughed as he opened it. "You brought your own coffeemaker with you?"

"If I were our diva I would have demanded that the theater buy me one," he said as he set it up, "but I like having my own things around. It gives me a little bit of home."

"Maria would never make coffee. She enjoys sending her lackey out for it too much."

Riccardo laughed. "I don't think Barbara would like being known as a lackey!"

There were a few seconds of silence. "Doesn't it keep you up at night, when you drink coffee during a performance?" As always she was trying to find a way to keep the conversation going without sounding as if that was what she was doing. She was afraid that if there was a lull, Riccardo might ask her to leave. At the same time, she feared that she sounded artificial.

"I'm too hyped up to sleep after a performance anyway. It doesn't make a difference." He pulled a packet of coffee and a box of filters from his bag. "So, if you're not here for the interview, what brings you here today? We're not called until tomorrow."

Gabrielle suffered a pang. He didn't want her there. "I just wanted to see the place. I got here yesterday, and I didn't have anything to do today. And I was curious about the theater. So I thought I'd come by and have a look around. Leave a few things in my dressing room. I get my own dressing room here, not like back home."

"What do you think of it?" He dumped the coffee into the filter and put it into the holder in the machine.

"It's beautiful!" she replied, her face brightening.

Riccardo laughed. "Don't let Maria hear you say that! She's already complained about it."

"How could she? There's nothing wrong with the dressing rooms, and we're guests here! Common courtesy would keep me from complaining about such a thing!"

Riccardo smiled. "Common courtesy is not something that comes naturally to Maria."

"It should! She's very lucky and she does nothing but take advantage of her good fortune. I don't think . . . Maria's not the diva she thinks she is!"

Riccardo turned to her, frowning. "Gabby, don't say things like that. Maria may lack grace, but she is a major talent. That's something I won't let you take away from her."

Gabrielle looked stricken. "I didn't mean . . . I just meant she thinks more highly of herself than she should."

"No. She's very good, and she knows it. Maybe it's better

for some people if they don't know how good they are, but part of Maria'a strength is that she knows herself. When she walks out onto the stage, she does it with a confidence that overwhelms the audience."

Gabrielle stared at him, open-mouthed. His face almost shone as he pictured his leading lady on the stage. Gabrielle could feel her hopes slipping away. She slowly lowered her face and her shoulders slumped.

"How can you?" she said softly.

"I beg your pardon?"

"How can you love her so much when she's so self-centered . . . and . . ."

He shrugged helplessly. "On stage as in real life, I'm afraid her personality is magnetic."

"Her personality is like a train wreck! You can't take your eyes away from it."

Riccardo smiled at her affectionately. "That is probably true."

She sniffed. "Don't you know how much I love you?"

He gazed at her sadly, then crossed the room and sat beside her.

"Gabrielle," he said softly, taking her hand between his, "I love you, too . . . but not in the way you mean. In the months we've been together, you've become like a sister to me."

"Yes," she said, drawing her hand away. "I'm everybody's sister."

"How bad is it?" David Cunningham said into the phone.

"Well, we're still in debt," his partner, William Stauffer, answered into the phone in his home office in Santa Marta. The Sheridan Center's budget hadn't allowed for both of the partners to come out to Chicago, so Stauffer had been left behind to deal with the bills and fund-raising. "I've been squeezing pennies 'til they bend, and I still haven't been able to pay everybody off. And I'm getting that old 'other shoe about to drop' feeling."

Cunningham rolled his eyes. He'd known that starting their company was going to be a challenge, but neither of them had quite realized exactly how costly it would be. For the partners the opera company was a labor of love: love of music, fine art, and their community, which they'd felt would be readily able to support the project. And to a great extent, the community had come through. The opera company had received a great deal of public backing, as well as the backing of several corporate sponsors.

But the expense of launching an opera company had far exceeded even the least conservative estimates of the neophyte partners, and the expense of taking the opera to different cities—a move that had originally raised their hopes—had almost cancelled out the benefits of doing it. Though the pockets of their sponsors were deep, they weren't bottomless.

That was the reason the offer from the Sheridan Center had been so opportune. It provided a modicum of cash for the company, and kept the cast entailed while the founders scrambled to finance the next project. The Center had agreed to pay a fixed rate to the opera company itself, as well as paying out a percentage of the box office. The Center was also bearing the expense of putting up the cast and crew. David wrinkled his nose at the sight of his own room at the Starlight Motel, a much less elegant home than those provided for the stars.

"David, are you there?" Stauffer's voice came through the receiver.

"What? Yes, I'm here."

"I said I have that 'other shoe' feeling."

"What other shoe? What are you talking about?" With his right hand, he swept the hair back out of his eyes.

"I don't know," Stauffer replied with a heavy sigh. "Murphy's law, I guess. I have a feeling that everything that can go wrong hasn't happened yet."

"Come on," David said with forced good humor, "we were a great success in the initial run. Lots of excitement! Remember opening night?"

"Yeah. It was really something." There was a smile in Stauffer's voice that quickly faded. "But where did that get us?"

"We didn't go into it for money, you know that."

His partner sighed. "Dave, there's not making money, and then there's not even being able to stay afloat. As it is now, we won't have enough money to do the next production, which will leave us looking like the Mickey Rooney and Judy Garland of the opera world. Twenty years from now we'll be looking back and saying, 'Gee, wasn't our *Carmen* great,' and trying to forget that we were a big failure."

"It can't be as bad as all that! What about the money from this gig? That's enough for seed money, isn't it?"

"Barely. A little tiny seed."

"We can go to our corporate sponsors again."

"Not if we still want to live in this city! They already think we've been to the well too often. It didn't look . . ." There was a hesitation over the line as Stauffer searched for the right words. "We didn't make ourselves look too good, flubbing the budget."

Cunningham rolled his eyes again. It was true, but it couldn't be helped. Every time they thought they'd had the budget settled and everything going their way, another union would come out of the woodwork.

"I know, I know," he said, "we weren't . . . very good about the budget. But I want to do whatever we can to get *Aida* up."

There was a deafening silence from the other end of the line. Finally, Stauffer cleared his throat. "Yeah, I know. Um . . . about that . . ."

"What?" David said irritably. He already knew what was coming.

"Dave . . . you've picked one of the most expensive operas to mount, if it's done right. And you know that after *Carmen*, everybody's going to expect us to do it right!"

"So, we will!"

"The money, Dave, the money!"

"I know. It'll come. Don't worry."

Stauffer knew better than to press his partner when he was

in a mood like this. It was all well and good to say the money will come; it was quite another thing to be the one to have to make it happen.

"Dave, I was thinking, maybe . . . maybe we should do something other than *Aida*."

"What?" He already sounded angry.

"Hear me out! Maybe we should put that one off for a while. Maybe, instead, we should do *Samson and Delilah*."

"Why?"

There was a beat before Stauffer answered. "Because it has a great role for Maria. A starring role."

David could feel a hardening in the pit of his stomach. "No."

"Come on, Dave. I know she's a royal pain in the ass, but she made a big splash in *Carmen*. You have to admit she's a draw."

"The company's the draw! The whole package!"

His partner sighed heavily. "Come on, David, you're not that naive. We're a little, tiny company that got a lot more press about their first production than anybody could've anticipated. Partly because of Maria."

David winced. His own words about their production being a stunt came back to him.

Stauffer continued. "The press has turned us into a big deal . . . a big deal with no money. *Aida* is just too much for us right now."

"That's exactly why we should do it!" Cunningham countered. "Even if we fall on our faces, people will admire us."

"All the way to the poorhouse . . ."

Cunningham was silent for a moment before answering. "We've already announced *Aida*. To back out now will make us look worse than anything we could do to the opera."

"*Delilah* would be great for Maria. It would really allow her to shine."

Cunningham let out a derisive "Huh! I think it's time for somebody else to shine."

Stauffer sighed again, resignedly. "Dave, you're going to

have to accept it. Maria has sparked a lot of interest. Featuring her will bring in audiences. We need all the help we can get at this point. We need her."

"I am not the star," Maria said expansively. "I am only a part of the opera. I have been surrounded by many, many marvelous singers."

Completely oblivious to her own contradiction, she leaned to the side and tapped the dangling ash from the end of her cigarette into the tray on the makeup counter. Even this simple action was performed with theatrical flair.

Heidi West was seated on the opposite side of the dressing room. The other chair was occupied by Riccardo Nuevo, who was also the subject of the interview. However, the placement of the tenor and the reporter in the guest chairs effectively turned them into an audience for the diva, who sat framed by the bright circle of lights around the mirror behind her.

"I was fortunate enough to catch a performance when I was out on the West Coast," said West. "I have to say you were very, very impressive. You're not just a singer, you're an actress."

"Thank you," Maria replied, inclining her head slightly.

"When you came out in that dress for the last scene—the long white dress—you know the one I mean?"

Maria inclined her head again.

"You were beautiful. And I just *knew* we were going to see blood."

The diva smiled. "It is very dramatic, is it not?"

"Yes, it is. The problem I've always had with *Carmen* is that it's so obvious that she's going to die. I think even someone who's being introduced to the characters for the first time knows that she's going to end up getting killed. It robs it of some of the . . . anticipation, if you know what I mean."

Maria shook her head slowly. "It all depends on how it is played, doesn't it?" She dropped her hands into her lap. The cigarette protruded from between the first and second fingers of her right hand. "I have heard a story—it may be true, it may not—that once, when Horne was performing the role, during the final duet when emotions are supposed to be running at their highest, a voice called out from the audience, "Oh, for Christ's sake, just stab her!" Maria sat back in her chair with a broad grin spread across her face.

West looked momentarily shocked—not by the story, which she dismissed as apocryphal—but by the fact that a woman so new to success would share it. She turned to Riccardo. "Fame for this production spread very quickly. I mean, Santa Marta isn't a very big place, yet there were features in several newspapers around the country, including my own."

There seemed to be an unasked question behind this statement, but Riccardo couldn't fathom what it was. "Yes, we were very fortunate."

"How did all that fame come to pass?"

"I believe when a performance is outstanding, word will spread!" Maria said matter-of-factly.

"I think most of it can be attributed to the fact that the *Los Angeles Times* did a glowing article about us," Riccardo explained professionally. "After that, a lot of other papers picked up on us. And David and Bill worked very hard to promote us."

West shifted her bulk in the chair that was dwarfed beneath her. "Not everything that was written about it was positive, though. I should point out before asking this that I thought the staging was incredibly exciting, but there was a lot of criticism of it. As a classical singer, how do you feel about that?"

"The staging?" He shrugged. "I think—"

"These are modern times!" Maria interrupted. "Not eighteen-seventy-five! It is only right and fitting that the opera should go with the times, otherwise it would be dead. Why should critics complain because the opera is done in a way that is exciting? *Exciting!* The beautiful words and the beautiful music are still there. The opera is still there!"

West raised her hefty shoulders. "Well, you have very little

to complain about yourself in
they've said about the produ
you."

"Except one," Riccardo s
glance at Maria.

"Whenever anyone is ver
"there will always be those wl
them down. It makes them feel
pigs."

"*I* am a critic, Ms. Cortez,"

There was another pause,
cigarette. As she blew out the smoke, she said, "I am, of course,
speaking of *bad* critics."

"Of course."

Riccardo smiled inwardly. If Maria kept tripping over herself, he wasn't going to have to worry about her leaving the
company: There would be nowhere for her to go.

"Is it true that you've been getting offers from other established companies?" West asked Maria.

"Not offers yet," Maria said. "But yes, there has been interest."

"But we're under contract," Riccardo said quickly. "For the
next two years. We have exclusive contracts with this company
and we owe our loyalty to them. They've given us an opportunity
we might not ever have gotten elsewhere."

"That may be," Maria said to him gravely, all but ignoring
the reporter, "but they owe us as well. They may have provided
the opportunity, but we provided them with the talent. We made
it possible for them to start their . . . little company, with a lot
more success than they would have had otherwise." She took a
long drag from her cigarette, exhaled, then turned a hardened
smile to Heidi West. "After all, I am—we are the ones up on the
stage, putting our reputations on the line, and bringing in the
notices that brought the acclaim you spoke of. Not Mr. Cunningham and Mr. Stauffer."

stand what they've done for us, and we
Riccardo said, shooting a warning glance at
go unnoticed.

tated before continuing. "You have to realize that
standpoint of a reporter, the idea of a pair of opera
pulled from obscurity and thrust into the spotlight is a
story."

Maria waved the cigarette in the air. "Much has been made of that idea. Too much. It's not as if we were plucked out of the chorus like so many Ruby Keelers. I was not masquerading as an opera singer. Isn't that right, Ricky?"

Riccardo didn't answer. His already dark skin reddened.

"Well," said West, "if something should come through for you with another company, do you think the Santa Marta Company would hold you to your contract? Would they stand in your way?"

Maria shook her head slowly. "I don't think anyone will stand in my way."

3

Steven Sheridan spent a very long day cooped up in the claustrophobic Wacker Drive offices of the Edwin J. Sheridan Foundation. His mother might believe in lavishing money on the arts and the needy in the name of his father, but her philanthropy ended when it came to the comfort of the minions whose job it was to administer the money. Even if one of them was her own son.

It hadn't been a good day. Aside from the piles of mail begging for money, there were the endless calls from the elite of society—or, at least, their assistants—who tried valiantly to make their prewritten spiels sound conversational. His answer was the same for everyone: Their requests would be taken under advisement, which meant that he would discuss it with his mother, the normal prerequisite for okaying anything over fifty thousand dollars.

Then there was the visit from Ben Weinstock, the foundation's chief accountant.

"May I speak with you?" he asked, opening the door to Steven's office a crack and poking his oily head inside.

Steven was on the phone. He looked up and waved the accountant in with an obvious lack of enthusiasm. Weinstock stood in front of the desk clutching a sheaf of papers. His wire-rimmed glasses were perched on the tip of his nose as if they had to be held away from his eyes in order for him to see.

Steven finished his call, then looked up. "Yes, Ben, what is it?"

The accountant cleared his throat. "I was just going over our statements and found a payment to the Sheridan Center that I didn't understand."

"What is it?"

Weinstock laid the top sheet from his bundle on the desk, slued it around so that Steven could read it, then pointed to a transaction underlined in red. Steven looked down at it, then up at him.

"Yes, I authorized that. It's fine. It's a payment for the orchestra."

"The orchestra?" Weinstock said with a puzzled frown. "It's very high. Is this for the rehearsals?"

"No. Ed Carnegie could explain it better than I can. It has something to do with—I think they call it a reserve, or a buffer, or something like that. Two weeks' worth of salary for the entire orchestra has to be put up in advance against the possibility of the production closing unexpectedly."

The accountant looked positively aghast. "Is there a chance of that?"

"Of course not. But it's the same for all the performance-oriented unions. It's a requirement."

Weinstock laid the tips of this fingers on the sheet as if to retrieve it, but held it in place. "Shouldn't we have made the check out directly to the union?"

"No," Steven said with a weary sigh. He felt like he'd had to explain this a hundred times already. "The Sheridan Center is a not-for-profit arts organization, so we donate the money directly to them. They'll keep detailed books on the expense for each project they decide to do. We have to keep our books separate from theirs. How on earth would we explain our foundation giving money to the musicians' union?"

"Will we get the money back . . . I mean, if nothing unusual happens?"

"The Center will get it back, and they'll have to account for it, just like everything else. Then they'll keep it in reserve for the next production. We don't come into it at all."

Weinstock shook his head as he lifted the paper from the desktop and placed it on top of his pile. "This opera certainly is costing us a lot of money."

Steven nodded dismally. "About four times more than it costs to mount one at the Lyric, from what I understand. But we're paying to bring the whole damn thing here, and then some. We had to greatly increase our contribution to the Center's initial operating budget, but, extravagant as it may be, it's what mother wanted. She'll spare no expense in my father's name."

Weinstock pursed his lips to one side. He had learned the truth of that statement in his two years with the foundation, but didn't know exactly what to think of it.

"I hope it's worth it," he said as he started for the door.

Like many people who feel they're under the thumb of someone else, Steven suddenly felt sorry for the harried underling. "Ben, if there's any other unusual payments that need to be made to the Center, I promise I'll let you know at the time so you don't have to ask. I should've thought of that before. I'm sorry."

And like many of the downtrodden, Ben was surprised and gratified to get an apology. He mumbled a thank-you, then left the room.

Steven decided to walk home that evening. It wasn't far from the Wacker Drive office to the Sheridan mansion, but he drew it out by first walking east to the lake before heading north.

He loved the lake. There was something about the wide expanse of water that made him feel as if there was a whole world out there for him to discover, were he ever able to break free of the life that had been fashioned for him. At the same time, as he watched the water washing up against the concrete promenade, he couldn't help feeling the irony. The waves, so free away from shore, seemed halfhearted as they buffeted lightly against the barrier, as if after years without success, they'd given up trying to erode the wall that held them back.

His mind distracted, Steven stepped into an indentation on the promenade where two parts of the walk had caved in slightly. The bottom of his right pant leg was splashed with the dirty water left in the hole by one of the more aggressive waves. He cursed mildly and brushed at the cuff. He straighten up, sighed, then went on.

Steven dawdled along the lakefront for a full hour, watching the joggers and bicyclists go by, feeling a sense of longing and envy for the freedom he imagined they enjoyed. After a while, he continued north to the Oak Street underpass, then up to his home.

"You're late tonight," his mother said as he walked into the front parlor. She sat in a wing chair sorting through a stack of letters on a low table beside her.

"Yes. I took a walk before coming home."

She glanced at him over the rim of her glasses, said a terse "Ah," then looked back down. "We've been invited to an opening at the Langley Gallery next month, on the twenty-third, so I'd appreciate it if you would mark that on your calendar."

"Yes, Mother."

"Also," she continued without looking up, "there's going to be a charity ball for the United Crippled Children's Fund. That's on . . ." She leafed through the correspondence for a moment, her forehead creased, and then found the letter she was looking for. ". . . the thirtieth. That's it. The invitation came directly to me rather than the foundation because this is Mildred Stein's pet project and she wanted to invite me personally. Please mark that on your calendar as well. She'll be expecting both of us."

"Yes, Mother."

"You'd better go in and eat now. Cook laid out your dinner ages ago. You're late, so I suppose you can't complain if it's cold. You can always tell cook to heat it up if you like."

I know that, he thought with an inward sigh. "Have you eaten?"

"I'm going to the Chestertons' for dinner this evening. It's supposed to be purely social, but I have a feeling they might have some cause they want to discuss with me. Alice Chesterton has been showing a great deal of interest in my work, which they usually do just before asking for money. We'll see. Now, if you're not busy tonight, you can—"

"I am busy."

She looked up. "You are?"

"I'm going to the hospital to visit Jerry."

"Jerry?" She said the name slowly. Her eyes narrowed and her hands tightened around the letters she was holding.

He clucked his tongue. "Mother, don't act like you don't know who he is."

"Oh! Yes, your friend." She contrived to look as if she'd just remembered this, then went back to leafing through the letters.

Steven watched her for a moment, feeling as if he would find her repulsive if only he could work up the energy to care.

"I'll give him your love," he said as he walked out of the room.

His dinner had gotten cold, but he didn't mind since he could barely taste it anyway. He ate as quickly as propriety would allow, then went upstairs and changed into a pair of designer jeans and a lightweight coral sweater.

Once again he decided to walk to his destination, since it wasn't that far to St. Joseph's. But this time he didn't take the long way. He crossed North Avenue, then made his way through the park to Diversey. From there it was then less than half a block to the hospital.

He knew his way around the hospital, having visited so many times already, and he knew most of the staff who were taking care of his friend. He got off the elevator on the eleventh floor and was halfway to the room when he ran into one of the nurses. She was a short woman with dark brunette hair. He knew her only as Judy.

"Hello, Mr. Sheridan," she said with a pleasing smile.

"Hi. How's he doing?"

Immediately her bright brown eyes dulled with sympathy. "He's doing a little worse, I'm afraid. We've had to put him on a morphine drip. He was in a lot of pain."

"I see." Steven betrayed no emotion.

"I just wanted you to know, so you wouldn't be surprised by how he is. It's hard to tell how morphine will affect people. Sometimes they become euphoric; sometimes they seem perfectly normal, at least for a while. Sometimes they just sleep."

"Okay," said Steven, walking away from her. He appreciated her kindness, but didn't want to have anything more explained to him.

When he reached the room, he found Jerry Parker lying in semidarkness, his eyes closed and his lips slightly parted. His young face was ravaged with illness, making him look twice his age, but his expression was untroubled. His breathing was a bit irregular, so that he sounded as if he had a mild case of apnea. Steven had never actually seen death, having been kept away from his father at the moment of passing, but even in his inexperience he could recognize the signs: His friend was almost gone.

Steven slowly crossed the room and stood for a moment next to the bed by the IV pole, shaking his head as he inspected the various bags of medicine. Then he pulled a chair up beside the bed. He watched its occupant for a while in silence, his hands wrapped around the withered fingers that lay against the bed rails.

"Jerry . . . Jerry . . ." he said softly. When there was no response, he sighed heavily. "I miss you already. You were one of the only people who could take me away from everything. . . ."

He waited, his head slightly bowed. He wasn't expecting a response (as much as he hoped for one), but was collecting his thoughts to the accompaniment of the steady sounds of the IV pump.

He raised his head and continued. "I can't believe it's come to this . . . but I wanted you to know that when it's all over, I'm going to go away for a while . . . take that vacation I always talked about. You were right . . . it's time. It's way past time."

Riccardo checked himself in the full-length mirror on the bathroom door. He was wearing his favorite suit, which was olive green and offset the dark creaminess of his skin. He adjusted his brown tie, tightened the knot at his throat, then grunted his approval. On his way out of his hotel room he patted his back pocket to make sure he had his wallet—sparing the thought that Maria would most likely have chosen an expensive restaurant for tonight's dinner—and then patted his right hand pocket for the plastic key card. He pulled the door shut behind him and headed down the hallway.

Halfway down on the right was an archway to the hall where Maria's room was located. When he came around the corner, he stopped suddenly: A man with long, dark, slick hair was knocking on Maria's door. Riccardo recognized him at once and drew back around the corner before the visitor could see him.

He heard the man knock a second time, then the door opened. Maria's voice cried out with a mixture of pleasure and surprise, "Tony!"

"Hello, darling!" Tony replied.

Riccardo peeked cautiously around the corner and saw the two of them exchange a very friendly kiss, then disappear into the room. Once the door was closed, he quietly made his way to it and pressed his ear close to it.

"I can't believe you came into town without telling me!" Maria said. "But I am so glad to see you! I'm so bored in this stupid town! Why are you here? What brings you?"

Tony Leonard had walked halfway into the room. He hooked his thumbs in his belt and displayed a sly grin.

"You flew in from New York just to see me? I can't believe that! Unless . . ." She stopped, realizing what the look on his face meant. "Unless you have news! Do you?"

"I sure do. It's news so good I wanted to deliver it in person. And it gave me an excuse to see you."

"What is it?" Her expression was so avid she looked almost vampirish.

"You know that next season the Met is slated to do *Il Travatore.*"

"Yes." There was a momentary flicker in Maria's glow. Good mezzo roles were hard to come by, and she wasn't exactly happy that one was put out of her reach before she could attain it. Azucena was a juicy role. And it would be years before the Met would do it again.

Tony noticed the disruption and his grin broadened. "Well, Renée Tabor has had to drop out, for reasons that have been unspecified, and they were having trouble finding a suitable replacement. It's hard to find a name so late in the game."

"Are you saying . . . are you saying . . ."

He nodded. "It looks like your publicity has finally paid off."

Her mouth dropped open. "You're joking!"

"No, I'm not. I've managed to get you the role, despite your youth!"

Maria let out a squeal of delight and threw her arms around him. "I can't believe it! I can't believe it!"

"It seems they're not above a little publicity-seeking themselves. Apparently having the hot new rising star in the cast—someone who's brought a lot of advance press with her—will be good for them as well."

She kissed him repeatedly on the cheeks and the lips, then pushed herself away from him. She clapped her hands together as she walked over to the window. "It is my dream!"

"It's our dream. You can be sure that I'll be sitting in the front row on opening night."

Maria looked so enraptured as she gazed out at the twilight through the sheers that Tony let her bask awhile in the news before continuing.

"Maria," he said at last, "I've assured them that you are available, but can we be sure of that?"

She turned to him. "Of course!"

"You're sure Cunningham and Stauffer will let you out of your contract?"

"Ha! By next season, the contract will mean nothing! I cannot remain a member of the Santa Marta Opera Company if the company no longer exists!"

Tony wasn't convinced. "Are you so sure they're in that bad of shape?"

"You told me the rumors yourself," she replied, almost accusingly.

"I know, but what I was hearing about the money problems was before they got the reprieve from the Sheridan Center. I would think they'd make enough money off of this to go on, at least for a while."

"They can't hold me!" Maria exclaimed in a burst of anger. "That damnable contract was unfair to begin with!"

"It was a very generous one for the position you were in when you signed it."

She made a noise through her nose. "I could take it to court! I could have it broken!"

He nodded. "And gain a reputation for not living up to your contracts? For being trouble? The opera world is very small, my darling. It wouldn't do to start out with a reputation like that."

She folded her arms across her chest. "Then what do you suggest I do?"

"I suggest that we talk to them. Dave and Bill are reasonable guys. I don't think they'd really stand in your way if they realized what a golden opportunity this is for you."

Maria smoldered silently for several seconds. "You give them too much credit. They're not fools! They know what they have in me. But they won't be any trouble . . . you let me take care of it!"

"Maria . . ."

"No, no!" She waved her hand dramatically. "No more talk about it right now! It is wonderful news about the Met! Instead of arguing, we should be celebrating!"

She held her hands out to him and smiled broadly. He stepped into her embrace. "How to you want to do that?"

"You know how." She kissed him deeply, and he responded in kind.

When they parted, Tony said, "Why don't we order room service and have a private celebration right here?"

She nodded her approval, and was about to kiss him again when she suddenly pulled back and grimaced. "Damn! I forgot about Riccardo! I was supposed to have dinner with him!"

Tony drew her forward and kissed her again, even more passionately than before. As their lips separated, Maria said, "I'll call him and tell him that I'm unwell."

Out in the hallway, Riccardo stepped back from the door. His face was flushed with rage. For a moment he glared at the door as if he might kick it down, flexing his fists several times. Then at last he took off down the hall, roughly loosening the knot in his tie.

4

Thursday afternoon the entire cast and crew, along with the local musicians who comprised the orchestra, gathered for the sole rehearsal the entire company would have on the stage of the Sheridan Center. It had only been a week since their last performance in San Francisco. With the cast already well versed in their roles, the orchestra prerehearsed off site, and primary lighting and crew members on hand from the original production, the producers felt that this could serve as a combination dress, pick-up, and tech rehearsal in the new space. Besides, they would have preview performances on Friday and Saturday night to iron out any problems before the Sunday opening.

"Children, children," Marc Berger cried out, this time addressing the adults who were bustling on the stage rather than the youngsters of the cast. "Everybody off! We're about to start. This is a complete run-through, so no stopping unless a piece of scenery falls on somebody's head!" He added half under his breath, "Which wouldn't at all surprise me."

David Cunningham was standing nearby in the aisle. He laughed. "Marc, if you weren't expecting disaster I would really be worried."

"Then you must be the calmest man on earth!" the director intoned.

Along with Cunningham, Edward Carnegie, several other members of the Center's staff, and the mothers of the children in the cast dotted the auditorium. All of them were happy to get the first advance look at the opera they'd heard so much about.

The crew and the straggling performers cleared the stage as the heavy maroon curtain descended. Members of the orchestra, clad in street clothes, chatted amiably with one another as they tuned their instruments. The musical director, who also served as conductor, emerged in the pit and took his place with a wave at Cunningham. He then turned back to the musicians, raised his baton, and without any preamble started the overture. The music sprang to vibrant, cohesive life in a startling contrast to the minor pandemonium that had reigned just a few moments earlier.

Edward Carnegie sat back in his seat with a deep, satisfied sigh. He loved it when everything came together.

Backstage, some of the men and women of the chorus and the supernumeraries arranged themselves on the set. The rest of the women—who were playing the workers in the cigarette factory—waited quietly in the stage-left wings, where they would enter through the archway that served as the entrance to the factory. The remainder of the men were either offstage right, or upstage behind the flats.

Maria Cortez had not yet emerged from her dressing room. Early on in the initial run the management had convinced her that although she had the most important role, her makeup should be done last, since she was the last of the first act principals to make an entrance. This would allow Sherman Dunston, the principal's makeup artist, to devote his full attention to her. The real reason for the move was that Maria, either out of inborn perverseness or the contrariness of a recent star, had demonstrated a tendency to delay Dunston in applying her makeup, never satisfied until he'd touched her up to her personal whims, so that he had to rush through doing the other performers. Putting her last gave Maria the illusion that she had him to herself, and that she had all the time in the world.

"Barbara!" Maria exclaimed testily as Dunston brushed her left eyebrow.

"Yes, ma'am," her assistant replied.

"Stop fussing with those costumes! I'm already dressed for the first act! Get out! I don't need you until the end of the act, and there isn't enough room in here for you to be flittering about! I'm claustrophobic enough and you're making it worse!"

"Yes, ma'am," the young woman said with the tired amusement of someone who has dealt too long with a child. She went out the door, leaving it open.

"Jesus! What I have to put up with!"

"I know, I know," Dunston purred. He smoothed her left eyebrow with his thumb, then stood back. The two of them looked at his artistry in the mirror while the orchestra continued the overture.

Maria cocked her head slightly at her own image, then reached for the cup of designer coffee that sat on the counter. She took a drink and then set it aside.

"The other doesn't look quite right, do you think?"

Dunston pursed his lips, trying not to smile. "I think you're right." He took a sip from his own mug of coffee, then set it on the counter and went to work on the offending brow.

Riccardo appeared in the doorway, looking quite dashing in Don José's uniform. "Maria, I haven't seen you all day. Are you feeling better?"

"What? Yes . . . yes, thank you, Riccardo." Her voice came to him from behind the makeup artist. "I feel a little better this evening. I'm so sorry I had to cancel our date last night, but it did help."

"Well, that's all that matters, isn't it? That's the important thing." His smile was a bit thin. He rested himself against the counter beside Maria's cup.

"I didn't know you weren't feeling well," Dunston "tsked" sympathetically. "You should've told me."

"It was nothing. I feel better now."

He leaned closer to her and peered into her eyes. "They look a little tired. Are you sure you're all right?"

"Of course," she replied irritably. "I've already said so." She pushed him back slightly. He shrugged and resumed his work. After a short silence, she said, "Oh, by the way Riccardo, Tony has come into town."

"Your manager?" He manufactured surprise. "What for?"

"To see the opening, I suppose. I'm an important client to him right now."

"I'll bet you are. And that's all?"

"What else?"

"It's a long way to come just to see an opera that he's already seen."

She craned her neck around Dunston so that she could see him. "Of course not. Why else would he come?"

Riccardo ignored this. "Well, I'm glad you're feeling better. I'll see you on stage." He left the room.

Dunston performed the same finishing touch with his thumb as he had with the other brow, then stepped out of the way so she could see herself in the mirror.

She tilted her head one way, then the other, then smiled at her reflection. "Ah! Perfection!"

She reached for her coffee.

"Energy, boys, energy!" Berger yelled from the audience.

In response, the chorus of urchins sang with a tiny bit more aggressiveness.

"Marc, we're not supposed to stop them, remember?" Cunningham said quietly as the director resumed his seat.

"I'm not stopping the anemic, no-talent little shits."

Cunningham couldn't help smiling.

The action progressed through the scene between Don José and Zuniga, who was being played by Jeffrey Baker, to the entrance of the girls from the cigarette factory. Then, on cue, Maria entered through the archway. Wearing a dingy white blouse and a long, ragged red skirt, she strutted across the stage as if she was in charge of everything and everyone. There was a flower in her hair, and a sheen on her skin that bore witness to the unbearable heat of the factory. Although it was a rehearsal, Maria still radiated electricity. Sparks seemed to fly from her eyes as she ogled the men, and the words dripped from her lips when she sang her opening lines.

Then the orchestra began the strains of "Habanera." When Maria started she seemed perfectly normal, swaying rhythmically with the music as she went from one man to the next, weaving her spell. But she faltered as she reached the far right of the stage. As the chorus took up the melody and Maria sang Carmen's seductive "L'amours," the sheen on her skin became beads of perspiration that quickly enlarged and ran down her face and neck. Her right hand went to her stomach.

> *L'amour est enfant de Bohême,*
> *Il n'a jamais, jamais connu de loi . . .*

She worked her way back through the men of the chorus, several of whom looked questioningly at her as she passed. It wasn't lost on them that something was wrong. She managed to make it to the other end of the stage, although not without noticeably wavering. When she came to a stop, she surprised one of the men by placing a trembling hand on his shoulder as she began the third verse.

> *L'amour est loin, tu peux l'attendre;*
> *Tu ne l'attends plus—*

Suddenly, Maria broke off and her hand flew up to her mouth. The blood seemed to drain from her face, then rush back up again. She frantically looked to the left and right, then ran off stage left.

The music sounded as if it were coming apart at the seams

as one by one the musicians realized that the conductor had stopped leading them. He gaped at the stage, then glanced over his shoulder.

David Cunningham was out of his seat like a shot. He ran down the aisle and across to the door on the side of the house that led backstage.

The usual behind-the-scenes activity had come to halt. The baffled crew were all standing stock-still looking off in the direction of the dressing rooms, forming a human wake through which the diva had fled. Before Cunningham reached Maria's room, he could hear the sounds of some very unladylike retching.

Sherman Dunston stood in the dressing room doorway twisting a makeup sponge between his fingers as if fascinated by what was occurring.

"What happened?" he said to the approaching producer.

"That's what I was about to ask you."

"Get out!" Maria bellowed from the bathroom with a gurgling cough. "I don't need an audience!"

"That's the first time madam has ever said that," Dunston said under his breath. If Cunningham hadn't been so worried, he would've laughed.

Barbara came out of the bathroom looking flustered and helpless. "I don't know what to do for her," she said, hurrying out of the dressing room as Riccardo joined the other two men.

"Is she all right?" he asked.

"We don't know," Cunningham replied. "Maria? Are you all right?"

The only reply was a renewed bout of vomiting.

"Hm," said Riccardo. "She said last night that she didn't feel well."

"That's right," Dunston acknowledged. "I mean, she said she felt better today. I guess she didn't really."

Cunningham's eyes became vacant, as if his worries were dancing before them and he didn't want to look. "This is awful! Maria's the . . . what are we going to do if she can't go on on Sunday?"

Riccardo looked as if he were trying not to smile. "I'm sure she'll be better soon."

The sound emanating from the bathroom ceased. After a lengthy silence, they heard the toilet flush. A few moments later, Maria emerged from the bathroom and leaned against the door-jamb. Riccardo and Cunningham went over to her.

"Maria, are you all right?" asked the producer.

"I don't know what happened," she replied languidly. "I just . . . my stomach suddenly felt queasy. Very, very queasy."

He helped her to one of the chairs. "How do you feel now?"

She thought for a moment, then looked rather surprised. "Better. Much better."

"Riccardo said you didn't feel well last night."

She answered after a beat, looking inexplicably confused. "Yes, that's true."

"Do you want us to call a doctor for you?"

"No. No, I feel much better now."

"Let me get you some water," said Riccardo. He went into the bathroom.

"I'll call a cab and we'll send you back to the hotel," Cunningham said.

A cloud passed over Maria's face. "No. I will be fine. I don't want to spoil the rehearsal."

"Your understudy can do it. We need you to be in good shape for the opening."

Riccardo came out of the bathroom carrying a glass of water, which he handed to Maria.

"No," she said to Cunningham. "There's no need for that. If you could just . . . if you'll let me rest for a few minutes, I'll be able to continue. Really, I'm feeling quite well now."

This time she sounded much more sincere than when Riccardo had questioned her about her health earlier.

Cunningham relented with the eagerness of someone who is grateful, for once, to not have his suggestion heeded. "Well, if you're sure." He looked over to the doorway. "Sherman, would you tell the cast we'll resume in twenty minutes?"

"Righto," the makeup artist replied as he walked away.

Maria took a tentative sip of the water and glanced up at Riccardo. "Why do you smile at me like that?" She would've sounded cross had she not been so weakened.

"Nothing," he replied. "I'm just happy you're feeling better."

The Friday-night preview performance was a sellout. As Marc Berger had secretly suspected, once his dreaded chorus of urchins got in front of an audience, they came to life, performing with more vigor than in rehearsal. Maria had fully recovered from her mysterious ailment, and played and sang her part so energetically it seemed as if she were making up for the lackluster rehearsal that had been all she'd been able to give the day before. Riccardo, Franco Giannini, and Gabrielle Charbonneau responded in kind, their own performances rising to Maria's intensity.

There was some initial skittishness on the part of the chorus that dissolved once they successfully got through "Habanera" without the leading lady having to flee the stage. Even the supers performed their mute pantomimes with an unusual amount of animation. It looked as if the Santa Marta Opera Company's production of *Carmen* had been remounted with all of its brilliance intact.

The entire performance went without a hitch until they reached the final scene, the duet between Don José and Carmen: the bitter quarrel that ends with the maddened Don José stabbing the woman with whom he has become obsessed. This was the one scene they had only sketchily rehearsed the day before. Since the cast knew how it worked, and since it didn't involve any of the supers, there seemed little reason for them to go through all the mechanics of it with Maria not feeling well. They had only sung it and gone through the motions of the business, ending with Franco and select members of the chorus entering through the gates in the massive wall that represented the outside of the bullring, finding Don José kneeling beside his victim.

At the preview, of course, the scene was performed in its

entirety, with all the effects of the original production. Maria was costumed in a beautiful, virginal white dress that signified that the love she had finally found in Escamillo, the toreador, had washed her clean. As always, Riccardo acted the part of Don José's descent into murderous rage so convincingly that it took the audience's breath away. At the same time, Maria so fully embodied the hated seductress that many of the same audience members would gladly have stabbed her themselves. She played the scene as if she not only detested Don José for not being the man she originally thought he was, but for coming back into her life once she'd found love and trying to drag her back down to his level. The scene was directed as an intricate, frightening tug of war between two obsessive people.

"*Pour la dernière fois, démon, Veux-tu me suivre?*" Riccardo sang, grabbing Maria's wrist as she turned to get away from him.

"*Non! Non! Cette bague, autrefois, tu me l'avais donnée . . . Tiens!*" Maria replied, wresting herself from his grasp. She took the ring from her finger—a ring that Don José had given to Carmen earlier—and flung it at him.

Riccardo caught her wrist again and twisted her around so that her back was to the audience. "*Eh bien, damnée. . . .*" He drew out his knife, raised it above her, and plunged it into her back. Her entire body seemed to stiffen in a surprised convulsion.

There was an audible gasp in the audience as a stream of bright red spread across the back of the pristine white dress. Maria slid down to the floor, her clawlike hands clutching at Riccardo, then relaxing.

The chorus could be heard singing from inside the bullring as Riccardo rose to his feet. Then the gates sprung open behind him and some of the chorus members rushed onto the stage, stopping in their tracks and crying out in shock when they saw what he'd done.

Riccardo looked down at the limp form and sang:

> *Vous pouvez m'arréter. . . . C'est moi qui l'ai tuée.*
> *Ah, Carmen! Ma Carmen adorée!*

The audience was already standing before the curtain had completely descended on the tableau. The applause was thunderous, punctuated by shouts of "Bravo!"

The cast remained frozen in place until the curtain touched the stage. Then the rest of the cast began to run onstage into their positions for the curtain call.

Maria sprang to her feet, glared furiously at Riccardo, and slapped him hard across the face.

"How dare you! How dare you! Stupido!"

One of the female supers, hurrying onto the stage, saw Maria's back and let out a scream.

"Shut up, you stupid girl!" the diva yelled. "It's a blood bag! Stage blood!"

One of the chorus members took the super by the hand and led her into place, whispering something in her ear.

"What in the hell is the matter with you?" said Riccardo, rubbing his cheek as they left the stage so that the curtains could be raised for the bows.

"You know what I'm talking about!" she said furiously. "You hit me so hard with that damned knife that I'll have a bruise tomorrow, you bastard! And you did it on purpose!"

"No, I didn't!" he said innocently. "If I did hurt you, it was a mistake."

The volume of the cheering crowd was raised with the curtain as the chorus took their bows.

"A mistake! You were able to do that scene for six months without hurting me! It was a mistake, all right! Only you're the one who made it!"

Riccardo heaved a sigh. "Maria, you will always take everything personally! I assure you that I didn't mean to hurt you, and I'm sorry if I did." He put his hands out to her in a theatrically pleading gesture. "Please forgive me, my Carmen."

"Oh, you are very funny," she said with increasing fury. On stage the secondary characters were taking their bows two by two.

"And on the other hand," Riccardo continued with a mock pout, "the slap you gave me you did on purpose."

"Shut up! You know what you did! And I know why you did it! You're trying to throw me off balance! But it's not going to work!"

There was a renewed cheering in the audience as Gabrielle, then Franco, took their individual bows.

Just before he went out on stage, Riccardo said, "I really have no idea what you are talking about."

He walked past her, and Maria stood in the wings seething, both at what had just happened and at the ovation the crowd was giving him. He bowed to the left, the center, and the right, then extended his hand in Maria's direction.

Some of Maria's fury died away as she walked out in front of the audience, whose ovation intensified even more at the sight of her. She came to a stop at center stage, faced the audience and inclined her head ever so slightly. It was a calculated move, one that she'd adopted very early on, that seemed to convey a sense of humility on the part of the diva and could send the audience into an absolute frenzy, as it did that night.

Far from allowing herself to be put off balance by what she believed was Riccardo's purposeful attack of the night before, Maria threw herself even more defiantly into her role at the Saturday night preview. The only alteration in her performance came during the final scene, when Riccardo grabbed her and turned her back to the audience. She glared into his eyes and stiffened her back ahead of time, bracing herself for the expected blow and almost defying him to try it again.

But the blow didn't come. Riccardo raised the knife above her and plunged it downward, but "pulled it" expertly, then pressed down on the blood bag concealed in the back of her dress.

The effect from the audience's standpoint was startling. It

looked as if he had viciously stabbed her, and was then pressing the knife further into her back. The blood spread across the white dress, drawing the usual shocked reaction from the audience.

It was about a half an hour after the Saturday night performance that Riccardo wandered into Maria's dressing room. He was dressed in a white shirt, unbuttoned halfway down, and a pair of black pants. He'd showered and his wet hair was slicked back. Maria had removed her stage makeup and was in the process of touching herself up for the street.

"Was that better tonight?" Riccardo asked.

"What?" She rather pointedly behaved as if she didn't know what he was referring to.

"The stabbing."

"Yes. At least you managed to do it without breaking any of my bones."

"I tried to do it even more gently than usual. I wanted to prove to you that last night was an accident."

She shot a glance at him that spoke volumes: She didn't believe him for a minute. "In other words, you managed to do it tonight the way you are supposed to. The way you did it for six months, without hurting me." She took up her own cup of coffee and took a sip, then replaced it.

Riccardo knelt beside her. Any artifice that might have been in his manner a moment before drained away. He took her hand in his. "Maria, I've told you before, again and again, that I love you. I would never do anything to hurt you."

"Of course you wouldn't," she replied curtly, snatching her hand away.

"How can you be so cold to me? You told me you loved me once."

"Poor Ricky," Maria said, brushing her hair. "My feelings haven't changed toward you."

He was caught in a moment of uncertainty. Her tone and

manner made it obvious that she was lying, as much as he would've liked to believe her. Despite what he'd heard a few nights ago through her hotel room door, and despite what he knew, he still harbored the dim hope that she loved him, and that he could hold on to her. But then it began to sink into his heart that perhaps she wasn't lying now. Maybe her feelings really hadn't changed toward him. Maybe she had never loved him.

"Would you like to go out for a bite to eat?" he said slowly, already knowing what the answer would be.

"I can't. Tony is waiting for me," she replied simply.

"Tony."

"I'm going to eat with him. He asked me earlier. What could I say?"

"Tomorrow night, then. Before the opening. An early supper?"

She hesitated as she laid her brush on the counter, then picked up her coffee cup and took another sip. "I'm afraid I can't do that."

"Why?"

She got up and went into the bathroom. Riccardo could hear her turn on the tap. She called out to him, "I'm sure you'll understand. Tony is in town just for a few days, and he's coming to the opening. I promised to dine with him."

"Suddenly you prefer him to me?" Riccardo replied, rising to his feet.

"Of course not! It's strictly business. He's my manager. I have to spend time with him. And he asked me first." She sounded as if she resented his doubts.

"Oh, I know what he is," Riccardo said meaningfully.

"Ricky, you are so ridiculous!"

He fought the urge to scold her for corrupting his name. "Am I?"

The taps were turned off and Maria appeared in the doorway of the bathroom, drying her hands with a small royal blue towel, just as Riccardo stuck his hands in his pockets.

She eyed him quizzically. "Yes, you are."

"What exactly is he managing for you?"

"My career."

"That is settled for the next couple of years, isn't it?"

"Mmm." She flashed a maddeningly coquettish smile and tossed the towel into the bathroom.

"I know Tony is . . . charming," Riccardo said, almost choking on the word, "but I think even he would have trouble breaking your contract."

She crossed the room and retrieved her coffee cup. "My contract? There will be no need for him to do anything—anything at all—about my contract."

"Really?" He knew that she had to get out of her agreement with the company, so she was lying again. But he couldn't for the life of him figure out exactly what she was playing at now, or when she was going to tell him the truth.

"None whatsoever." She downed the remainder of her coffee in one gulp. "Now, if you'll excuse me . . ."

"Certainly," he said, a smile spreading across his face. "Enjoy your dinner."

He walked out of the room.

5

Sunday brunch in the Sheridan household was eaten with the reverence with which Margaret Sheridan felt everything should be done on the Sabbath. Not that meals were ever joyous occasions at the Sheridan table, but there was an additional, oppressive solemnity about them on Sundays, as if God himself were at the table casting a pall over the proceedings. It was an attitude that Steven had never been able to understand, since his mother was otherwise an irreligious person who, he believed, would take the existence of God as an affront to her own supremacy. She attended church out of social responsibility rather than belief. But like everything else in his life, Steven went along with it.

On the Sunday morning of the day the Sheridan Center was set to open, Edward Carnegie was invited to partake of the sacred brunch. It was more of an edict than an invitation. He arrived about a quarter of an hour before the appointed time wearing a crisp navy blue suit and was shown into the dining room by a gray-uniformed maid. Although she directed him to the seat he would occupy during the meal, he preferred to remain standing until he was joined by his hostess and host.

The table was set with fine china and silver. There was a round platter of sliced fresh fruit, separate serving dishes of scrambled eggs and bacon, and a rack holding diagonally sliced toast.

Carnegie didn't have long to wait. Steven had heard his arrival and hurried downstairs to greet him.

"Edward! It's nice to see you," he said with awkward formality.

Carnegie took the extended hand and shook it. Their hands lingered together a little longer than strictly necessary.

"How are things going today?" he asked quietly.

"We'll see in a minute."

Margaret Sheridan's heavy perfume reached the dining room before she did. She was wearing a deep purple suit and a thin gold bracelet. Her antique clips were framed by stiff curves of hair around her ears.

"Good morning, Mr. Carnegie," she said without looking at him as she crossed the room.

"Good morning, Mrs. Sheridan. It was nice of you to invite me."

Mrs. Sheridan took her place at the head of the table. "Be seated, please."

Edward and Steven took their places, Edward at her left and Steven at her right, directly across from each other.

"Steven will pour," Mrs. Sheridan announced.

Her son complied, serving out coffee from the silver pot.

"Help yourself," she added as she spooned some eggs onto her plate.

"Thank you," Carnegie replied.

"I assume that everything is in readiness for this evening."

"Everything is going quite smoothly."

"I'm very pleased to hear it. I must admit, I had some reservations about your appointment as director."

"That's understandable."

"You are, after all, rather young. But so far, you've certainly delivered on your promise."

"Thank you."

"I also should say that with my reservations, if it hadn't been for my son's glowing recommendation, I wouldn't have sponsored you."

Something resembling a smirk flashed across Steven's face. "Mother isn't being entirely straightforward. My opinion has never held that much weight with her."

Mrs. Sheridan's head pivoted in his direction, and she stared at him coldly for several seconds. Then she turned back to her guest. "My son is quite correct, Mr. Carnegie. I would not have proceeded on his word . . . alone. Of course, I had you looked into myself."

Carnegie was in the process of scooping some fruit from the platter. He stopped with his spoon in midair. "I beg your pardon?"

"I had you investigated," she repeated without inflection. "By the Lazar Detective Agency."

Carnegie glanced at Steven, who appeared completely unmoved by this revelation.

"I don't know that I like that," said Carnegie.

Mrs. Sheridan turned to him with a faintly surprised look on her face. "I had never heard of you, and you were being considered for a position of great importance. Of course I had you looked into." She glanced at his spoon, which reminded him that he was still holding it suspended over his plate. He resumed serving himself.

"And what did this investigation of yours turn up?"

"Nothing of any significance. Nothing I didn't suspect."

"Suspect?"

"Perhaps that was a poor choice of words. I should say, nothing that I didn't already believe."

"Such as?"

She chewed for a moment, swallowed, then dabbed the corners of her mouth with a cloth napkin. "Steven told me that he knew you from college. He led me to believe that the relationship ended there."

"That's not exactly accurate, Mother," Steven said dispassionately. "I didn't say anything about whether or not I'd seen Edward since graduating college."

"Exactly," she replied.

"It didn't have anything to do with his qualifications for the job."

"On that we agree. His actual qualifications were outstanding, as far as they went. There was no doubt at all about that."

"As far as they went?" Carnegie asked.

"You were experienced, but perhaps not quite so much as I would have preferred."

"Then why did you hire me?"

"Given your relationship to my son, I thought perhaps it might be best to have you close at hand. Especially since Steven has seen fit to remain silent about it."

Carnegie started to serve himself some eggs, then changed his mind and re-covered the plate. "It wasn't a secret that we knew each other, Mrs. Sheridan. Steven and I have remained in touch. That's how he knew enough to recommend me."

"I see. I just thought it was odd that I had never heard anything about you before."

"I don't know why you would have. We don't see each other that often."

Mrs. Sheridan paused in her eating and turned toward him, her expression positively frosty. Either she didn't believe him or she knew that wasn't true. "Frequency doesn't concern me so much as the nature of your relationship. We are a very old family, Mr. Carnegie, with a very important, prestigious name."

Carnegie found the attention a bit disconcerting. "We're friends, Mrs. Sheridan."

"I trust that you understand just how precious I believe our family name to be, and behave accordingly," she said pointedly. She then resumed eating.

There was nothing overtly threatening in her tone. There didn't need to be. Carnegie knew that she held his future in her hands, and that with her local power and her money, she could probably destroy him if she wanted to. At least, she believed she could.

Edward looked over at Steven, who still seemed unruffled by the proceedings. Steven gave an almost imperceptible shake of his head.

"So, you watched the rehearsal," Mrs. Sheridan said conversationally, tacitly letting him know that the subject was closed. "Was it everything you had hoped it would be?"

"It's very impressive," he replied blankly.

"Good. I want the opening of the Center to be a memorable event."

"I promise you, it will be unforgettable."

Tony Leonard turned over on his side and propped himself up with his left arm. "Are you feeling better?"

"Yes," Maria replied wearily. "I felt better right after . . . right after I finished being sick. I don't know what's been wrong with me lately."

"Maybe it's the excitement."

"Don't be stupid. Opening-night jitters are for amateurs!"

He laughed ruefully. "I meant the excitement of being with me."

"We haven't really been able to be together . . . that much."

He pushed back the covers and climbed out of bed. "Do you want to get something to eat?"

"I don't know," she mewled. "I'm ravenous, but I don't know that I trust my stomach yet."

Tony paused in the act of slipping his arms into the sleeves of the white terry bathrobe. "Are you sure you feel all right?"

"Yes, yes," she said testily. "I don't understand it. It's as if I've never been sick at all."

He pulled the robe over his shoulders, closed it, and tied the sash at his waist. "I should probably call room service, then. You have to keep up your strength." He started for the phone, but was stopped by a loud pounding on the door to the room. Maria was so startled by the noise that her body gave a violent jerk.

"Maria!" David Cunningham's voice boomed through the door. "Maria! Are you in there? Open the door!" There was a pause during which Tony shot a questioning glance at Maria, who was looking at the door with a wicked half-smile.

"Maria!" David yelled, renewing his assault on the door, which sounded as if it might splinter. "Open up, dammit!"

Tony crossed the room and turned the knob. "What the hell are you doing?" he asked as Cunningham came into view.

David screwed up his face with distaste. "Leonard! I should have known you were behind this!"

"What?"

"This!" David waved a very wrinkled section of the newspaper so close to the manager's face that he fell back a step. David stormed past him and went directly to the bed. Maria was now sitting up with her back against the headboard. She drew her legs up and wrapped her arms around them like a happy child.

"What's the meaning of this?" he said, shaking the paper at her.

"What are you talking about?" she replied casually.

"This! This!" The section he was holding was Arts and Leisure, the front page of which was devoted to the anticipated Heidi West article about the opera company and the opening of the Sheridan Center. He angrily tapped his index finger against a paragraph that had been circled in red. "It says here that next season, you're going to be singing at the Met!"

"Let me see that," said Tony. He took the paper from David's hand and quietly scanned the paragraph. Then he looked at Maria over the top of the paper and pursed his lips disapprovingly.

"What does this mean?" Cunningham demanded again.

"I think it is very clear."

"You're not going to be at the Met next season! You're going to be in Santa Marta, singing with our company!"

"You see it there in black and white," she said with a shrug. "The paper tells you where I will be."

He turned on Tony. "And you! I thought more of you than to pull something like this!"

"I didn't know anything about it." When David raised his eyebrows in disbelief, the manager amended his statement. "I mean I didn't know anything about it being announced in the paper. I don't know how they got hold of it. Yes, Maria does have an offer from the Met. I thought we would discuss it with you. I told Maria that you are a reasonable person, and that you wouldn't stand in her way."

"Stand in her way! You think it would be standing in her way to expect her to honor her contract? To expect her to give something back to the people who gave her her opportunity? Without us, she wouldn't be getting calls from any other god-damn company!" He turned to Maria and found her smiling up at him. "And let me set you straight! I hope you haven't signed anything with them yet, because we're going to hold you to your contract! If you don't, I'll haul your ass into court so fast you won't know what hit you!"

"No, you won't," Maria said calmly.

"What?"

"You will not haul me into court." She sounded so confident that some of Cunningham's anger faded in confusion.

"I've got news for you—"

She cut him off. "If you take me to court, the only thing you will do is make yourself look bad. You will make your little opera company look even smaller than it is, and pettier. You'll look like you are desperate to hold on to the *real* talent for your survival, as if your foolish little company couldn't survive without me. Worse yet, you'll look like you are selfishly trying to hold back a great talent! A talent that *made* your little company!"

David sputtered. "That's . . . that's absurd!"

"No, it is not. And you know it! Do you think that in these months I haven't learned how to use the press? Do you not think I could sit with a reporter, all dressed in white, and hit the right note of simpering so effectively that they will look at me as your helpless victim? I will look like the injured party!"

Cunningham drew back as if slapped. "No. I think it's entirely possible that you could do that."

"Then it would not be advisable for you to cross me, or that is exactly what will happen."

"Do you know how quickly word of this will spread?" Cunningham said after a stunned pause. "Within a month, every opera company in the world will know you pulled this. I'll see to it!"

"Please do. A difficult diva! That will be news to them all! All they will do is believe that I must be worth the trouble."

Cunningham started for her, almost as if compelled to attack against his will, but Tony anticipated him and managed to grab him by the shoulders.

"No! I think you'd better leave."

Cunningham continued to glare at Maria for several seconds. "You unholy bitch of a fishwife! I could kill you!"

"Please," Tony said with a measure of gentleness. He sounded as if he could understand the impulse, but still would have none of it.

Cunningham made a sharp, frustrated gesture with his hands, then turned and walked quickly from the room, slamming the door behind him.

"Jesus Christ! I've never seen him like that," said Tony as he sat on the edge of the bed. He looked down at the paper. "I wonder how this West woman found out about the Met deal."

"That's easy," said Maria. "I called her and told her about it."

"You what?"

"I told her myself. I wanted it in the article."

"But why? You must've known what it would cause!"

"What do I care about these people!" she said with a dismissive wave of her hand. "In another year, their company will no longer exist!"

Tony sighed. "Why couldn't we handle this like . . . gentlemen?"

"Gentlemen! Wrangling back and forth for months to no purpose! That is what behaving like 'gentlemen' would get me! I don't have the time or the patience for such stupidity!" She pointed at the newspaper. "This is the best way. It's public from the first. This way, anything that they try to do to me will be public. You'll see. Soon David will realize that it is futile to pursue the matter, and then he will give us no trouble at all."

Tony shook his head slowly. "Maria, I wish you had let me handle it. It's not good to leave bad feelings like this behind."

"It's better this way. The wound is cauterized immediately." She snapped her fingers. "We are rid of him."

Tony eyed her for a moment. Although he was drawn to her by her obvious beauty and vitality, and nobody admired her talent more than he did, until this moment he hadn't realized just how dangerous it was to trifle with her. "I hope you never want to be rid of me."

She smiled. "That will never happen."

The lobby of the Dover Hotel was a sea of activity. A line of people were waiting to check in and check out, while others rushed by with a variety of luggage and garment bags, pausing momentarily to drop off keys and drop paperwork in the express-checkout box on the front desk.

Gabrielle Charbonneau stepped off the elevator into the minor mayhem. She paused for a moment to get her bearings, finding the bustle a bit daunting, then nodded to herself with decision. She went into the hall to the right of the elevators, which led to Superella, the hotel's restaurant. She was so lost in thought that she almost collided with Franco Giannini.

"Oh!" she exclaimed, coming to a halt when she saw him.

"Franco! I just knocked on your door. You weren't there."

"No, we were just having breakfast."

She could barely hide her disappointment. "You've already eaten. That's why I stopped by your room, to see if you wanted to have breakfast."

"I'm so sorry. That's a shame. We just now finished. You remember Paul Chamberlain?" He indicated the gentleman standing to his left.

"How do you do?" she said halfheartedly. It was difficult for her to master up any enthusiasm for introductions as her plans crumbled before her eyes. Having failed to find Franco in his room, she'd hoped to catch him in the restaurant and join him. Now she'd have to eat alone.

"Did you hear what happened?" she said, turning back to Franco.

"I read about it in the paper this morning."

"In the paper? Anything she does makes news now, doesn't it?"

"It's fairly important news, at least for us."

Gabrielle's eyes widened. "Is she that sick?"

Franco and Paul glanced at each other with some confusion, then Franco said, "What are you talking about?"

"Last night. I got back from the theater before she did. I was in the bar when she arrived. She was white as a sheet. Her manager was with her—that Tony What's-his-name. I went to see what was wrong, and he said that they had been going to go out to eat, but she became ill on the way to the restaurant and they'd had to hurry back here. I asked if she wanted help up to her room, but she just cursed at me."

"That, at least, is typical," Franco said with a sympathetic smile. "But that's not what I read about in the paper. It seems our diva is leaving us."

"What!" Gabrielle's jaw dropped open.

He nodded. "She's gotten a surprise offer from the Met for next season, so it looks like she won't be with us."

"But . . . but . . . what will we do?" From the conflicting

emotions crossing her face, it was apparent she couldn't decide whether the detrimental aspects of this announcement out-weighed the positive ones.

"Well, Gabrielle, to paraphrase the song, we will survive. I should think our happy little company will be a lot more peaceful if we don't have to suffer the dubious charms of our resident prima donna."

She wasn't looking at him. Instead, her eyes were trained on the floor, and she was shaking her head in disbelief. "No . . . no, she can't do this. I have to talk to Riccardo."

She hurried away from them, back toward the elevators, without another word.

"That girl is really a study," said Paul Chamberlain, who had remained silent during this exchange.

"Oh, leave her alone," Franco said, laughing.

The slightly dulled sense of anticipation of the preview perform-ances gave way to a full-blown, festival-like feeling of expectancy on opening night. Twin searchlights scoured the sky, their beams rippling across low hanging clouds. Red velvet ropes stretched from the stone lions to the parkway, forming an entryway where cabs, cars, and limousines could disgorge their elegant passen-gers. And a red carpet had literally been rolled out down the stairs.

The media was out in force. Crews from all the local stations were set up in strategic locations so that the staircase and arriv-ing first-nighters could serve as the backdrop for their taped sto-ries. The print media was also on hand, bulbs flashing at such a rapid-fire rate that the whole scene looked as if it were being showered with oversized glitter.

With so much action and so many important people in at-tendance, none of the reporters noticed the dignified, bright-eyed elderly woman who was helped from a cab by a young female escort. Emily Charters held Lynn Francis's arm lightly as they slowly ascended the steps. The commotion didn't really bother the old woman: She was too preoccupied with getting into the theater safely to pay the lights and the crowd much mind. With her free hand she kept the hem of her long black dress slightly raised as a precaution against tripping, which she thought was a danger given that the temporary carpet, though a nice touch, didn't look particularly stable.

The glass doors were held open by a pair of young blond men in grayish blue uniforms. They greeted the ladies with almost identical, charming smiles, and the one nearest Emily raised two fingers to the brim of his cap in a respectful salute.

The outer lobby was crammed with bodies: A long line of people trying to pick up their tickets snaked away from the box office, while the rest of the crowd became the human equivalent of sand in an hourglass, seeping through the four doors where their tickets would be checked. Emily and Lynn edged forward carefully, all the while being jostled by the throng of people eager to see the inside of the newest jewel in the city's crown. When they reached the door, a sober young woman took their tickets, glanced at them, tore them in half and said "Aisle three on your right" as she handed the stubs to Lynn.

"Oh, dear!" Emily exclaimed, wide-eyed, as they stepped into the inner lobby.

Inside there was the steady roar of a thousand milling people, all talking at cross-purposes and trying to be heard over one another, amplified by the hollow echo off the polished marble walls and floor of the cavernous room. On the landing at the halfway mark of the sweeping main staircase, a string quartet vainly tried to be heard above the crowd. As a special treat for the occasion, exotic-looking hors d'oeuvres, most of them in colors that didn't occur naturally in food, were circulated by very young, pleasant waiters and waitresses who appeared to be enjoying themselves immensely.

"Are you all right, Emily?" Lynn asked.

"Yes, of course. I just don't think I've ever seen so much conspicuous affluence in one place in all my life."

Lynn laughed attractively. "Yeah. You can smell the money. Look at that." She discreetly gestured at a woman who was passing nearby. The woman was wearing a white evening gown, cinched beneath nonexistent breasts, and a necklace made up of several rows of large diamonds. "If there's a power failure, she can lead us all to safety."

Emily chuckled quietly. Her attention was then drawn to a rather pudgy man, standing about fifty feet away, who was engaged in conversation with a small cadre of people.

"Isn't that the mayor?" she said.

Lynn craned her neck. "Yep. You're out with the luminaries tonight, Emily."

"I didn't think he went out on Sundays."

Lynn frowned. "The tickets must've been free. Would you like something to drink?"

"Oh, no, my dear. I think I'd like to find our seats, if you don't mind."

"Not at all!" She offered the old woman her arm.

Lynn carefully shepherded Emily through the mass of people to a door above which was a faux antique lantern embossed with AISLE 3. Lynn handed the stubs to the usher who was waiting in the doorway. He glanced down at them, said, "Follow me," and took off down the aisle.

"Come along, Emily," Lynn said loudly. "We have to hurry. The usher seems to be in a footrace."

He didn't stop or turn around, but he slowed down considerably. Still a bit ahead of them, he came to a halt by row eleven and waited with a surprising degree of chagrin. When they reached him, he handed them each a program and said very softly, "Sorry, ladies. The place is mobbed and I wasn't thinking. I didn't mean to rush you. Seats one-oh-one and one-oh-two."

"That's quite all right, young man." Emily's opinion of him rose a notch.

He smiled and went back up the aisle. Emily and Lynn took their seats, which were the first two on the aisle.

"My, my!" said Emily as she smoothed her dress. "Your friend certainly got us very good seats!"

"She got us the very best she could. The first ten rows were reserved for VIPs and friends of the cast."

Once they'd settled themselves, they spent some time taking in the surroundings.

"What do you think?" Lynn asked.

"It's a lovely theater. Very grand."

Lynn pursed her lips and pushed her hair back behind her ears. "All right, Emily, out with it. What are you thinking?"

Emily returned an impish smile. "Just that this theater has been made to look—on the inside, at least—like the beautiful old theaters, like the ones we have downtown. It's grand, but it's imitation grandeur, if you know what I mean."

"Um-hm."

"Oh, there's nothing wrong with it. It's like furniture that's been designed to look like antiques. They're lovely in their own right, but they're not the real thing."

They fell silent for a while as they perused their programs.

"I really don't know what you'll think of this," Lynn said, flapping the program closed.

"Of what?"

"This opera. Everything I've read about it said that it's very innovative. I don't know how promising that is."

"I'm sure I'll enjoy it," Emily said brightly. Her gaze traveled to the box seats on the right side of the auditorium. "Ah! The benefactress of the theater has arrived."

Lynn followed her gaze and saw the woman just entering the box. She was dressed in a black gown with a matching wrap draped over her shoulders. As she came into view, there was a noticeable rise in the roaring murmur of the audience.

"Who's that?" Lynn asked.

"That is Margaret Sheridan, wife of the late Edwin Sheridan for whom this theater is named. I believe the young man is her son."

They watched as Steven lifted the wrap from his mother's shoulders and hung it on a hook out of sight. He then held the back of her chair as she sat. He leaned down and said something to her, then left the box.

"Interesting." Emily sighed as she went back to reading her program.

Lynn glanced at her watch. "Fifteen minutes to go."

The atmosphere backstage was highly charged. As on most opening nights, the tension made everyone feel as if they were in the midst of controlled chaos. Added to this were the discordant sounds of several individuals vocalizing, which seemed to be coming from everywhere at once.

The members of the chorus, in reaction to the kinetic energy of the locally hired supernumeraries, were overcompensating with a blasé attitude that none of them really felt. The effort to appear perfectly calm caused some of them additional stress. At the same time, this display of confidence on the part of the chorus made the already anxious supers feel more underrehearsed than they really were.

When Riccardo arrived at the Center he put his sports bag in his dressing room and went next door to see Maria. There were several vases of roses, two of them on stands, and one box of flowers that had yet to be opened was lying on the counter. The perfume was thick and overpowering. Maria wasn't there yet.

The knot in Riccardo's stomach tightened. It had been there since he'd read the paper that morning, and had done nothing but twist and turn over the course of the day as he'd tried to get Maria to answer the phone or the door. He spat on the floor and went back to his room.

Once there, he picked up one of the packets of coffee that were lying on the counter, put a filter in the top compartment of the coffeemaker, then emptied the packet into the filter and shut the lid. He then took the pot into the bathroom, filled it with water, came back to the coffeemaker, and poured the water into its receptacle. He switched on the machine.

"Oh, good, you're here!" Sherman Dunston said as he bustled into the room. "Would you mind if I did your makeup now?"

"No."

Riccardo sat down in his chair and Sherman went to work on him. After a couple of minutes, the makeup artist paused and frowned. "Are you nervous?"

"Why do you ask?"

"Your face is very taut."

"I am not nervous," Riccardo replied slowly.

Sherman shrugged and went back to work.

They soon heard the diva's arrival. Through the wall came a squeal of delight as she entered her dressing room and discovered the wealth of floral tributes. She then chattered excitedly to her assistant as she read the cards.

Then, unexpectedly, there was a shriek.

"What the hell was that?" said Sherman.

"The excitement of opening night," Riccardo said without concern.

Next door, Maria flung the now-opened box to the floor. "Bastard!"

"What's the matter?" Barbara asked.

"Look at them! Lilies!"

"They're beautiful."

"Beautiful?" Maria spat back with contempt. "Idiot! Lilies mean death!"

"Well, they're kind of odd for an opening-night tribute," Barbara said, kneeling and gathering the scattered flowers back into the box, "but I don't think they're supposed to mean anything."

"You don't think! That is the problem! These flowers are a warning!"

There was a gentle tap at the door. Maria barked "Come in," and the door opened, but not far. Carl Watson, the stage manager, poked his head in. "Is everything all right, Ms. Cortez?"

"Of course it is!" Maria said after a beat.

"I thought I heard you scream."

Maria glared down at the flowers, then back up at Watson. "Everything is fine. The stupid girl just dropped my flowers. That's all."

After a pause, Watson said, "Oh!" and withdrew, looking suitably perplexed.

"Do you want me to throw them away?" Barbara asked.

"No. I will not give him the satisfaction!"

"Who?"

Maria narrowed her large eyes. "Whoever sent them, of course. I want you to find a vase and put them over there where I can see them always!"

"Whatever you say."

Sherman applied the finishing touches to Riccardo's makeup. "Well, time for me to do madam." He picked up his coffee mug and started to gather up the rest of his paraphernalia.

"No!" Riccardo's voice wasn't particularly loud, but it was authoritative enough to stop the young man.

"What?"

Riccardo got up. "I want to talk to her first."

He brushed past the little man, went directly to the adjacent room, and flung open the door. Maria and Barbara were so startled that they froze for a second.

"Barbara, leave us!" said Riccardo.

She hesitated, looking to her mistress. Riccardo's tone was all Maria needed to slap her awake.

"How dare you order her about!" she said indignantly.

He didn't falter. "Get out!"

Barbara jumped, then hurried from the room. He closed the door behind her.

"I suppose you are responsible for this," Maria said, fingering one of the lilies.

"What?" His determination was momentarily diverted with surprise.

"I suppose it was meant to scare me. If that's the case, you've failed again!"

"I don't know what you're talking about! I didn't send you any flowers."

"Of course you didn't," she said with a superior smile. "You would never try to to frighten me, just as you would never try to hurt me!"

"Enough!" he yelled, taking control. "I'm not here to talk about your ridiculous suspicions!"

"Then why are you here?"

"You know why! If you didn't, you wouldn't have been avoiding me all day!"

"I've done nothing of the sort. I haven't even thought of you all day."

"Oh, yes you have," he said evenly. "You must've known I would see the article in the paper this morning."

She flashed a malicious smile. "It was a nice article, I thought."

He stepped closer to her. "Until this morning I tried to believe that you wouldn't do it. That we had something together and you wouldn't throw it away. But now I know you mean to leave me!"

"What of it? We're both adults! I have to take the opportunities as they come to me. I can't wait around for you to be asked to the Met, if that ever happens!"

"I would never have held you back! Even if we had to be separated for a while, I still would have loved you . . . if only you had loved me!"

"This again!" she said loudly, throwing up her hands.

"But now I know you don't. You were going to go away without even telling me."

She looked at him for a long moment, then said simply, "As you say, I expected you would see the article."

"And Tony? Your manager? Will he be going with you?"

"Tony lives in New York."

He stared down at the seated woman, who did little more than calmly take a sip from her paper cup of coffee while she trampled his heart.

"You told me you loved me," he said.

She shrugged. "Maybe I did, once."

This was too much for him. His face flushed, and he exploded. "I won't let you go!"

"You won't *let* me!" she replied shrilly, rising from her chair. "You won't stop me! I'm sick of you! You turn my stomach! You act like a child!" She screwed up her face and mimicked him. " 'You said you loved me'! That's something that a child would say! If I did, then it's over and done with! If you want someone to love, why don't you go to that fat, lovesick cow of a girl who always moons over you!"

"What?" His voice was hollow with confusion.

"Gabrielle!" She spat the name back at him.

"She's like a sister to me."

"That's not what she'd like to be to you!"

His face hardened. "I don't want Gabrielle, I want—"

His fury was interrupted by a tentative rap on the door.

"Come!" Maria said unceremoniously.

The door was opened by Edward Carnegie, who had Steven Sheridan by his side.

"I'm . . . I'm sorry to interrupt," Edward said. Both men looked terribly embarrassed by the scene they'd walked into. "We've met before. I'm Edward Carnegie."

"I remember," Maria said with a cordiality that seemed impossible to the two men given what they'd heard as they'd approached the room. Riccardo grunted something unintelligible.

"This is Steven Sheridan. His family funded this Center."

"I'm pleased to meet you," said Maria.

"We just wanted to stop by and officially thank you all for lending your talents to the opening of the Center."

"On behalf of my family, I can second that," said Steven. "We're grateful to have such a renowned production as our opening."

Riccardo had been standing to the side, fighting to remain civil. When the pause occurred in the conversation, he blurted out, "Excuse me, I must get ready" and left the diva and the two bewildered guests behind.

He stopped in his tracks as he entered his dressing room. Gabrielle was seated in his chair at the counter. She was looking down at her hands, folded in her lap. Tears were streaming down her face.

She slowly raised her reddened eyes to him. "I just wanted to wish you luck."

He started to say something, but she bolted from the room.

Emily took note of Steven Sheridan's return to his mother's side. The auditorium was now almost completely filled, with only a few stragglers left hurrying to their seats. Her attention was drawn to a sullen young man who came out the door on the right side of the auditorium near the stage.

"Oh," she said to Lynn, "I believe that's the man who formed the opera company. His picture was in the paper this morning."

"Hmm," said Lynn. "He doesn't look very happy, does he?"

"Indeed."

David Cunningham slumped across to the second aisle and sat in the empty seat at the end of the third row.

As the lights dimmed, the excitement in the air was so tangible it was as if live wires were dancing over the heads of the audience. The houselights faded away. When the conductor, bathed in a spotlight, ascended from the low entrance in the pit and took his place, the audience broke into enthusiastic applause. He bowed to the audience, turned around, raised his baton dramatically, and with a single swift swipe, the orchestra, the production, and the new theater officially sprang to life.

When the curtains opened, there was an audible gasp from the audience at the sight of the massive set.

"Dear God!" Lynn whispered to Emily. "That looks like real stone!"

Emily nodded.

The slightly increased tempo at which the opening was played might not have pleased purists, but it enhanced the sense of activity in the square. Then Gabrielle entered as Micaela. Her makeup had been hastily repaired, and anyone would have thought that the anxiety she showed as she asked after her love, Don José, was the result of excellent acting.

The audience was equally impressed with Riccardo's Don José. Although he radiated a handsome and masterful presence, he managed to seem forlorn, conveying a man who was more lost than a soldier should be.

But the real sparks started to fly when Maria hit the stage. As she sang "Habanera," her deep, full-bodied voice caressed every man who came within her reach. She wandered among them, dripping sensuality, fully aware of the effect she was having and yet uncaring of the outcome.

True to Marc Berger's vision, the chorus had been carefully choreographed in a way that naturally punctuated the music. When they took up the melody, the women moved forward in a gently twirling motion, each on the hand of the men. The effect was of slowly increasing perpetual motion: something that would have been little more than an interesting gimmick were it not for the fact that the vocals didn't suffer in the least. Rather, it seemed as if Carmen was casting her hypnotic spell over everyone in the square, and they were all too willing to go along. The dance continued, the formations becoming more intricate and complicated, with Maria weaving her way through it all. When the song came to its end, the audience cheered.

The rest of the performance built from there. In the scene at the inn of Lillas Pastia, the "Gypsy Song" was accompanied by a lively flamenco dance, in which many of the chorus members, and finally Carmen herself, joined.

But even that was topped by the arrival of Franco Giannini as Escamillo, the toreador. His straight-backed bearing and confidence matched the dynamic music. His booming baritone took instant command of the revelers at the inn, and the audience as well, whose sense of decorum was the only thing that kept them from leaping to their feet at the end of the song.

There was no doubt in the minds of the audience that the prepublicity for the opera had not been an exaggeration. The cast as a whole, unknown though they might have been, were outstanding, and Maria Cortez in particular was a force to be reckoned with. Not only was her voice rich and vibrant, she could also dance and act. In the later scene when she taunted Don José for wanting to run back to his barracks at the sound of the bugle, her contempt for him seemed to emanate from the core of her being.

During the second intermission, Lynn and Emily went out into the lobby to stretch their legs and enjoy a cold drink. The atmosphere in the lobby was positively joyous. Apparently the general consensus among the audience was that they were seeing something truly remarkable, and nothing quite equals the pleasure of witnessing a fine performance.

"What do you think?" said Lynn as she took a sip of ginger ale.

"It's being very well sung," Emily replied, "which is the most important part. But I don't think I've ever seen it more well acted."

"You don't mind the so-called 'innovations'?"

She shook her head. "I don't know that it's quite as innovative as they would like us to believe, but the way it's being performed really is rather exciting."

The atmosphere backstage was quite different from the front of the house. In the common dressing rooms, the chorus were tempting fate with early congratulations on another triumph, and the supers seemed almost stupefied by the success they were enjoying. But the principals had come off the stage and retreated separately to their dressing rooms without uttering a word to each other, both in the first intermission and in the present one.

Riccardo sat alone, nursing his festering pride. He refilled his coffee cup and took some sips from it while trying to decide what to do. Then he reluctantly took himself down the short hall to Gabrielle's room. He knocked lightly on the door, and heard her call "Come in."

She looked up as he entered. When she saw who it was she immediately lowered her head and said, "Please, Riccardo, I—"

"I just wanted to say . . . I'm sorry."

She raised her eyes to him. "So am I."

The last act opened with the festivities in front of the outer wall of the bullring. The costumes alone were enough to take the audience's breath away. Everyone was dressed in white with slashes of color: red sashes and brightly hued fans, hats, and accessories. Fruit vendors and wine merchants mimed selling their wares, while the ladies danced with delight as they sang.

The apex came when Escamillo entered with Carmen on his arm. In her pristine white dress, Maria fairly glowed in the spotlight. The chorus then went through the upstage gates into the arena.

The tension that had built as Carmen rejected Don José, who in turn became increasingly obsessed with her, was absolutely palpable when he appeared for their fateful, final duet. When Riccardo entered he was also dressed in white, though his clothes were soiled and his vest tattered. His hair was dishevelled and he was sweating heavily. As the horrifying, emotional tug-of-war played out, Don José seemed to be falling more and more out of control. It was so immediate and believable that at one point Emily uttered a quiet "Oh, my!"

Riccardo was almost panting and the sweat was streaming down his face as he caught Maria's wrist, which caused a visible wince throughout her body. When she tried to get away, he twisted her around violently. But instead of allowing her back to be turned to the audience, Maria continued to struggle to get away. All the while they continued their impassioned singing.

When the moment came, Riccardo pulled the knife from his belt with his free hand.

His voice cracked as he sang: *"Pour la dernière fois, demon, Veux-tu me suivre?"*

"Non! Non! Cette bague, autrefois, tu me l'avais donnée . . . Tiens!"

"Eh bien, damneé!"

Maria looked positively terrified as Riccardo swung the knife upward. She struggled with all her might to pull herself away from him. Then, without warning, he let go of her wrist and sent her sprawling backward to the floor of the stage. No longer panting, Riccardo was gasping for breath. The knife fell from his hand and he hunched over sharply, slapping his chest with his palms. He released several heaving coughs, and for a brief moment he stopped moving entirely. Then he crumpled to the floor.

The music stopped prematurely and the curtains were hastily closed. The entire audience was stunned into silence.

Lynn leaned over to Emily. "Now *that* was an innovation!"

6

On Monday morning the media, which had been planning to report on the success or failure of *Carmen* in the entertainment sections of their papers and programs, instead found themselves with front-page news about the dramatic death of Riccardo Nuevo.

Late in the morning Detective Jeremy Ransom was finishing a case report when his partner came into the office and dropped onto the ancient Naugahyde couch that was pushed up against the wall.

"Don't tell me," said Ransom.

"It's a suspicious death," Detective Gerald White answered.

"Of course it is."

"Respiratory failure. The ME says the pulmonary edema isn't in keeping with a healthy thirty-year-old man. So it could be—"

"Poisoning. Alkaloid poisoning," Ransom interrupted. "So we have, what? Cocaine, morphine, nicotine, and any one of a thousand other types. Any sign of drug use?"

"Uh-uh."

Ransom tossed his pen on the desk and rose from his chair. "There wouldn't be. How long had it been since he'd eaten?"

"Several hours. Where to first?" said Gerald, following him out of the office. "The theater?"

"No, I think our first stop should be Emily."

"Emily? Why?"

"Because she was there last night."

"You're kidding!"

"There was a murder in the theater, Gerald. Of course Emily would be there."

His partner laughed.

"She and Lynn were supposed to be at the opening."

"So they were in the audience? What could they have seen?"

"Knowing Emily? Everything."

"Jeremy!" Emily exclaimed with pleasure when she opened the door. Although it was her custom to sound surprised to see him, in this instance the reaction was genuine. "And Detective White. How nice to see you! How is your wife and those two little girls of yours?"

"Not so little anymore."

"I was just making some tea. Come along." She led them back to the kitchen, although neither of them needed a guide. Over the years Ransom had become more or less a permanent fixture in Emily's tidy little house, and Gerald had visited there on several occasions as well. "Please, sit down. Would you like some tea?" The detectives politely declined. "What brings you here this morning?"

"The death you witnessed last night," said Ransom.

Emily paused in the midst of switching off the burner under the kettle. "Really?" she said with interest. "Then Riccardo Nuevo was murdered? Hm. Yes, well, that would explain it."

Ransom shot a glance at his partner. "It explains what, Emily?"

She came over to the table and rested her hands on the back of her chair. "Well, Mr. Nuevo collapsed right at the end of the opera, when he was about to stab Carmen. The curtain was rung down immediately. Of course, the audience was stunned, as you might imagine. There was a very short period of complete silence, then quite a bit of . . . I don't know what you'd call it. Buzz?"

"Um-hm?"

"Then a gentleman came out in front of the curtain and introduced himself. He said his name was Edward Carnegie and that he was the head of the theater. He told us that it seemed Mr. Nuevo had had a heart attack. He thanked us all for coming to the opening, then asked us to go home. Given the circumstances, he did it quite calmly. He seemed very poised."

She stopped and Ransom waited for a few seconds. When she didn't continue, he said, "I'm sorry, I still don't understand what that explains."

"Oh!" Emily exclaimed, her cheeks turning a delicate pink. "Forgive me, it's just that Mr. Nuevo didn't look like he was having a heart attack, so I was surprised when Mr. Carnegie said that."

"It didn't look like a heart attack?" Gerald asked.

"No. He looked like he couldn't breathe."

"I would think someone having a heart attack would look that way," said Ransom.

"Perhaps. But a sudden heart attack is very painful. I would've expected him to . . . maybe clutch at his heart, or put his hands to his chest. Mr. Nuevo was gasping for air, but he didn't seem to be in that much pain. What he did do was slap at himself . . . like this." She pantomimed the action on her own chest. "As if he were trying to beat air into his lungs."

Ransom once again marveled at the old woman's acuity. "As always, you're correct. It seems he died of respiratory failure."

"That healthy young man?" said Emily as she pulled out her chair and sat down. "Not that it would have been any more unusual for him to have had a heart attack . . ."

"That's just the thing. As far as the medical examiner can tell, he was a little too healthy for that type of death. He suspects it was poison. So they're going to have the tissue samples tested, but that will take quite a while. In the meantime . . ."

"In the meantime you have a group of potential suspects who are not exactly tied to this city."

"Right. The doctor mentioned alkaloid poisoning."

Emily raised her thin gray brows. "I see."

Ransom cleared his throat. "We have no idea how it might have been administered, so I was hoping you could tell me a little about the performance. Do you remember him drinking anything?"

"You mean onstage?" She shook her head. "No, no he didn't. But that doesn't mean anything."

"Hm?"

"Well, it's been a long time since I've been in school . . . I think schools were better when I was a young girl, so much more comprehensive. I remember one teacher who talked to us about poisons in a way that was quite titillating. Personally, I always thought she just enjoyed scaring little girls . . ."

"Emily . . ." Ransom said with gentle impatience.

"Oh, yes, I'm sorry. It's just I seem to remember that alkaloids can be very slow, can't they?"

"I don't know that much about them."

"Well, if I'm remembering correctly, they can. And if that's true, then it could've been given to him much earlier . . . which would take in everyone onstage and off."

"Mm-hmm," said Ransom. He didn't much like the prospect of having the time frame widened. "Before he collapsed—do you remember if there was a change in him at any time during the performance? Did he seem ill?"

Emily sighed. "It's very hard to say, given the nature of this particular opera and the production. It was acted with more of a sense of realism than I've ever seen before. It was a startling production. You see, the trouble is, Don José becomes increasingly obsessed with Carmen. Mr. Nuevo seemed more and more distressed as the opera went on, but then, he would. He was breathing very heavily and perspiring quite a bit in the final scene. But again, it was right for the part."

Gerald jotted these things down in the small spiral notebook he kept in his breast pocket. Free as she was of a guilty conscience, Emily paid him no mind.

"Thinking back," said Ransom, "now that you know there was something wrong, can you hazard a guess at when he started to behave differently?"

Emily gazed past Ransom and into the previous night's performance. The detectives watched and waited. After a long silence, she straightened herself in her chair and said, "Jeremy, how familiar are you with the opera?"

He shrugged. "*Carmen*. I've seen it."

"There are four acts. However, the Santa Marta people are doing it in three. . . ."

"Are they trying to do it faster than everyone else?" he asked with an impish grin.

She returned an indulgent smile. "No, my dear. *Carmen* isn't a terribly long opera, and sometimes the second and third acts are combined so that there are only two intermissions. That's the way this company is doing it. All of Don José's exchanges with Carmen are rather heated, particularly in the latter part of the opera, so it's difficult to tell. I would say . . ." Once again her expression became far off. "I don't think that he began to falter until the last act, after the second intermission."

Ransom laid his palms on the table. "Did you notice anything else unusual during the performance?"

Emily eyed him cannily. "*Carmen* is a very volatile story. I was rather taken aback by how realistically it was performed. . . . Of course, I suppose that is the point, and the reason there's been so much publicity about it. The two leads were quite believable. . . ."

She stopped again and her smile became more pronounced.

"Yes?" said Ransom.

"Particularly Maria Cortez. She played her part so well that you would have sworn she really was contemptuous of Don José."

"I see," said Ransom.

Ransom and Gerald arrived at the theater about twenty minutes after taking their leave of Emily. As Gerald brought the car to a stop in front of the steps, Ransom exhaled a heavy cloud of smoke through the open passenger window.

"My God, look at that," he said.

Gerald titled his head sideways in an attempt to see past his partner. "What?"

"The Edwin J. Sheridan Center for the Performing Arts," Ransom answered sardonically. "I wonder if it was purposely built to look like a mausoleum." He crushed out the remainder of his cigar in the ashtray and popped open his door. "Shall we?"

Gerald sighed inwardly as he climbed out of the car. Something in his partner's tone told him it was going to be one of those days.

The box-office attendant directed them to Edward Carnegie's office. Their footsteps echoed as they crossed the marble cavern to the elevator that was discreetly tucked away behind the main staircase. When the doors slid open on the third floor, the detectives stepped out into the plush silence.

"The lady in the box office said the door was on the right, but I don't see any," Gerald said.

"There's no need to whisper," Ransom replied.

"I'm not whispering."

Ransom realized with surprise that Gerald was correct: It wasn't that he was speaking softly, it was that the moment they said anything in the midst of the thick carpeting, heavy curtains, and fabric-covered walls, their words were swallowed in the plushness.

They were about to examine the wall to find the promised door when they heard a muffled click and one of the panels opened outward. A young woman in a dark blue business suit came out and smiled at them.

"Are you the detectives?" Her voice barely carried the short distance over to them.

"Yes. I'm Detective Ransom, and this is Detective White."

"Sadie down in the box office called up to let me know you

were on the way, so I could look out for you. People can get lost looking for this office. I'm Bonnie Payton, Mr. Carnegie's secretary. Step this way, please."

She ushered them in and closed the door, then led them to Carnegie's office.

"Is this about last night?" she asked.

"Yes."

"We're all very shocked about what's happened," Bonnie said, not sounding at all shocked. "This isn't exactly the type of publicity the Center was looking for for our opening. The papers this morning said that the cause of death was unknown, but . . ." She came to a halt in front of Carnegie's door with her hand poised to knock. "But—I don't mean to sound nosy—but since you're here, does that mean there's something wrong? I mean other than that Mr. Nuevo died?"

"His death appears to be a bit complicated," said Ransom. "Were you at the performance last night, Ms. Payton?"

She lowered her hand. "Yes, I was."

"Did you notice anything unusual about Mr. Nuevo before he died?"

"What do you mean, unusual?"

"Did he seem sick before it happened?"

She thought for a few seconds. "No, not really. He seemed like he was really acting his part. I guess I would make something out of that now that I know he was dying, but it didn't seem unusual at the time."

"By acting the part, I take it you mean he was agitated, upset . . ."

She was nodding. "Yes. Like I said, it didn't seem out of the ordinary for the role he was playing; it's only looking back at it now that I could believe it was more than that."

"Hmm," Ransom said thoughtfully. "Tell me, did you get to meet the members of the cast?"

"You mean the principals? Only in passing. I'm a secretary, detective. People don't usually take any notice of me."

Something about her smile told Ransom that one took no notice of Ms. Payton at one's own peril.

"So you can't tell me anything about them or their relationships?"

She shook her head ruefully. "Only second hand, and only rumors. I heard they fought like cats and dogs, but I never saw it myself."

Ransom emitted another "hmm" then glanced at the door. Ms. Payton picked up her cue and rapped on the door with her knuckles, then opened it and showed them in.

"Mr. Carnegie, these are the detectives that have come to see you. Ransom and White."

Carnegie came out from behind the desk and shook their hands in turn, while Ms. Payton quietly made her exit.

"Have a seat, gentlemen," he said with a sweeping gesture to the chairs in front of the desk as he resumed his seat behind it. "I was surprised when Bonnie told me you were on your way up. I mean, I take it for granted this is about Riccardo's death, but . . ." He allowed his voice to trail off.

"We believe that Mr. Nuevo was murdered," Ransom said matter-of-factly. Gerald withdrew the notebook from his breast pocket and laid it on his knee, his pencil poised above it.

Carnegie's expression didn't change. "How is that possible?"

"What do you mean?"

"Well . . . Riccardo fell down and died at the end of the opera. He'd been onstage for quite a while. How could . . . what killed him?"

"We believe he was poisoned with something that acted fairly slowly."

"Uh-huh." Carnegie sat back in his chair as if this was explanation enough for him.

"Forgive me," said Ransom, "but you don't seem very surprised."

Carnegie knit his eyebrows. "Why should I be?"

Ransom smiled. "I think the question is why *wouldn't* you

be? Do you know of any reason someone would want to kill Mr. Nuevo?"

"Not at all. I guess . . ." He laid one hand on top of the other on his desk and sighed. "I guess I'm just a hard person to surprise, that's all."

"Apparently. I assume you've met the members of the company."

"The principals, yes."

"What can you tell me about them?"

Carnegie spread his palms. "Nothing, really. I only met them; I didn't get to know them at all."

"So you wouldn't know anything about their relationships to one another."

"Not really."

Ransom considered the man for a moment. Although Carnegie seemed blissfully ignorant of the internal workings of the opera company, Ransom found it hard to believe that the manager of an important new theater wouldn't be keeping a fairly close watch on the company on which so much of the Center's first impression was riding.

He said, "So, you don't know of any . . . unpleasantness among the company members?"

Carnegie shook his head. "I don't really have that much to do with the company itself. David Cunningham is the man you need to talk to. He's their manager. Well, actually, he's one of the two men that founded the company. He's my main contact with the opera company. If they were unhappy about anything, or if they wanted anything, I heard about it through David."

"And were they?" Ransom asked after a beat.

"Were they what?"

"Unhappy about anything?"

Carnegie laughed lightly. "I heard that Marie Cortez didn't think her dressing room was large enough—which in the opera world means there was enough room for her, but not for her ego—but that's about all."

"I see." There was a silence during which Ransom seemed to be studying his fingernails. He suddenly looked up and said, "Did you, by chance, go backstage last night?"

Carnegie drew back in his chair. He looked surprised and a bit affronted by the question. "As a matter of fact, I did. I went back to wish them good luck. I thought it was something I should do as the—" He broke off, his eyebrows rising. "Oh! I just thought of something. I went to greet Maria first, since she's the star. When I got there she was having an argument with Riccardo."

Ransom flexed his right hand. "Do you know what it was about?"

"Not really," Carnegie said, slowly shaking his head. "The door was closed. I heard them inside. I would've just gone away, but . . ."

"Yes?"

He continued with reluctance. "But the opera was starting in about ten or fifteen minutes, and I thought it might be best to interrupt them, if you know what I mean."

"I'm afraid I don't," said Ransom. Gerald silently smirked at his notebook.

"A fight just before going on isn't very good. I thought maybe I should try to stop it and maybe smooth it over. But they stopped the minute I knocked on the door."

"You didn't hear anything they said?"

Carnegie shook his head slowly. "No . . . wait! I heard Riccardo say something like, 'I won't let you go,' and Maria yelled back at him, but . . ." He gave a helpless shrug.

Ransom crossed his legs and folded his hands on his knee. "What will this mean to your opera?"

Carnegie hesitated. "I don't understand."

"The loss of Riccardo Nuevo. Will you be forced to cancel the rest of the run?"

"Oh, no. Of course not. Nuevo has an understudy. He'll go on."

"His name?"

"I'm sorry, I don't know it. David Cunningham just told me they had one, and that he'd be able to go on."

"You've already spoken with Mr. Cunningham about it?"

"Of course I did," Carnegie replied defensively. "There's a lot of money involved in this. Of course we've already discussed it."

"I'm so sorry," Ransom said with calculated sheepishness. "I didn't mean to imply anything. It was just that Mr. Nuevo only died late last night."

Gerald surreptitiously glanced at his partner.

"Well, thank you very much," said Ransom, rising abruptly. For once Gerald was caught off guard by his partner's move. He fumbled the notebook, almost dropping it before slipping it back into his pocket.

Ransom looked at his watch. "It's almost one o'clock. Now, Mr. Carnegie, what time does the opera begin?"

"We're dark on Monday nights," he said, rising uncertainly.

"Ah. Good. We'll need to have our evidence technicians in to go over the backstage area. It will probably be the least trouble to you if we do it right away."

"Yes . . . of course."

"Could you show us to the dressing rooms?"

"I'd be glad to."

Carnegie preceded them out of his office. He paused at Ms. Payton's desk and said, "Bonnie, I'll be back . . . directly." He then led the detectives back to the elevator.

As they rode down, Ransom said, "Excuse me for saying this, but you seem a bit young to be the head of a place like this."

Carnegie smiled. "I take that as a compliment. It means I've achieved more than people expect someone to by the age of thirty."

"I suppose it does."

Ransom's enigmatic smile caused the Center's director some

inner turmoil, which he tried very hard not to show. He wondered if Ransom's reply had been as innocent as it seemed, or if he knew more than he was letting on.

They got out of the elevator at the lobby and Carnegie led them down the nearest aisle to a door on the left of the auditorium near the stage.

"This is the quickest way," he explained.

Ransom stopped at the door and pointed to the corresponding one on the opposite side of the house. "Does that one go backstage as well?"

"Yes. But the stars' dressing rooms are offstage right."

"Right?" said Gerald, glancing at the other door confusedly.

Carnegie smiled. "Yeah. Sorry. Stage directions are backwards. They're from the actor's point of view. So offstage right is actually the left if you're sitting in the audience."

They went through the door and up a fairly steep concrete ramp to the side of the stage. Ransom stopped, and the others followed suit.

Gerald let out a low whistle. "Jeez! It's bigger than it looks from the audience."

"Suitable to every occasion," Carnegie said, mustering up a note of pride that was rather unsuitable to the occasion. "This theater can house everything from grand opera to those godawful Webber extravaganzas."

The stage was set for the first-act curtain, the Spanish square. The artifice used to deceive the audience was evident: Whatever the frame of the huge set might be, it had been covered with irregularly formed Styrofoam and painted in varying shades of tan and gray. Even at this close proximity it resembled stone. From the distance of the audience it would look thoroughly realistic.

It takes so little to create an illusion, thought Ransom. His gaze traveled up to the flies, in which were suspended four gigantic backdrops that looked as if they could easily crush anyone who had the misfortune to be underneath them. He shook his head. He would have preferred that the victim had been killed that way. It would have been much less problematic.

He turned to Carnegie. "And where are the dressing rooms?"

"Over here."

They crossed the stage-right wing to a hallway partially hidden from view by a mass of cleverly faked boulders, which Ransom assumed would be for the scene in the mountains.

Carnegie stopped by the first door. "This is Riccardo's dressing room. Maria's is next door. There are two more a little ways down there." He pointed toward the end of the darkened hallway. "Those are being used by Franco Giannini and Gabrielle Charbonneau. There are two larger ones at the end used by the secondary players."

"And the rest?"

"The rest?"

"The rest of the dressing rooms."

"Oh, yes. There's a staircase at the end of the hall that goes down to them. There's two big communal dressing rooms."

"Well," said Ransom, "thank you very much, Mr. Carnegie."

Carnegie looked quite surprised. There was no doubt he was being summarily dismissed. "You don't want me to stay?"

"No, we won't keep you any longer. We need to have a look around, and then we'll be calling in the evidence technicians, which will all take quite a while. I'm sure you have a lot of work to do. But I must ask you to keep everyone away from this area for the time being."

"Oh. Okay. Could you let me know when you're done, so I know the theater is clear?"

"Certainly," Ransom replied pleasantly.

Carnegie started to walk away, but Ransom stopped him. "Oh, one more thing. Could you tell me where the cast is staying?"

"The principals are at the Dover Hotel, and the chorus is scattered around in less expensive accommodations. I can get you a list if you want it."

"That would be very helpful. How many chorus members are there?"

"About thirty. And there's twenty supers, but they're all local. I'll get you a list of their addresses as well."

"And the crew?"

"Most of them are local. A few came with the company."

"We'll need their addresses, too. Where is David Cunningham staying?"

"He's at the Starlight Motel, on Belmont."

"Hmm?" Ransom replied questioningly.

Carnegie glanced down at the floor. "We couldn't very well put everyone up at the Dover. Mr. Cunningham is the company manager, not one of the stars." He looked up at them and smiled. "And as their manager I'm sure he understands the need to conserve money."

"I see," Ransom said with a slight smile. "Well, thank you again."

When Carnegie left them, Ransom said, "That hardly seems the way to treat the founder of the feast."

"Uh-huh," said Gerald. "What are these supers he mentioned?"

"Supernumeraries," Ransom replied offhandedly. When he noticed the look of puzzlement on Gerald's face, he added, "Spear carriers."

"I thought you said this opera takes place in Spain."

Ransom curled his lips. "You know, Gerald, sometimes I wonder how we've been able to stay partnered for so long. Supernumeraries are the opera equivalent of extras."

"Oh."

"Now, call in for the techs, will you?"

Gerald pulled the cell phone from the right-hand pocket of his dark brown jacket and complied while Ransom went into Nuevo's room. Nothing seemed out of the ordinary. A red silk robe with gold piping hung on a hook on the bathroom door, and Don José's uniform was on a hanger in the closet. Riccardo's sports bag was on the floor. Ransom crouched over it and gingerly looked inside. It contained a pair of black denim pants and two white T-shirts, along with a couple of silver bags of coffee.

At the far left end of the makeup counter was a coffeemaker. The pot was empty. It had been used but not cleaned. He lifted the lid with the end of his cuff and looked inside. It was full of used grounds. He dropped the lid back into place and sat in the chair that had been pulled out from the counter.

In the center of the counter was a makeup case that resembled a tackle box. It was filled with various tubes and pots of color, as well as several brushes and flat sponges. To the left of the box was a hairbrush and a metal comb. To the right was a coffee mug that was empty except for a few dregs. Ransom peered over the rim and sniffed. There was an evident aroma of coffee, but nothing else.

Ransom sat back and fought the urge to drum his fingers on the counter. He didn't think that fingerprints were going to help their investigation much, since he was assuming that Nuevo was killed by someone in the company, and it would be natural for their prints to be there, but he still didn't want to add his to the mix. It was then that he noticed a paper coffee cup set off to the side. It was about half full. He stood and bent over the cup. As with the mug, it smelled only of coffee.

"They're on their way," said Gerald. He snapped the phone shut and shoved it back into his pocket as he came into the room. "Is something wrong?"

"We have our work cut out for us, Gerald. It'll take four to six weeks to get results back from the lab. Poison!" he exclaimed disdainfully, as if he took the mode of murder as a personal affront.

"How long is this thing supposed to be in town?"

"Eight weeks."

"Anything interesting in here?"

"Just one little tidbit. It looks like Mr. Nuevo had a visitor." Ransom indicated the cup.

"That could be from anyone."

"Thank you, Gerald," Ransom said flatly.

They left Riccardo's dressing room and went next door to Maria's.

"Good grief!" Gerald said even before elbowing the light switch. "It smells like a funeral parlor in here!"

As the lights flooded the room they saw the reason for the smell: The room was filled with flowers that were beginning to wilt.

"Well," said Ransom. "It would seem the diva is very popular."

Aside from the flowers, the contents of the dressing room were roughly the same as the first, except for the absence of a coffeemaker. A glass of water was on the counter, next to a makeup case that was significantly more expensive and elaborate than Riccardo's. All of her costumes were neatly hung in the closet.

They went on to the other dressing rooms. Nothing seemed out of the ordinary; at least, there was nothing that looked overtly like poison. There were a couple of coffee mugs in Franco Giannini's room. They'd both been washed and laid on a paper towel on the counter to dry. Gabrielle Charbonneau had left several tissues wadded up and scattered on her counter. Three Styrofoam cups had been crushed and tossed in the small garbage can. A half-empty pitcher of water sat on the far end of the counter. In Jeffrey Baker's dressing room there was a single paper cup tossed in the garbage.

When they'd finished with the principals' dressing rooms, they checked the larger ones, then went down the stairs and scanned in the two communal rooms used by the chorus. Ransom sighed heavily at the sight of it: cups and glasses were everywhere, as were makeup cases, brushes, and various items of clothing. At the end of the room there were racks of costumes, each of which had a label pinned to the sleeve with the name of the person who would wear the costume.

When the evidence technicians arrived, Gerald showed them where the dressing rooms were located, and Ransom instructed them to make sure they took samples of any liquids found backstage. The detectives then left the technicians to their work. They picked up the extensive lists of addresses from Carnegie's secretary on their way out.

"You think it's something he drank, then?" Gerald asked as they headed back to the car.

"I think we can safely assume that Mr. Nuevo didn't sit still while someone injected him with poison."

"Well, whose cage do you want to rattle now?"

Ransom laughed. "I think we'll start with Mr. Cunningham. Since he's the head of the company, he can probably fill us in on the relationships among the cast."

The Starlight Motel had been built on Belmont during the mid-fifties. Nobody could remember why there had ever been a need for a motel in what was essentially a residential neighborhood, nor could they understand why anyone would stay there for anything other than a quick tryst, except for the fact that it was far enough west that its inconvenience made it one of the cheapest places to stay in the city.

In the intervening years, a small candy factory had been erected directly to the east of the motel, and at least three days a week the air was tinged with the odor of burnt chocolate. To the west was an ancient apartment building the length of a full city block. The row of retail spaces at its base housed junk shops that made halfhearted attempts to raise themselves up, with hand-lettered signs that said ANTIQUES in the few remaining, unboarded windows.

Gerald steered the car into the alleylike driveway, narrowly missing the motel's signpost. From the amount of scratched paint and dints on the post, it was apparent that he was one of the few people who managed to avoid hitting it. The sign at the top had a dark blue background with the motel's name emblazoned in pink neon, along with several small white neon stars, half of which had been permanently extinguished.

The hotel itself was a dusty rectangle with eleven rooms on two levels. The twelfth space was taken up by the office.

Gerald pulled into what appeared to be a parking space. It was hard to tell since only the barest remnants of yellow lines remained.

Ransom waited by the car while Gerald went into the office. When he came out, he said, "Cunningham's in number eleven. End of the line."

"Lucky man," Ransom replied through curled lips.

They went down the walk to the room, passing a sun-blistered Coke machine to which an out-of-order sign had been affixed. The tape holding the sign had yellowed and was peeling off, and the words had all but disappeared. When they reached the room, Gerald rapped lightly on the door with his knuckles.

"Who is it?" a voice called from inside.

"Mr. Cunningham? It's the police. We'd like to talk to you," said Gerald.

"The police?" Cunningham said as he opened the door. His brows had arched into crescents over his eyes, making him look thoroughly astonished.

Ransom introduced himself and his partner. "May we come in?"

"Yes! Sure." He stepped aside to allow them to pass. Ransom was fairly impressed by the interior of the room. Although the meager furnishings were obviously old, the place was quite clean. It seemed what little care was given to keeping up the Starlight Motel was limited to the inside.

"Is this about last night?" Cunningham asked.

"Yes," said Ransom.

He motioned them to the chairs on either side of a very low, round table by the windows. Gerald took out his notebook and touched the tip of his pencil to his tongue.

"What's wrong?" Cunningham asked as he sat on the edge of the bed.

"From the results of the autopsy, it seems that Mr. Nuevo was poisoned."

"Poisoned? You mean he was murdered?"

Ransom nodded.

"That's crazy! Who would do that?"

"That's what we're trying to find out."

Though it didn't seem possible, Cunningham looked even more astonished. "You mean you think it was one of us?"

"We don't know yet," Ransom replied patiently. "Did Mr. Nuevo know anyone in Chicago?"

He stared at Ransom blankly for a moment, then his head moved slowly from side to side. "Not that I know of. I don't think so. He didn't say."

"Would he have?"

Cunningham blinked. "I don't . . . what do you mean?"

"I was just wondering if you and Mr. Nuevo were on friendly terms."

"Yes, yes, of course," the manager said, going slightly pale. "We didn't have any problem with each other. Ask anyone."

Ransom's smile showed Cunningham he would do just that. "I think it's most likely, given the type of murder it was, that it was done by someone close to him. At least, close enough to have access to him. If he didn't know anyone in the city, that pretty much narrows it down to your company."

"I don't believe it!"

Ransom sat back in his chair and slid one leg over the other. "Tell me, Mr. Cunningham, were you backstage last night?"

The manager's face went blank for a split second. "Yes. Why? You don't think I—"

"I merely thought that you would've noticed if there was a stranger there."

"Oh. Well, I wasn't back there that long—just to check and make sure everything was all right. I didn't see anybody who didn't belong there."

Ransom shrugged. "So once again we're left the company. Would you tell me about Mr. Nuevo's relationships with the other members?"

"I don't . . . I mean, I wouldn't really know about his personal life. That much, I mean."

"Do you know if there was anyone who didn't like him?"

"No . . . no. Everyone liked him. As far as I know. But like I said, I don't really know that much about their relationships. I try to stay out of that sort of thing."

Ransom's right eyebrow escalated. "Surely in an opera company there are personality variances to deal with. As head of the company, you'd be the one to do that, wouldn't you?"

"But there wasn't with Riccardo!" Cunningham said firmly.

There was a short silence, then Ransom said, "Were there problems with other members of the cast?"

He hesitated and his cheeks reddened. "Not really."

"Hmm," said Ransom. "We spoke with Edward Carnegie a little while ago." He turned to Gerald. "How many people did he say are in the opera?"

Gerald flipped a page back in his notebook and did a quick calculation. "Between the company itself and the local people they're using, around fifty."

Ransom turned back to Cunningham. "Around fifty. It's difficult for me to believe that that many people could be together for any length of time and maintain perfect harmony. Especially given the egos involved."

This struck a chord with the company manager. A certain hardness crept in around his eyes. "Well, Maria is a little hard to deal with."

From the way he said this, Ransom suspected he was dabbling in understatement.

"What was Ms. Cortez's relationship to Mr. Nuevo?"

"They were . . . quite friendly, I understand."

"So it said in the papers," Ransom replied wryly. "Was it true?"

"As much as anything like that can be."

"I beg your pardon?"

Cunningham had been staring at this own hands. He looked

up guiltily. "I don't . . . nothing. I just didn't think Maria was as serious about it as Riccardo was."

"I see," said Ransom. He waited a beat, then lightly asked, "Did she have any reason to kill him?"

"No!" Cunningham exclaimed indignantly. Ransom thought perhaps this reaction stemmed from Cunningham fearing that he'd allowed his dislike for the diva to get the better of him. The one thing Ransom was sure of from the obvious hedging was that the company's manager was none too fond of the company's star.

"Do you know of anyone who would've wanted to kill Mr. Nuevo?"

"No one," Cunningham replied. "Riccardo was a very, very sweet man. He was never any trouble."

Ransom considered this for a moment, enjoying the discomfiture the silence seemed to be causing the man. Finally he said, "Who is Mr. Nuevo's understudy?"

"What?" Cunningham said with surprise. "His understudy? Patrick Laramie. Why?"

"What does Laramie do while waiting for a break?"

"He sings in the chorus. Why?"

"So in one broad stroke Laramie is made a star?"

"You're not . . . that's just crazy!" Cunningham said. He started to rise but caught himself at the last minute and sat back down on the bed. "We've been performing this opera for six months. Why would he do it now?"

Ransom spread his palms. "I'm just looking for possibilities."

Cunningham sighed. "Patrick will be playing Radames in our next production, *Aida*. He doesn't need to step on anyone to get a starring role."

"Hmm. So the show will go on without a pause."

"Well, it might seem unfeeling," Cunningham said quickly, "but we can't help it. We can't afford to miss a performance. We can't lose the money. We need it. It's a matter of survival for us."

"I see." Ransom allowed a long pause, then said, "This has been a very bad week for your company, hasn't it? You've lost two of your stars."

"Two? What do you mean?"

"Didn't I read that Maria Cortez is leaving your troupe?"

Once again the manager's visage hardened. "That remains to be seen."

"He's right," said Gerald as they got back into the car, "the understudy thing doesn't make any sense. Not now. It might have six months ago."

"I didn't say it made sense," Ransom replied as he pulled a plastic-tipped cigar from the pack in his inner pocket. He pressed the dashboard lighter. "I said it was a possibility. I was just trying to give Cunningham a 'for instance' because he wasn't very forthcoming. I can't believe this opera company gets along as well as he'd like us to think."

Gerald pulled the car to a stop at the mouth of the driveway, waiting for an opening in the busy Belmont traffic. "The Dover Hotel?"

Ransom nodded. The lighter popped out of the dash, and Ransom pulled it out, lit his cigar, and then slid the lighter back into place. The car quickly filled with a heavy cloud of smoke. They both rolled down their windows.

At the first cough in the stream of cars, Gerald hung a right and they headed east.

"What did you think of Cunningham?" Gerald asked.

"I think he has something to hide."

"Really?"

"I can't imagine what it is, if he didn't have anything to do with the murder."

"Come on, Jer. You know that some people just act guilty when they talk to the police. They can't help it. It doesn't mean anything."

Ransom took a deep drag from the cigar, then aimed a stream of smoke out the window. "He was lying about how well these people get along together, I can feel that much in my bones. I don't see the need for it. I'm also sure that he was soft-soaping the relationship between Nuevo and Cortez. I don't see the reason for that, either. I can't believe he'd be afraid that she'd be implicated in Nuevo's murder. I got the impression that he wasn't very fond of her."

"Yeah," said Gerald. "Especially when you mentioned the fact that she was leaving."

"Ah, well," Ransom sighed. "Maybe we'll learn more from the diva herself."

They parked in the loading zone in front of the Dover Hotel—much to the dismay of the doorman, whose protests were cut short at the sight of Gerald's badge. The concierge directed them to the hotel manager's office.

The manager was a dignified gentleman named Harvey Bakersfield. He was in his midfifties and had an air of unflappability. He didn't blink at the news that one of his guests had been murdered, although that might have been due in part to the fact that the guest had had the decency to do it away from the premises. Bakersfield provided them with a key card for Nuevo's room, along with the room numbers of the other principals in the company.

"He didn't bat an eye," said Gerald as they waited for the elevator.

"I imagine he's been managing this place for a lot of years," said Ransom. "I'd be willing to bet he's seen it all."

They rode up to the fourth floor, where all of the company members' rooms were located. Their first stop was 412, Riccardo Nuevo's room. Gerald slipped the card in the slot below the doorknob and the lock opened with a loud snap. He turned the knob and opened the door.

Despite the fact that the room had been occupied by hundreds, if not thousands, of guests before Nuevo, the fact that the most recent occupant had died suddenly seemed to hang there. A stillness had settled in the air as if the disruption in the natural order of things had left the room in limbo.

Their search didn't take very long, because there was nothing much to see. The usual personal items were found on the bathroom sink. In the closet were a pair of suits and several shirts and trousers in various colors. The latest edition of *Newsweek* lay unopened on the bedside table. There was nothing else to give the room any personal touch. Ransom slid open the large white doors on the left wall of the room, which hid the Pullman kitchen. It didn't look as if Nuevo had ever used it.

"Let's go," said Ransom as he slid the doors shut.

Their next stop was Room 401, where Maria Cortez was housed for the run of the show. Gerald knocked on the door and they waited. The detectives were surprised when it was opened by a rather handsome man of around forty with long, dark, curly hair. He looked equally startled to see them.

"I beg your pardon," said Ransom. "We're looking for Maria Cortez. I'm Detective Ransom, this is my partner, Detective White."

"Oh. I'm Tony Leonard. I'm Maria's manager. Come on in."

They found Maria languishing in bed, propped up on a pile of pillows, and wearing a flowing white dressing gown that Ransom thought would be more appropriate to a corpse in a vampire film. Her dark red hair was attractively disarranged.

"Did you say you were detectives?" Maria said weakly.

"Yes," Ransom replied, then made the introductions again.

"I am sorry," Maria said. "I cannot . . . I feel all of the strength has gone out of me. It is like that when death has had you in his hands."

Tony had pulled chairs up beside the bed for the visitors, then went over to the window and stood watching her. Ransom and Gerald were seating themselves when Maria made this startling pronouncement. Both stopped for a split second, then lowered themselves onto the chairs. Gerald pulled out his notebook with a bit more alacrity than was his norm.

"I'm afraid I don't understand," said Ransom.

Maria's eyes widened in remembered terror. "He was clutching me when he died! He had me in his hands! I tried to break away from him, but the grip of death is strong."

Ransom said, "So Mr. Nuevo was holding you when he begun to convulse?"

For a moment Maria seemed to waver uncertainly, as if she half suspected that he was making fun of her.

"Have you ever been in the hands of death before? It is not something you will soon forget."

"Perhaps not," Ransom said lightly. "Why don't you tell us what happened?"

"What happened? You know what happened!"

"Yes, but we're trying to put together the details. Was there anything unusual about Mr. Nuevo's performance last night?"

"Unusual? Other than the fact that he threw me to the floor and then died? Other than the fact that he almost twisted my wrist off the end of my arm?" Apparently her strength was coming back to her. Or at least, she appeared to have forgotten that it had gone. Her eyebrows took a dive toward her nose. "No. Not for him. Ricky was a very erratic performer."

"In what way?"

"You simply never knew what he was going to do on the stage from one night to the next. Sometimes it was very good, other times . . ." She let her voice trail off suggestively, the implication being that she didn't want to speak ill of the dead.

Ransom said, "It was reported to us that he seemed to be having difficulty breathing during the last act. Can you confirm this?"

"I suppose it is true."

"Can you tell us when you first noticed it?"

Maria slowly moved her head from side to side, keeping her eyes on his. "No. I didn't notice it as if something was wrong. I noticed it only as another change—that perhaps Ricky was more 'into his part' than normal. He did that sometimes, got into his part." She suddenly became more animated. "The other day, when he went to stab me at the end of the opera, he did not 'pull his punch,' as they say, and hit me full force in the back with that damned trick knife! I have a bruise from it! Right in the middle of my back!" She turned to her manager. "Don't I, Tony?"

He was caught off guard and cleared his throat. "Yes. Yes, you do."

"You see?" she said, turning back to the detective. "And I challenged him backstage! I yelled at him! I accused him of trying to hurt me! But what does he do? He claims he was just taken away with the part. That he forgot himself. That it was an accident! But I know better. He did it out of spite!"

Ransom allowed the words to hang in the air, then said, "Now, what did he have to feel spiteful about?"

Maria wavered again. Some of her anger had dissipated when she replied. "It was only jealousy."

"Really?" Ransom said with an undisguised glance at Tony.

Maria pointedly ignored this. "He was jealous because I am a star while he was merely a tenor."

"Hmm. Is that why you argued with him last night?"

Maria went saucer-eyed and her mouth dropped open. "What?"

"We heard that you had an argument with Mr. Nuevo just before the opera began."

"Who told you—?" She stopped and her face relaxed with understanding. "Ah yes, those men."

"Men?"

"The men from the theater, who came back to see us. They must have told you. They came in while we were arguing. Well, what of it? Why do you ask me about this? What business is it of yours if I argued with Ricky?"

"I'm sorry," Ransom said with rather insincere self-effacement. "I should have said this at the outset: We're asking questions because Mr. Nuevo was murdered."

"No!" Maria bellowed. Her right hand flew out to the side. "Tony . . . Tony . . . please!"

Tony was at a loss as to what was expected of him, so it was with some confusion that he reached out to her. She grabbed his hand and clutched it so tightly that her knuckles went white. Tony stood stoically by her side, trying not to wince.

"No! It's not true!"

"I'm afraid it is. Mr. Nuevo was poisoned sometime during last night's performance."

"But how is that possible? He stood! He sang! How could he have been poisoned?"

"That's one of the things we're trying to figure out. Most likely through something he ate or drank."

Maria stared at him for a while, then frowned and pushed Tony's hand away. "I don't believe you!"

"What you believe is of little consequence at the moment," Ransom said with elaborate patience. "What concerns us is the subject of your argument with Mr. Nuevo."

For a moment she looked as if she might refuse to answer, but instead she flapped her right hand and said, "It was nothing. It was only that he was upset about my plans to leave the company."

Ransom raised his right eyebrow. "Had he just learned of your plans?"

"Yes. He read about it that morning, like everyone else."

There was a longer pause. "He read about it? Forgive me, Ms. Cortez, I was under the impression that you were fairly close to Mr. Nuevo."

"Where do you get such an idea?"

He shrugged. "From the newspapers."

"Ah! So you see? You really can't believe what you read in the papers! These things that reporters cook up so that they can have a story!"

"You're saying that there was no truth to the stories?" Ransom asked slowly.

"None at all! They were just for publicity."

Ransom gazed at her. "Ms. Cortez, he was heard saying to you 'I won't let you go.' You have to admit, that does sound as if there was something between you."

Maria caught herself just short of letting her temper run away with her. She shot a hasty glance at Tony, who was looking out the window, pretending to hear nothing. She sighed dramatically and lay back against the pillows. "I am sorry, Mr. Detective. There is no reason to protect him anymore."

Gerald looked up from his notebook in surprise.

"Protect who?" Ransom asked.

"No, no, protect is the wrong word. I mean . . ." She made a show of searching for just the right words. "Ricky had an infatuation with me, that is all. It sometimes happens. It was not reciprocated." She said this without any outward sign of hubris, as if infatuated men were a tiresome fact of life with which she would always have to deal.

"I see," said Ransom.

Gerald stopped writing and looked over at him. There was something unsettling in his tone. Ransom was staring at the woman through narrowed eyes as she absently straightened her dressing gown. Suddenly, he uncrossed his legs and put both feet on the floor. "Ms. Cortez, I feel there are a few things I should point out to you."

"Yes?"

"First, this is not an opera, this is real life, and a man has been murdered. I would appreciate it if you would reserve the drama for the stage. Secondly, it's likely that Mr. Nuevo was killed by someone close to him—in proximity, if not emotionally."

"What has that to do with me?" Maria demanded hotly.

Ransom smiled. "There have been cases in which a person with an infatuation has been killed because that infatuation has caused difficulties for someone else."

In the periphery of his vision, Ransom saw the corner of Tony Leonard's mouth crook upward.

"I had no need to kill Ricky!" Maria's normally dark skin had flushed an even deeper red. "If you are looking for someone who did, why don't you talk to his little puppy dog?"

"Who would that be?"

"Gabrielle Charbonneau!"

"Why would she want to kill him?"

"Because she couldn't have him!" Maria exclaimed. "Because he wanted me!" If she had originally intended to play down the nature of her relationship with the deceased, she'd failed. The jubilance in her voice made it sound as if she considered her victory over Gabrielle to be a triumph.

"We intend to talk to everyone," Ransom said. "As soon as we're done with you. At the moment I'm concerned with how much of a problem Mr. Nuevo was going to be to you."

"He was no problem!" Maria answered with frustration.

"He said he would not let you leave the company. How did he intend to do that?"

"He couldn't! He was only speaking from his hurt pride! Ricky was not a problem for me! He could do nothing to stop me from leaving this company!"

"Why is that?"

"Because I knew the truth about him!" She smiled triumphantly at the detective.

"Yes?" he said with infuriating calm.

She leaned forward. "Riccardo Nuevo, who was so handsome, so exotic, and soooo Spanish, was really very plain, very ordinary Ricky Novak from Laredo, Texas!"

"Really."

"He thought he would like to succeed in the opera, and that nobody would take him seriously because of his roots! So he left Texas and re-created himself. He was dark enough that he decided to become Spanish. He was fluent in the language, as many are in southern Texas. He adopted the name Riccardo Nuevo—'New Ricky'—very funny, no? And then auditioned for opera companies far away from Texas."

"How do you know all this?" Ransom asked.

She leaned in closer to him. "Because he told me! He told me in a—"

She broke off suddenly and drew back, the blood draining from her face.

"In a romantic moment?" Ransom said lightly.

"He told me for reasons of his own," Maria replied curtly. "I do not know what they were."

In the silence that followed, Ransom noticed that Tony had turned from the window and was staring down at Maria as if he'd never seen her before.

Finally Ransom said, "Ms. Cortez, did you by chance go into Mr. Nuevo's dressing room last night?"

Her brow furrowed. "Yes, I did. I went to . . ." She looked down at her hands. "I went to apologize."

Tony looked perfectly astonished at this. "You did?"

She turned her face up to him and gave a self-deprecating laugh. "I know, it is not like me. But . . . you were right. I should not have given the story to the papers. I should have talked to them all first, tried to smooth things over." She turned back to Ransom. "I saw how much I had hurt Ricky. I went to apologize. How did you know?"

"It was just a hunch. We looked through the dressing rooms earlier. There was a ring from a coffee cup on your makeup counter, but no sign of a cup. We found two in Mr. Nuevo's room: one mug and one paper cup."

"I must have forgotten my cup in his room."

There was a beat, then he asked, "How long were you there?"

"Not very long. Why do you ask this? What does it matter?"

"I just wondered. Riccardo's mug was empty, and the cup was only half full. It looked as if you'd stayed for some time."

"That is not possible," said Maria. "I didn't get a chance to drink it. I had a fresh cup of coffee. Barbara, my maid, is to have this for me for the intermission. I took it with me when I went to talk to Ricky. I don't remember drinking any of it. He must have drunk it himself, or someone else did."

All three men stared at her. There was a tingling in the air that could be felt on their skin.

Maria looked from one face to the other, her confusion causing her to grow angry again. "What is it? Why do you look at me like that?"

Ransom was the one to explain. "Because, Ms. Cortez, if Riccardo Nuevo drank your coffee, it is possible that he wasn't the target of the murderer."

7

You must be insane!" Maria said in a failed attempt at haughtiness. From the way she was goggling at the detectives, she clearly didn't dismiss the idea.

"On the contrary," said Ransom, "it's a very definite possibility."

"But you say you don't even know how Riccardo was poisoned yet!"

"Exactly. So it could've been from his own coffee, or it could've been from yours, if he drank it."

Maria was silent for several seconds, then flapped a hand in the air again. "No! No, this is crazy!"

"What a minute, Maria," said Tony Leonard, who had almost been forgotten during the diva's display of emotion. "Think about what's happened to you this week!"

She turned her eyes to him and blinked once. "What do you mean?"

He explained to the detectives. "These past few days, during the rehearsals and previews, twice Maria became violently ill for no reason at all."

Maria waved him off. "But that was only—"

"No, Maria, listen to me! Don't you see? You were very sick, but you were fine right after—"

He stopped when he noticed how she was glaring at him. He realized that she would consider it a serious breech of her dignity for him to graphically explain the results of her illness: Divas do not vomit. He struggled for the proper words.

"She was . . . ill, but she was perfectly fine . . . right . . . afterwards. Doesn't that mean—couldn't it be that somebody tried to poison her earlier?"

Ransom looked over at Maria. "The trouble was with your stomach?"

She looked down at her folded hands. "Yes."

"Do you have any idea who would want to kill you?"

Maria sighed. "When you are very talented . . . when you are in the limelight, many people can become jealous. I suppose there are some who would want to see me dead."

"Anyone in particular?"

"No," she replied, giving him a coy smile. Apparently she was satisfied to cast suspicion on everyone.

"I can name one person," Tony said. "David Cunningham! He stormed in here yesterday morning and threatened to kill her!"

"Did he?" Ransom replied, his right eyebrow sliding up again.

"It was nothing," Maria said casually.

"And why would he do that?"

"Because—" Tony glanced at Maria uncertainly. Then he turned back to Ransom. "Cunningham was upset about Maria leaving the company."

"I see. Did he learn about the decision the same way that Mr. Nuevo did?"

"Yes," Maria said innocently.

My, but you've been a busy little thing, haven't you? thought Ransom. "I think that will be all for now," he said, rising from his chair. Gerald followed suit.

"What? Wait!" said Tony.

Ransom ignored him. "I take it that your plans to leave the company don't include abandoning this production, so it won't be necessary to tell you all to stay in town."

"Of course not!" Tony answered for her. "But wait! Aren't you going to do anything to protect Maria?"

"So far we don't know that there's any real threat to her."

"But you said yourself—"

Ransom interrupted him with a shrug. "That is just another possibility. One of many. But we have to remember that Riccardo Nuevo is the one who's dead."

"What does it matter if Ricky is dead if *I'm* the one they're after!" Maria exclaimed viciously.

"I demand you do something to protect her!" said Tony.

The right edge of Ransom's lip curled. "We don't have any food tasters in the department." He turned to the diva and said, "Good afternoon, Ms. Cortez."

"Just a minute!" Tony followed them out into the hallway, closing the door softly. "That wasn't very funny, detective."

"It wasn't meant to be. But what would you have us do? There is no way we could guard her against being poisoned, and I doubt very much that she would take the necessary steps to ensure her own safety, even if I told her what to do."

This brought Tony up short. The concern that had been on his face fell away, leaving his expression somewhat empty. "What do you mean? What steps?"

"The safest thing for her to do would be to stay away from the theater until we've sorted this thing out."

"You mean let her understudy go on for her? She'd never do that."

"Barring that," Ransom continued with increasing impatience, "she should not eat or drink anything at the theater that she didn't prepare or provide with her own hands."

"Okay," said Tony, "okay, I'll see to it that she does that."

He moved toward the door. Just as he was about to grab the knob, Ransom said, "Oh, Mr. Leonard, one thing: Did you happen to go backstage last night?"

"Me? No, I didn't. I've been backstage a couple of times since I got here, but not last night."

"When did you get into town?"

He answered slowly. "Um . . . a few days ago. Why do you ask?"

"That would be . . . just before Ms. Cortez began suffering her mysterious illnesses?"

"What are you driving at?" Tony said, more in shock than in anger. "You don't think I'd hurt Maria, do you?"

Ransom cocked his head. "She mentioned that you had a certain familiarity with her body. You were able to confirm the bruise on her back."

Tony sighed. "I'm in love with her, Mr. Ransom. I admit that. Why would I want to hurt her?"

"I don't know," Ransom said with a smile, "unless the stories about her and Nuevo were true."

"They weren't!" Tony exclaimed. "And even if they were, I wouldn't kill *her,* I'd—" He broke off abruptly when he realized what he was about to say. He blushed deeply and looked away.

"But you weren't backstage last night," said Ransom.

He and Gerald walked away, leaving Tony Leonard gaping after them.

"That was certainly enlightening," said Ransom, pausing by the elevators. "People are lying to us already."

Gerald frowned. "You mean Cortez?"

"I mean Edward Carnegie."

"What?"

"When I pressed Ms. Cortez about the argument, she wondered how we'd heard about it. Then she said, 'those *men* from the theater. *They* told you.' Plural. I got the impression from Mr. Carnegie that he was alone."

"I guess," Gerald said doubtfully. "Who do you want to talk to next?"

"The sweet, innocent Micaela."

Gerald glanced at the list in his hand. "Who?"

"Gabrielle Charbonneau. She's the woman playing Micaela in this opera."

Gerald found the name on his list. "She's in four-oh-eight."

They went to the end of the hall, where a sign indicated that Room 408 was to the right. It was the second-to-last room.

Gerald's knock was answered by an attractive young woman with long brown hair. Her round face was streaked with tears and her eyes were bloodshot.

"Yes?" she said with a quavering voice. "Are you the detectives?"

"You knew we were coming?" Ransom asked.

She nodded, causing the tears on each cheek to run down and converge on her chin. "David called me."

She showed them into the room, which was a bit smaller and less elaborate than Maria's.

"He didn't call to tell me you were coming—it was about the rehearsal. He wants us to come in tomorrow and rehearse with Patrick, Riccardo's understudy. But . . . how we can . . ." She interrupted herself with a fresh onslaught of tears. "I don't know how I'll be able to do it. I was up all night. I couldn't stop crying. I finally did this morning. I didn't think I had any more tears left in me. And then . . . and then . . ." She stopped again and buried her face in her hands.

"Mr. Cunningham told you we suspect that Mr. Nuevo was murdered."

She dropped onto the edge of the bed and nodded without looking up.

Gerald took a seat at a small writing desk by the window, and Ransom pulled up a chair to face Gabrielle.

"I take it you were fond of Mr. Nuevo?" he said gently.

"Riccardo was the sweetest man! He was always kind to me. He would take time out from whatever he was doing to say a few words, which is more than I could say for a lot of people in this company."

"Miss Charbonneau, we're trying to establish what Mr.

Nuevo's relationships were like with the rest of the company. Can you help us with that?"

"I can try." She sniffed loudly and drew her wrist across her eyes to wipe away the tears.

"Did he have any friends in the company?"

"Everybody liked him. Everybody!"

Ransom was silent for a moment. His certainty that Gabrielle needed to be treated gently was warring with his desire to point out that perhaps someone had not liked Nuevo. He tried again.

"Was he particularly close to anyone?"

A cloud passed over the young woman's face. She absently caught a strand of hair between her thumb and forefinger and began to fiddle with it, averting her eyes from the detective.

"He was close to Maria."

"Anyone else?"

"I don't think she left time for much else."

Ransom took note of the hardness in her tone. "What about his relationship with you?"

Her hand froze with the strand pulled out to the side, and she looked directly at him for the first time.

"I was like . . . I was like a sister to him." Tears brimmed over her lower lids and coursed down her face. She wiped them away with trembling fingers, then laughed ruefully.

"Do you know if there was ever any trouble between him and anyone in the company?"

"Only with Maria. She was born to make trouble."

"What kind did she make for Nuevo?"

Gabrielle let out a rippling sigh. "She kept him on a leash . . . like a dog that you don't care for but you think might come in handy some time."

"I don't understand."

"When we started rehearsals, she went after Riccardo right away. You could see it. She monopolized his time, and if anyone else talked to him, any woman, I mean, suddenly Maria would be there, interrupting, putting her arm through his as if she wanted me to know that she owned him."

Ransom noted the switch to a personal pronoun.

"But that changed once we opened. We made a big splash, you know. I don't think any of us expected it. Of course, Maria would have everybody believe that she knew it would be like that all along, and that she was the whole reason we were so successful. But it's not just her! We're all a part of this production! We all worked together to make it good!"

There was a beat, then Ransom said, "And her relationship changed toward Riccardo once you opened?"

She nodded. "Tony Leonard came on the scene. I suppose he recognized a good thing when he saw it, and he got her to hire him on as her manager."

"Well, that seems to have been a good move on her part," Ransom said. "He's managed to get her into the Met."

Gabrielle's pale cheeks turned red. "I guess she knew that he could do things for her. She never would've had anything to do with him if she didn't think she could use him. But the minute he showed up, she dropped Riccardo . . . but not completely. She kept him on that leash, just in case she needed him again."

"Did he realize that was happening?"

"I think . . . I think he could feel that she had slipped away. But he loved her." Gabrielle managed to make it sound as if she wouldn't even find fault with him on this sore point. She frowned. "I hated the way she treated him."

"Hmm," said Ransom. "How does Ms. Cortez treat the other members of the company?"

"She treats anyone she can't use like dirt."

"Does that include you?"

She sniffed. "Maria is especially hard on women. At least, the ones with solo parts. She acts as if we're her competitors, but that we're no competition, if that makes any sense."

"Yes, it does. You seem to be a very observant person."

She shook her head sadly. "I don't have very much else to do. I don't really have any friends here. Maybe I played my part too well. Have you ever seen *Carmen*?"

"Yes."

"Micaela is the woman that Don José should marry, but doesn't. Their relationship is so . . . I don't know, I think half of the audience leaves thinking that she was his sister." She laughed again, this time bitterly. "I'm the little sister to the whole company. I've tried to make friends, but I'm afraid I'm not very good at it."

"I'm sure that isn't true," Ransom said kindly, trying to draw her out. In reality he thought it probably was true: It would be difficult to make friends while pitying oneself.

"Yes it is," Gabrielle said. "They say it's always that way for a middle child. I was the second of three. My older sister and my younger brother were adored. I was just sort of there, helping out. Doing whatever I was asked to. Ignored."

"Miss Charbonneau, there are fifty people in this company. Surely there are friends for you."

"I hardly had any chance to get to know anyone other than the principals. I didn't have very many rehearsals with the chorus because the only time I'm on with them at all is in my first scene, and even then it's not singing with them."

Ransom didn't point out that she'd been backstage with them for the past six months. He already knew why she hadn't mixed with them: She wanted Nuevo.

"The only other person who's nice to me is Franco." Her face lit up a bit when she mentioned his name. "He's very sweet to me. But . . . he's nice to everybody."

They fell silent. They'd gone farther afield than Ransom would have preferred, but he had sensed that letting her ramble a bit would get them something useful. He decided it was time to get back on track.

"About last night, did you see anybody out of the ordinary backstage? Anybody who didn't belong there?"

"No."

He glanced at his partner. "You didn't see anyone from the Sheridan Center?"

She shook her head.

"Did you go into Mr. Nuevo's dressing room at all?"

"Yes," she said, her eyes brimming at the memory. "Just before the opera."

"How did he seem to you?"

She hesitated. "He . . . I didn't . . . he wasn't there."

"I see," Ransom said with interest. "Is it possible he was next door, in Maria's room at the time?"

She nodded, and the tears overflowed.

"You heard them arguing."

"Yes. She was being her usual . . . beastly self. I felt so sorry for Riccardo!"

Both of Ransom's eyebrows elevated. "You could hear what they were saying?"

Gabrielle sniffed and averted her eyes. "Yes. You can hear everything through those walls. He was—he was angry because she was leaving the company. And she hadn't told him! That's just the way she treated people!"

"There was nothing more to it than that?"

"No," Gabrielle replied hesitantly.

"You're sure?"

"Yes, I'm sure!" She buried her face in her hands and wept.

"I really hope she didn't do it," Gerald said once he and Ransom were out in the hallway. "She's already had more than her share of trouble."

"You think so?"

"Yeah! You heard her!"

Ransom sighed wearily. "Yes, I did. It seems to me that all of her troubles are self-imposed."

"Have a little compassion, will you?" Gerald said, coming close to losing his patience. "She hasn't had it easy."

"She was a middle child, Gerald. She didn't lose a limb in a car accident."

"Everybody has their own problems. If her parents really did ignore her like that, I can see where that would hurt her."

"But she's an adult now. A rather wet adult."

"What's the matter with you?" Gerald said after a beat.

"What do you mean?"

"Well, you're being really . . ." He searched for a word that wouldn't set his partner off. ". . . cranky, even for you. What's wrong?"

He sighed. "Sorry, Gerald. I don't like this kind of case."

"You mean poisoning?"

"I mean one where I'm faced with suspects whose drama has to be waded through in order to get the facts."

"You think Charbonneau is a suspect?"

"I'm not as susceptible to tears as you are. I think she's a possibility if Nuevo was the target. I think she's a definite possibility if it was Cortez."

Gerald pursed his lips and shook his head. "I can't imagine that girl killing somebody. Look how broken up she is."

"Yes, she's very distressed," Ransom said pointedly.

"She just lost someone she loved!"

"Perhaps. But how do you think she'd be if she accidentally killed the object of her affection while attempting to rid herself of a rival?"

Gerald's face melted into a frown. He didn't like the idea, but couldn't deny that it made sense. It was also the type of suggestion that would cause him to cast doubts on his original interpretation of what he'd just witnessed.

Their next stop was Franco Giannini. His room was almost identical to Gabrielle's, but at the opposite end of the hall.

"I've already heard about the murder," Franco said as he showed them in. "David called a little while ago."

Ransom was immediately struck by Franco's bearing, which was confident and unassuming at the same time. He was also surprised to find another man in the room. Without pause, the baritone introduced him.

"Gentlemen, this is my partner, Paul Chamberlain. Paul, Detectives Ransom and White."

They shook hands formally, which seemed to be expected, and Franco offered them seats.

"It's a terrible thing to have happen. Riccardo was a nice guy," said Franco.

"How well did you know him?" Ransom asked.

He shrugged. "As well as you'd know any coworker you've been with for half a year."

"Do you know of any reason someone would want to kill him?"

"Good God, no! He's the last person I would think anyone would want to murder."

"Who's the first?"

There was nothing malicious in the smile that this elicited from him. "Have you spoken with Maria Cortez yet?"

"Yes, I have," Ransom replied, returning the smile. "And since then I have gotten the impression that most people would agree with you. What would you say if I told you it was true?"

"What was?"

"That Maria was the intended target."

"Oh my God," said Paul, who had seated himself on the dresser to Franco's left.

"You mean Riccardo was killed by accident? That's terrible! I mean, it's bad enough that he was murdered, but to think he was murdered in place of that—" He stopped abruptly and produced a sheepish smile. "Should I plead the fifth here?"

"Disliking Ms. Cortez wouldn't exactly make you a prime suspect, unless you have a reason for going beyond that that we don't know about."

Franco laughed. "I don't think so. Maria is the type of prima donna that would get laughs on the screen, but in real life is really just tiresome, like a noisy, bratty child."

"Frank knows the perfect way to handle people like that," said Paul. For a split second the detectives were at a loss as to who he was referring to, which was cleared up when he shot an affectionate glance at his partner. "When Maria starts one of her tantrums, he just sits back, crosses his arms, and watches her, like an audience, until she's done with her performance."

"I see," said Ransom. He turned back to Franco. "Do either of you know anyone who would want to kill her?"

Franco and Paul looked at each other, then back at Ransom.

"Oddly enough," the baritone said, "the only person I can think of is Riccardo."

"Why is that?"

"Because she treated him like garbage," he replied, with none of the venom that Gabrielle had had when she said virtually the same thing. "She strung him along. God knows why. I don't think Riccardo could have helped her career any, as good as he was."

Paul chimed in. "Riccardo was underrated. At least, he didn't get the notice he deserved in this opera. But that was because Maria stole the spotlight."

Franco nodded in agreement. "Not just onstage. I've seen them interviewed together. She dominated everything. He came off looking like sort of a sad sack. Led-around-by-the-nose type of thing." Franco shook his head, then asked, "Do you know how it was done?"

"We think he was poisoned."

"I can't imagine Riccardo trying to poison her and accidentally killing himself. He wasn't terribly bright, but he wasn't *that* dim."

"Why do you say he wasn't bright?"

His partner answered. "He got mixed up with Maria."

"How about Tony Leonard, her manager? Would he have a reason to kill her?"

Franco gave a rueful shrug. "Sorry, but I don't know him at all. I suppose he had reasons—probably most people that knew her did—but I wouldn't think he'd kill his meal ticket, would you?"

"Well," said Ransom after a short silence, "the idea that Maria might have been the target is only one possibility that we're pursuing. Of course, we're taking into account that Riccardo may have been the intended victim all along. Are you sure you don't know of anyone who would want to kill him?"

They both answered in the negative.

"Not even Maria Cortez?"

"Now *there's* a pretty idea," Franco said, brightening at the prospect. "Except I don't know why she'd need to. She's a climber. I don't think there was any way he could stand in her way, was there?"

"Not that we know of."

"I mean, if there was," Franco continued, "then I wouldn't put it past her."

Ransom considered him for a few moments. Franco obviously had little time for Maria Cortez, but although the things he had to say about her might be quite harsh, from all outward appearances he didn't harbor any rancor against her.

"Forgive me for asking this," said Ransom, "but Ms. Cortez doesn't strike me as particularly tolerant. . . ."

Franco laughed pleasantly. "That's an understatement. I pity poor Barbara."

"Barbara?" Ransom said with some surprise.

"Barbara Kean. Her maid. Madam runs her to distraction."

Ransom glanced at Gerald, who was in the process of jotting down the name.

"That's not exactly the kind of tolerance I was referring to."

"I know. She didn't harass me in any way, if that's what you're driving at. Which either means she thought I was beneath her notice, or she begrudged me the good reviews I've gotten."

"I don't think it's that, Frank," said Paul. "I think with that voice of yours—" He turned to Ransom. When he spoke, his admiration for his partner was obvious. "Have you seen the opera yet? Frank has a fantastic voice. It's clear and powerful—great tone, without the flashiness that *some* people resort to." He turned back to Franco. "Between your voice and the fact that you weren't going to be one of her conquests, she knew she didn't have any power over you, so she steered clear."

"Interesting," said Ransom. "Where does Gabrielle Charbonneau fit into all of this?"

Both men rolled their eyes.

"Poor Gabby!" Franco exclaimed. "Our little wallflower. She always seems to fall for the wrong people. She was absolutely besotted with Riccardo, who had no time for her because he was so besotted with Maria. My God, it sounds like a cheesy soap opera, doesn't it?" He paused and grinned. "Or maybe just an opera."

"Then she set her cap for you," Paul said, also grinning.

"Not seriously."

Ransom raised his right eyebrow. "Didn't she know that you weren't available?"

Franco gave a sad laugh. "Gabrielle is one of those women who willingly put blinders on. I don't make an issue of my sexuality, but I don't hide it, either." He glanced at his partner, who looked anything but happy. Apparently this was a bone of contention between the two of them. Franco added apologetically, "Of course, it wouldn't exactly do to make an issue of it, given the part I'm playing."

"I see," Ransom said slowly. "Do you think Gabrielle could've kept herself from seeing that she didn't have a chance with Nuevo?"

Franco sighed. "I don't see how she could've maintained that particular fantasy. But if you're implying that she might've had a reason to kill Riccardo, or Maria, you're way off base. Gabby couldn't hurt anybody."

Gerald looked up from his notebook and smiled thoughtfully.

"One last thing," said Ransom, "did you see anyone backstage who didn't belong there?"

Franco shook his head.

"No one at all? Perhaps Tony Leonard?"

"No, he wasn't there. Oh, wait, that guy from the theater was there. I can't remember his name."

"Edward Carnegie?"

"Yes. He was there with his partner. I don't remember his name, either." He looked to Paul, who shrugged disinterestedly.

There was a pause, then Ransom said, "When you say 'partner,' do you mean it in the same way you do when you introduce Mr. Chamberlain?"

Franco smiled with surprise. He looked as if he hadn't realized what he was saying. "As a matter of fact, I believe I do."

"Do you have any basis for thinking that?"

"Just a feeling," Franco replied with a shrug. "Really, Mr. Ransom, it's not like I'm implying some sort of unholy alliance. It was just a thought. What does it matter?"

"As far as I know, it doesn't."

"You don't want to question anyone else today?" Gerald asked as they rode down in the elevator.

Ransom shook his head. "It's getting late. I want to get back to area headquarters. We can turn the lists of the chorus and supers and crew over to the next shift. They'll have to be interviewed. I don't know what good it'll do. The chorus at least would know the other members of the company, so they could probably tell if a stranger was back there."

"You don't think a stranger could've done this, do you?"

Ransom turned to him. "A stranger to *them*, Gerald. They wouldn't be expected to know Edward Carnegie and his mysterious partner. They probably don't know Tony Leonard, either. They can also be asked if they saw anyone go into Nuevo's dressing room. We should concentrate on the last half of the opera, because I can't believe that the poison, whatever it was, took four hours to work."

"What'll we do next?" Gerald asked.

"Tomorrow we need to talk to Barbara Kean, Maria's maid. I don't know where she was today, since she wasn't with Maria, but she might have heard or seen something that will help us. At least, she might know if anyone has a particular grudge against the diva. And we need to talk to Carnegie again. I want to know why he lied to us . . . by omission."

8

Jeremy Ransom's relationship with Emily Charters had begun as a professional one, when Emily served as a vital witness in what Ransom would always refer to as "The Pennington Players Case." Ransom had grown to respect the elderly woman, somewhat grudgingly at first, then with the unswerving devotion one might have for a beloved professor. He had an especially high regard for her mental acumen and her uncanny insight into people, both of which had helped him on several occasions. Over the years she had become a surrogate grandmother to the emotionally distant detective, one of the few people with whom he ever allowed his guard to be down.

Ransom had seen to Emily's care after her bypass surgery, and once the initial threat to her health had passed he took to visiting her often to check on her. It wasn't long before "often" became nightly, and in an unspoken natural progression, their visits came to be centered around dinner.

The table was set that evening with cream-colored china bordered with vines. Emily often referred to them as her "old-lady china" with a twinkle in her eye.

"When I was a girl," she once explained to Ransom, "I always thought of this type of china as something that would only appeal to old women. I suppose that's because my own grandmother had a set quite like it that she kept in a glass cabinet in the dining room of her home. The only time I ever saw china of this sort was when we visited her. This set was willed to me by Beverly, a dear old friend, several years ago. I don't know why she thought I would want it. When I came into possession, I must admit I was tempted—only for a moment, you understand—to think of myself for the first time as an elderly person. But somehow I found the idea amusing rather than threatening. I don't use these plates very often, but they never fail to bring a smile to my face."

In the center of the table was a large serving bowl filled with cauliflower florets and a smaller bowl with peas and pearl onions. Emily served the breaded pork cutlets directly from the broiler.

"Please, don't wait for me," she said, as she did every evening, when she placed the plate in front of him. She went back to the oven to retrieve her own portion.

As always, Ransom waited for her before starting his meal. He had already explained to Emily everything he and his partner had learned so far. She returned and placed her plate on the table, then seated herself. "So what you're saying is that you have no way of knowing who the intended victim really was?"

"On the face of it," Ransom said as he helped himself to some cauliflower. "But we normally proceed on the assumption that the person who was killed was the intended victim." He spooned some of the vegetables onto her plate. "The trouble is, nobody seems to have wanted Riccardo Nuevo dead, while everyone has something against Maria Cortez."

She clucked her tongue. "My goodness, she seems to have gone out of her way to make enemies."

"Exactly. Which is why this is one of those rare cases when I think the wrong person really may have been killed." He replaced the serving spoon in the large bowl, then picked up the other and served out the peas and onions. "There's also this business of Cortez's mysterious illnesses."

"Which doesn't strike me as a good sign," said Emily. "Is it possible that someone tried to poison her before, unsuccessfully?"

"That's a possibility. If true, they didn't use nearly enough. She only reported being nauseated, not short of breath."

Emily considered this. "I suppose if she wasn't given very much of it, it might have upset her stomach to the point that she didn't notice the shortness of breath."

"That's all assuming that Cortez was the intended victim. It's early days yet. Someone may have had a perfectly good reason for wanting Nuevo out of the way."

Emily smiled at him playfully. "You mean a good reason as far as motives for murder go."

"Yes, Emily," he replied. "And people are lying to us already. Cortez told us that Nuevo had no hold over her, and yet we know that he told her he wouldn't let her leave the company. He must've had something he could use."

"Not necessarily. A jilted lover isn't the most rational of persons. He could merely have been saying what he wished could be true."

Ransom replaced the second serving spoon. "Yes, but if he really did have something to hold over her, it would give her a motive to murder him. Then there's Gabrielle Charbonneau. She completely broke down when I asked her about the argument between Nuevo and Cortez. She told us what we already knew, but I have a feeling there was more to it, that she heard something else she's not telling us."

"I feel sorry for that poor girl," Emily said as she cut a slice of pork. "I don't know if there's anything quite so sad as someone who has created phantoms for herself."

Ransom looked at her. "What do you mean?"

"I once knew a woman who I believe was like your Miss Charbonneau. She was a member of the church for a very short time. She was the first to volunteer whenever anyone was needed, the first to offer her services on committees, and the first to arrive at any function at which she was scheduled to serve. But this heightened public spirit of hers didn't really stem from a willingness to serve, at least that wasn't what I felt. It came from a loneliness so acute that one had only to speak with her for a few minutes for it to become evident. Her need for friendship, her loneliness, was so desperate that it could be sensed by virtually anyone with whom she came into contact, even in the most casual way. Desperation is never attractive and it drove away the very people whose friendship she desired. I don't know what had happened to her that caused that desperation, but her belief in her utter friendlessness became a self-fulfilling prophecy." Emily speared the piece of meat with her fork and put it in her mouth.

Now that she had taken her first bite, Ransom started on his own meal. "You say she was only a member of the church for a short time?"

Emily nodded. Once she had swallowed, she said, "Yes. She moved on very quickly. I think people like that often do. They try one place, and once they've exhausted their opportunities for companionship there, they move on to somewhere else."

"Hmm. Well, getting back to the matter at hand," he said lightly, "aside from the principals, we have Edward Carnegie, who conveniently failed to mention that he wasn't alone when he came backstage before the opera. He was accompanied by another man."

"Really? I wonder . . ." Emily's gaze traveled off into the distance.

"What?"

"What?" she said, suddenly coming back to the present. "Oh! I was just thinking, the Sheridans were there last night. Of course, they would be there at the opening of the Center, since it bears their name. By the Sheridans, I mean Margaret Sheridan and her son, Steven. Right after they entered their box, I saw her son say something to her, then he left. He was gone for quite some time."

"Do you happen to know when that was?"

"As a matter of fact, I do. It was fifteen minutes before curtain. Lynn just happened to mention it."

Ransom considered this for a moment, then shook his head and resumed eating.

"He could've gone anywhere. He could've gone to the bathroom, or to get his mother a drink."

"Yes, but . . . I seem to remember—of course, it was several months ago, so I may be mistaken—but I seem to remember reading, back when Mr. Carnegie was appointed the head of the center, that he had some connection to the family? Or that he had the family's support?"

"Yes?" Ransom said with interest, knowing Emily well enough to know that there was more to come.

Her shoulders elevated slightly. "What would be more natural than for a member of the family who built the theater to stop backstage to wish the company well? After all, it wasn't just the opening of the opera, it was the opening of the theater."

Ransom gazed at her while he thought about this. "If that's the case, then there seems to be even less of a reason for Carnegie to neglect to mention it."

"It does seem rather odd," said Emily as she took a sip of tea.

Tuesday morning Gerald came to Ransom's office with the reports from the evening shift.

"A big zero so far," he said. "Most of them were questioned, and 'nobody knew nothin' about nothing.' They didn't hear or see anything unusual."

"Nobody noticed anyone going into Nuevo's dressing room?" Ransom asked.

"The cast was too hyped up and the crew was too busy. That's the long and the short of it."

"Well," Ransom said with the type of heavy sigh that's usually reserved for later in the day, "let's get at it."

They arrived at the Sheridan Center at ten o'clock with the intention of questioning Edward Carnegie first, but were diverted by the sound of singing coming from the auditorium. They went in through the aisle-five entrance and stood at the back of the house.

Onstage was a young man who was the image of Riccardo Nuevo, once removed: His hair was shorter and not quite so dark, and he was thinner and paler than Nuevo, which left him with none of Nuevo's European allure. In fact, he looked quite ordinary. But there was nothing ordinary about his voice. He had a solid tenor that filled the auditorium. He was accompanied solely by a piano, whose music floated up from the orchestra pit.

Unfortunately, the power of his voice was mitigated by his obvious lack of confidence. He wandered the stage as he sang as if he had no idea where he was supposed to be.

"Patrick Laramie, the understudy, I presume," Ransom said.

Laramie was in the middle of the first-act duet with Carmen when the detectives arrived. As he sang his part, Maria Cortez stood with her arms folded defiantly beneath her breasts, watching him with scorn that would've been more appropriate to the latter part of the opera. This did not go unnoticed by the tenor, and it seemed to add to his discomfort.

He sang, *"Ah! si je t'aime, Carmen, tu m'aimeras . . . Chez Lillas Pastia, tu le promets? Carmen . . . tu le promets . . ."*

Instead of taking up her part, Maria strode across to him and slapped him hard on the back.

He spun around, startled. "Wha . . . ?"

"You are supposed to be facing me, idiot! You are supposed to be untying the rope from around my wrists, you fool! This is a love duet! Even if you are stupid enough to forget that I have to be unbound at the end of this song, the least you could do is remember that you are supposed to be falling in love with me, and *look* at me, you imbecile!"

She strutted to the foot of the stage and glared down at a man who was seated in the center of the seventh row. "You have to be insane if you expect to do this! This fool will never be ready! I won't do it!"

With this she stormed off the stage.

"Oh God," said the tenor. "I'm sorry, John."

The man said, "It's not your fault. You'll be fine. We'll go on without her for now."

"Excuse me," Ransom called out as he and Gerald came down the aisle. The man in the audience turned around, and a head popped up just beneath the stage, peering over the rim of the orchestra pit like a modern-day Kilroy.

The man stood up. "Who are you?"

"Detectives Ransom and White. We're looking into the murder of Riccardo Nuevo."

"I talked to the cops last night," the man said, "and we've got a lot of rehearsing to do."

"And you are?" said Ransom.

"John Turner. The assistant director."

"The assistant director?" Ransom repeated with some surprise. "I would've thought an event like this would've called for the director to be on hand."

"Marc Berger, the *real* director, went back to the coast the minute the previews started." He emphasized the word *real* to convey his displeasure at Ransom's tone of voice, which he'd taken as a slight to his position. "I'm the assistant director, and I'm in the chorus, so I stay with the production."

Ransom ignored him and spoke to the man on the stage. "I take it you're Patrick Laramie?"

"Yes," he replied apprehensively. "I talked to the police last night, too."

"I'm sure you did," said Ransom, "but if you don't mind, we'd like to have a word with you."

"You would?"

"Jesus Christ!" Turner interrupted. "We're rehearsing here! He has to be ready for tonight!"

"He was rehearsing a duet," Ransom said with a half-smile. "One can't do that alone."

"Yes, he can! He was—" Turner stopped when he saw the unmoving expression on the detective's face. He threw up his hands. "Oh, what's the use! Take five, Terry!" This was apparently directed to the pianist, who disappeared into the pit. Turner then turned to Ransom. "That's five minutes, detective! No more!"

"Yes, sir," Ransom replied, the smile spreading to the rest of his face. The assistant director found this so maddening that he turned on his heel and banged out of the auditorium through the door on the right.

"I would just like to have a quiet word with you," Ransom said to Laramie impassively. "If you could join us?" He gave a nod in the direction of the door on the left.

"Sure. I'll be there in a sec."

The detectives waited by the door and were joined almost immediately by the tenor. "What can I do for you?" he asked anxiously. "I mean, I really did talk to the police last night. They came to my hotel, and I—"

"There's nothing wrong," said Ransom. He considered the young man for a couple of seconds, then said, "First, I wanted to say that we arrived here a few minutes before Ms. Cortez's outburst. I was very impressed with your voice."

"Thank you," Laramie replied, obviously flattered.

"I understand that you're going to play Radames in *Aida*."

"Yes," he said, looking unaccountably relieved. "I'm looking forward to it. I've been preparing for a long time."

"You have?"

Laramie's face went blank. "Of course! It's the chance of a lifetime, and I have to make the most of it! Just look what that kind of chance led to for the leads in this production." He stopped, then gasped and quickly added, "I don't mean the murder! I meant all the publicity and what it's done for their careers and everything!"

"I understood what you meant," Ransom said. "I was just surprised that you'd been spending so much time on *Aida*. From what I heard of your singing just now, it sounded to me as if you'd been preparing for this role."

Tiny frown lines at the corners of Laramie's mouth signaled

the return of the anxiety he'd shown before. Ransom suddenly realized that the cause of the momentary relief had been getting away from the subject of the present opera.

"Thank you," Laramie said, turning pink. He seemed unaware of the implication of what Ransom had said. "I already know the role. Vocally, I mean. But when it comes to this production . . . all this business . . . all this staging . . ." He shook his head, clearly overwhelmed. "They gave me two rehearsals when we opened six months ago, and I've never had to go on as Don José." He lowered his voice. "And between you and me, I didn't pay much attention during the rehearsals I did have. I mean, hell! I'm starring in the next opera, and Riccardo was young and healthy. I didn't think I'd ever have to go on. I sure didn't expect him to die!" He sounded a bit awestruck at the idea of dying.

"Well," said Ransom as he started for the door, "I just wanted you to know I think you're doing a very good job."

"Really?" Laramie said, completely bewildered. "Didn't you have anything you wanted to ask me?"

Ransom paused in the doorway and looked back at him. "Come to think of it . . . no, I must've been mistaken."

It was Gerald's turn to look surprised, but he said nothing until they were halfway up the ramp to the backstage area.

"I take it that puts an end to the idea of the understudy as the murderer."

"Oh, I think so," Ransom answered wryly. "This murder was orchestrated by someone who is clever, and Mr. Laramie seems to be a bit of a dim bulb."

"Why? Because he doesn't know his part? That's not really fair! He only had two rehearsals, six months ago. You can't expect him to remember any of that."

"Perhaps," Ransom said, his tone giving no indication of conceding the point. "However, I would expect him to retain some of it after spending six months watching it, even if he wasn't playing the role."

"I suppose . . ." Gerald said reluctantly.

"And I hate to agree with the alarming Ms. Cortez, but I would also expect him to know when he's singing a love song."

While the detectives were talking to Laramie, a much more heated discussion was taking place backstage.

"It is barbaric!" Maria announced at the top of her lungs. "Barbaric! Ricky's body is still warm, and you have us going on as if nothing has happened! How can you live with yourself? How can you sleep at night?"

David Cunningham was seated on the makeup counter, watching her as she paced back and forth gesturing wildly with her arms to punctuate her indignation. Up until a few days earlier, he would've taken a conciliatory approach with her. But since he now knew that she intended to abandon the company with no compunction as to their fate, he found it very difficult to handle her with kid gloves.

"Exactly when do you think it would be proper for us to reopen?" he said flatly.

She stopped in her tracks and glared at him. She wanted to yell "Never!" but she decided against it. She shook her head vigorously and sliced the air with her palm. "I do not know! I can't make a decision that is at war with my heart! That's something for you to decide!" She resumed her pacing. "It is just unfortunate that such decisions are left to an unfeeling man who had no conscience whatsoever!"

"I find it very hard to buy this . . . *remorse* of yours, Maria, since you treated Riccardo like a dog."

"How dare you!" she screamed. "How dare you say such a thing about me! You know nothing about my feelings for Ricky!"

"Of course I do," he said. "You were indiscreet enough with Tony that everybody in this company knew exactly how you felt about Riccardo. Not only that, but from what I hear, you didn't tell him, this man you say you cared about, that you were leaving the company, either, did you? Funny way to treat someone who you want me to believe you felt so much for!"

Maria wavered as she paced. She wasn't used to being talked to in this fashion, and Cunningham's sudden self-possession threw her slightly off balance. "It doesn't matter what my feelings were for Riccardo . . . or how they might have . . . changed. What matters is common decency!"

Cunningham laughed. "Be careful, Maria, you may be struck by lightning."

"I know what decency is! And I know that to continue with this opera right after Riccardo has died is indecent! Have you no feelings?"

"Sure I have," he replied calmly. "Riccardo is the last person I would've wanted to see dead."

Maria stopped short and looked at him quizzically. Then the corners of her mouth curved. "You should be careful yourself, David. The police are not convinced that someone wanted to kill Ricky. They think I might have been the one whose life was attempted."

"I don't want you dead," Cunningham said after a beat. "I want you tied to me for the next two years, honoring your contract, standing on that little stage in Santa Marta, singing in the chorus."

"What?"

"I want you to miss every opportunity you've hoped for, and by the end of those two years for you to be forgotten. And if I can't have that then I'm going to spend that time dragging you through the courts until your name is so vilified in the opera community that nobody will have you!"

Maria stood in the center of the room, her eyes wide like a startled animal. This kind of attack from the normally mild-mannered company manager was so uncharacteristic and unexpected that it had the effect of dousing the diva with cold water. But the effect was short-lived. When she realized exactly what he was proposing, she reared back with her right hand.

"Bastard!" she cried as she swung at him.

But he was too quick for her. In one swift movement, he grabbed her wrist before her palm could come in contact with his cheek.

"Not this time," he said coldly. "And I'll tell you what you're going to do now! You're going to get your ass out on that stage and go through with this rehearsal without any more trouble, or in five minutes I'll have the Met on the phone and explain to them that you're trying to breach your contract with us, and that if they go through with their plans for you they'll get dragged into court along with you!"

For the first time Maria looked afraid. Her rigid body went limp and she pulled her hand away from him, dropping it to her side.

"You wouldn't. How could you keep me from doing this?"

Cunningham went to the door. "When have you ever played fair with anyone, Maria? I've put up with a hell of a lot from you because of your talent. But now I'm fighting for the life of this company. And I'm not going to have everything I've worked for destroyed by some . . ." He looked as though he knew exactly which word he wanted to use, but even if he'd allowed his temper to sway enough to openly threaten her, he still couldn't bring himself to use the first word that had come to mind. He said quietly, "You think that the company can't survive without you? Maybe you're right. That's all the more reason for me to fight. You never should've forced me into this."

Cunningham emerged from Maria's dressing room just as the detectives arrived backstage. When he saw them, he rolled his eyes and went straight to them.

"Look," Cunningham said without preamble, "we have a really important rehearsal going on here today if we have any chance of performing tonight, so I hope to God you're not going to disrupt it."

"I assure you," Ransom replied, his mouth curved in the way

that made him look like a malicious elf, "we will try to see to it that this murder will cause you as little trouble as possible."

The bravura Cunningham had marshaled to deal with Maria began to vanish. "I didn't mean . . . I know you have to do your job, but you've got to understand that we can't afford to be dark for even one night."

"So you've said."

He glanced over the company manager's shoulder. Maria Cortez was making her way from her dressing room to the stage. She was doing it slowly enough to make her reluctance evident, but still, she was doing it. Cunningham turned to see what the detective was looking at, then turned back.

"We had a difference of opinion about the rehearsal."

"It would appear you won."

Cunningham flushed guiltily. "Well, yeah. Sometimes these people—their egos get away from them, and you have to remind them of what's important."

"Sometimes you have to do more than that, wouldn't you say?"

"What do you mean?"

"In the course of our investigation we've turned up some information that leads us to believe that Nuevo might have been killed by mistake. The killer may have been after your leading lady."

"What?"

Ransom eyed him for a moment. "Mr. Cunningham, you really should stick to management and stay away from acting."

Cunningham's face went a deeper red. "I don't . . ." he started, but stopped and sighed wearily. "All right, you're right. I've already heard about that. Just now, in fact."

"Why did you want to pretend it was news to you?"

He looked down at the floor, which was dusty despite the newness of the theater. "I don't know. It's just the idea of talking to the police, I guess. Maria just told me that she might've been the one who was meant to die, while we were arguing. I don't doubt it. But . . . she made it sound like an accusation." His pulse quickened when he glanced at Gerald, who was taking notes.

"How could she do that?" Ransom asked.

Cunningham stared at Ransom for several seconds. "Oh, what's the use! I should tell you before she does because she'll make it sound worse than it really was. She's such a . . ." He struggled with himself, then fully gave in, shaking his head dismally. "That woman is just plain unreal. Sunday morning I read in the paper—in the paper!—that she's leaving our company and going to the Met. I couldn't believe it! Not that she wouldn't do it—I mean, try to walk out on her contract. I couldn't believe she would tell the papers instead of talking to me and Bill . . . Bill Stauffer, my partner. I was furious! I confronted her in her room. Her manager was there. I said . . . I said I could kill her! I wouldn't have done it! It's just the type of thing you say when you're angry."

"It's also the type of thing some people *do* when they're angry," Ransom said without any particular inflection.

"You've got to believe me," he said miserably. "I couldn't kill anybody!"

The diva and the understudy had resumed their duet on the stage. Maria's deep mezzo filled the silence that followed Cunningham's revelation.

"Well," Ransom said at last, "you're right about one thing. Ms. Cortez did make it sound a lot worse than that."

Cunningham's eyes widened. "She already told you about it?"

"Oh, yes. She would have us believe that you tried to attack her . . ." He looked at his partner. "Like a wild animal, isn't that what she said, Gerald?"

"That's what she said."

"I just—I just forgot myself for a minute." Cunningham stammered.

Ransom sounded surprisingly conciliatory when he said, "We all forget ourselves now and then. It's just fortunate Mr. Leonard was there, isn't it?"

Cunningham didn't reply.

"Tell me something," said Ransom, his tone indicating he

was changing the subject. "Both times we've been here we've come in through the auditorium. I assume there's a stage door entrance?"

The company manager perked up a bit. He pointed to the left. "Yeah. Over there. The cast and crew have to use it."

"I take it it's guarded."

He nodded. "On days that there's anyone in the theater. Otherwise it's locked."

"Is the guard there now?"

"Yeah."

"Thank you, Mr. Cunningham," Ransom said as he walked away. He left the manager to wonder how much damage he'd done to himself.

Gerald followed Ransom down the hallway to the door Cunningham had indicated. They went through it and found themselves in a small anteroom. The bulk of the room was partitioned off behind a wall of protective glass, and directly across from them was a door leading to the outside. Behind the glass sat a man whose youthful face belied his graying hair. He wore a red flannel shirt and a pair of denim jeans. When the detectives entered, he looked up from a copy of *People*.

"Can I help you?" He sounded a trifle surprised that they had come from the theater rather than the outside.

Ransom showed him his shield and made the introductions. "We're looking into the murder of Riccardo Nuevo."

Before he could say anything else the outer door opened and a young woman breezed in. She had black hair that reached almost to her waist and had a navy blue bag slung over her shoulder. She was carrying a large paper cup of coffee from one of the trendy coffee shops.

"Hi, Pop!" she said, paying no attention to the detectives.

" 'Morning," he replied. He pressed a button on his desk and the lock on the inner door clicked. The woman went through.

"Who was that?" Ransom asked once the door had closed.

"Barbara Kean. She works for Maria Cortez."

"Ah," said Ransom. Then he smiled. "Pop, hmm? You're a little young for that nickname. So is this theater. Do they just automatically call the stage door guard 'Pop'?"

The man behind the glass grimaced. "It's worse than that! Has nothing to do with the theater, believe it or not! My name's Bert Wiesel. Pronounced 'wise,' but ever since I was a kid people have pronounced it 'wheeze.' Pop Weasel! Get it?"

Ransom cleared his throat. "Everyone who comes through here has to be buzzed in by you, is that correct?"

"That's right. The people I know belong here get buzzed in. Everyone else has to sign in after being okayed by whoever they're here to see."

"And this is the only way to get in backstage?"

Wiesel shrugged. "Except through the house. 'Course, if someone came backstage through there, they'd be sure to be seen."

"We'd just like to make sure that nobody outside of the company members and the theater staff got in on Sunday night."

He shook his head. "Not this way, they didn't. You think maybe some kook killed off Mr. Nuevo?"

Ransom spread his palms. "We're just making sure. Do you keep a log?"

"Sure do." Wiesel opened a drawer and pulled out a clipboard that held a small stack of forms. "Won't make any difference, though. I can tell you now that nobody came in this way that didn't belong." He lifted the top sheet, scanned the one beneath it, then pulled it off the clipboard and held it up to the window. "See? Only people who were here were delivery men from florists. Six of them. All for Maria Cortez."

Ransom read down the list. "Did they leave the flowers here or go backstage?"

"Left them here. I have one of the stagehands take them back." He turned the page around and looked at it. "But, like you see, I log them in."

"I see," Ransom said slowly. "Would you buzz us back in?"

"Sure."

Wiesel pressed the button and the lock clicked. Gerald opened it and started to go through, but Ransom stopped and turned back to the guard. "Oh. One thing: When Ms. Cortez came in on Sunday evening, was she alone?"

"Huh? Yeah. She was."

"Do you remember if Tony Leonard came in later?"

Wiesel looked thoroughly confused. "Who?"

Ransom smiled. "Never mind."

He and Gerald went through the door.

"Well, maybe we've finally been told the truth about something," Ransom said wryly. "At least now we know that Leonard really didn't come back here that night."

"Unless he came in through the auditorium," said Gerald.

Ransom shook his head. "Mr. Wiesel is right. I don't think anyone who was planning to commit a murder would risk being seen by the audience."

"But he could've come in earlier—before the audience got here."

"And done what? Left a poison trap for Nuevo? It doesn't work, Gerald. The only thing we know he drank backstage is coffee. There were no signs that he had anything else to drink. We can safely assume that's where the poison was. Unless the murderer has a degree in toxicology, I hardly think he or she could've come up with a poison so tasteless that it could've been hidden in water, if there is such a thing. I just wish it didn't take so damned long to get results from the lab."

As always when frustrated, Ransom reached for the pack of cigars in his breast pocket. Then he remembered where he was and dropped his hand with a heavy sigh.

"That's the way it is when they don't know what they're testing for," Gerald said.

Ransom shot him a glance to let him know he didn't need the explanation. Gerald shrugged.

They could hear the voices of Maria and her new partner

wafting from the stage. They were going through the rigors of another duet, which Ransom recognized as coming from the latter part of the second act.

"While the cat's away, let's talk to the maid," said Ransom as he headed for Maria's dressing room.

When they stepped through the doorway, Barbara Kean leapt off the diva's makeup chair.

"Oh!" she exclaimed, putting a hand to her chest.

"I'm sorry, we didn't mean to startle you."

"No, it's not that," she said, calming herself down. "I thought you were Maria. It would never do for me to look comfortable."

Barbara Kean had an ingratiating smile and high, prominent cheekbones. She was dark enough that Ransom thought her ancestry could be American Indian. She wore a simple, beltless, pale yellow dress that was rather tentlike despite the fact that it was fairly short, and she had silver bracelets on each wrist. Ransom suspected that the shapelessness of the dress was due to the danger of appearing at all attractive in the diva's presence.

"Are you the police?" she asked.

"Yes, Miss Kean. Detectives Ransom and White."

"You know who I am?"

"Yes. You're Ms. Cortez's maid, aren't you?"

Barbara grimaced. "I was hired as her personal assistant. She likes to call me her maid. It makes her feel superior. I should say more superior."

Ransom tilted his head slightly. "It doesn't sound like there's any love lost between you and your employer."

She laughed. There was no bitterness in it, only amusement. "Do you have any children, detective?"

"No," he replied, his brow furrowing.

"Well, I don't either. But I have nieces and nephews, so I know how to deal with children. You either spend all your time yelling at them, or you ignore them and go about your business."

"And you choose the latter?"

She shrugged. "Yelling would get me fired. Listening to all

her whims would get me crazy. So I just let her talk, and I do my job."

"And part of your job is getting her coffee?"

She laughed again. "Oh, Lord! The coffee! Yes, that's part of my job. I could make her coffee here, but that would be too easy. She claims that LaMont's is the best, so she insists on having it from them. But if you'd ever seen her eat or drink, you'd know she's not that discerning. She just likes saying, "Barbara, run out and get me some coffee.""

"And you don't mind doing it?"

"Why would I? The weather's nice, I get to take a walk. And it's a break, if you know what I mean. Do you want to sit down?"

"Thank you, no," Ransom replied. "I only have a couple of questions to ask you. I assume on Sunday night you were sent out for coffee?"

She nodded. "I brought some in with me, like I usually do. She sent me out later for more."

"When was that?"

She looked upward and sucked her lips in until they almost disappeared. "Um . . . it was during the first intermission that she asked me to do it, so I went once the second act started. Took me about half an hour. Why do you ask?"

"It's possible that whoever killed Mr. Nuevo was actually trying to kill Ms. Cortez."

She lowered her eyes to him and knit her brows. "Hey, wait a minute! You think there was something wrong with her coffee?"

"It's possible that it was poisoned, yes."

The implications of this took a few moments to register. "Not by me!" she said warily. "I bought it, brought it back, and put it right here on this counter. I never touched it again."

"Was this room ever left unattended?"

"Well, sure it was! Maria's onstage a lot. There's no reason for me to just sit here."

"What do you do?"

"Sometimes I stand in the wings and watch the performance. Sometimes I talk to people."

"Who is there to talk to once the opera starts?" Ransom asked.

"Most of the chorus are offstage for really long stretches. And of course, Sherman doesn't have anything much to do but touch-ups once the first act is underway."

Here was a name the detectives hadn't hear before. "Sherman?"

"Sherman Dunston," Barbara said. "He's the makeup man for the principals."

Ransom glanced at Gerald, who duly noted the name in his notebook.

"So, when you're out of the room, would it be possible for someone to slip in here unnoticed?"

She wrinkled her nose and answered slowly. "I suppose so. But . . . there's always so many people backstage. I'd think somebody would notice."

Ransom considered this. Then he said, "You know, Ms. Kean, given the volatile nature of your employer, I'm surprised you didn't already know about the possibility that the killer was after her rather than Nuevo. I would think she would've told you."

Barbara smiled. "I didn't see her at all yesterday. Her manager's in town. She doesn't like me around when he's here."

"Why is that?"

"No idea," she said with a shake of her head that caused her hair to spread into a web across her back. "Probably didn't want me to know they were having an affair."

"Are they?" Ransom asked with a raised eyebrow.

She lowered her voice to slightly more than a whisper. "Excuse me, you can hear everything through these walls. Of course they are. She might be able to fool other people, but how's she going to keep it from her assistant?"

"You know this for a fact?"

She nodded. "I've seen enough. Even if I didn't know it for

a fact, I'd still *know* it. Maria's one of those women who feels that sex is the perfect way to control a man." She smiled. "It works for her."

"Why would she try to keep it from you?"

"Who knows? She might've been afraid it would get back to Riccardo, but he wouldn't have heard it from me. A job like mine, silence is part of what you're paid for."

Ransom couldn't help registering a mild bit of surprise at this. Barbara laughed. "Hey, my loyalty ends with police intervention!"

"I understand," Ransom said with a smile. "I have one more question for you. We've been told that Mr. Nuevo and Ms. Cortez had an argument just before the opera began Sunday night. Were you here for that?"

She looked heavenward and sighed. "Oh, that! I was sent out of the room. But I didn't go far. I could hear them. You already know what they were arguing about, right?"

"Why don't you tell us?" said Ransom.

"It was about her leaving. In typical fashion, putting it in the paper was her way of announcing it to the company. Riccardo was furious. Hell, everybody was. I felt sorry for him. You know, men are really stupid sometimes. I don't know how anybody could fall for Maria's game, but a lot of them do. He loved her. Poor idiot. And she was vicious to him. And to Gabrielle."

Gerald looked up in surprise.

"Ms. Charbonneau came in during the argument?" Ransom asked.

"No, thank God! I meant Maria was vicious *about* Gabrielle. Gabrielle had a crush on Riccardo. When they had that fight, Maria told him he should go to Gabrielle. Well, that's not exactly what she said: It was something like 'why don't you go to that moon-faced cow' or words to that effect."

"What did Nuevo say to that?" Ransom asked.

"He said he didn't want her."

9

Just what we need," Ransom said as they went up the aisle toward the lobby. "More people backstage! We'll have to talk to the makeup artist, especially since he was hanging around the dressing rooms during the performance."

Gerald said nothing. He was lost in thought, his fleshy face puckered.

"What is it, Gerald?"

"I guess Ms. Charbonneau moves up a notch on the suspect ladder," he replied.

"Ah, yes, the sweet Micaela. At least we know now what she wasn't telling us."

"Yeah. She must've heard what they said about her."

"Don't take it too much to heart. I doubt if she would kill Maria Cortez for calling her a cow."

"I wasn't thinking of her. I was thinking of him."

They passed through the black-curtained doorway into the lobby. Ransom stopped and looked at his partner. "Very good, Gerald. If she heard what Nuevo said, she might have wanted to murder him. But there's still a problem with that: The argument took place just before the opera began. I don't think even a woman scorned would just happen to have poison on hand."

Gerald looked almost relieved at this. "Where are we going now?"

"To do what we came here to do in the first place: talk to Carnegie."

Bonnie Payton was seated at her desk, intently scanning a sheet on the stand to the left of her PC while her fingers moved rapidly across the keyboard.

"Hello, detectives," she said, without any physical indication that she'd noticed them.

"We need to see Mr. Carnegie. Is he in?"

She stopped typing and looked up. "Yes, he is."

"Don't bother to announce us," Ransom said as he and Gerald went past her desk.

Instead of protesting, Payton flashed a curious smile. "That's all right." She went back to typing.

Edward Carnegie was seated at his desk reading a letter when the detectives came into his office. He looked up, surprised, and failed to catch himself before a trace of displeasure crossed his face. Unlike on their first visit, he didn't rise, apparently feeling that the sudden intrusion didn't demand professional courtesy.

"Gentlemen," he said, "I didn't know you were here." He placed the letter facedown on his desk.

"Forgive us for barging in like this," Ransom said without a hint of sincerity, "but I have a few more questions to ask you."

"Me?" There was genuine surprise in his voice.

Ransom took a seat facing the desk without invitation, and Gerald sat next to him. "Yes. Well, one question in particular: Why didn't you tell us that Steven Sheridan accompanied you backstage Sunday night?"

Gerald looked at his partner, trying not to let his own amazement show.

Ransom was taking a gamble, because he had no proof whatsoever that Sheridan had been the man with Carnegie, only

Emily's suggestion that it would've been understandable for him to have done so, and the connection to the Sheridan family.

The gamble paid off. Carnegie froze for a split second, just long enough to give himself away.

"I didn't think it was important."

"You seem to be a reasonably intelligent young man. I didn't think it was necessary to point out to you that this is a murder investigation."

Carnegie sat back in his chair and folded his hands in his lap. "The Sheridans are one of the most prestigious families in Chicago. There's enough scandal as it is with a murder being committed in their theater on opening night without needlessly bringing one of the family into it. Steven simply came backstage with me to wish the players good luck on their opening. His presence doesn't have any bearing on your case."

Ransom shrugged nonchalantly. "He may have seen something."

"He didn't see anything that I didn't see," the director replied, fighting to keep the sharpness out of his voice.

Ransom leaned forward. "Mr. Carnegie, this is not a theatrical game, it's a murder. And you're not in charge of the investigation, I am. I decide what's important and what's not. And withholding information is the type of thing that will lead me to believe you have something to hide."

Once again there was a moment where Carnegie seemed to have turned to stone. Then he laid his palms on the desk and pulled his chair forward. "Of course. I'm sorry. I was just thinking in terms of protecting the family."

"Is there some reason they need protection?"

"No! Of course not! I meant I was trying to keep their involvement in this to a minimum."

Ransom sat back and crossed his legs. "I can understand your desire to spare the Sheridans any trouble, since they've been so good to you."

"What?" Carnegie said blankly.

"You have a close relationship with them, don't you?"

"Not . . . particularly. How do you mean?"

"I thought I heard that you had the Sheridans' backing in getting this job."

"I didn't need anyone's backing," Carnegie replied, his back stiffening. "I was more than qualified for it."

Ransom smiled. "But you did have the Sheridans' support, didn't you? Or, at least, one of the Sheridans."

There was a long silence during which Carnegie appeared to be deciding which avenue of response would cause the least amount of trouble. He decided to fall back on total—or near total—honesty, with a sense that he was treading on very thin ice. He produced his most ingratiating smile.

"I met Steven in college. We were quite close." He paused. "Do I need to explain that?"

"No, I don't think so."

"We drifted apart after college, but we stayed in touch. Meeting every now and then. Steven put me forward for this position because he knew me and knew I was right for it. But the decision to support me for the job was his mother's, not his. And I can tell you that she had me very thoroughly checked out before doing it. If anything, my relationship with Steven worked against me."

"Really?" Ransom said, sensing that the last part of the director's statement had been a bit forced. "I wonder why she decided to do it, then?"

Carnegie faltered. "I . . . couldn't say."

I'll bet you could, thought Ransom. Then he said, "Steven Sheridan is the head of the Sheridan Foundation, isn't he?"

It seemed to the detective that Carnegie had again frozen for a split second, although for the life of him he couldn't understand why. Sheridan's position was common knowledge.

"Yes, he is."

"So I assume you've been working fairly closely with him since being hired. What is your relationship like now?"

Carnegie huffed disgustedly. "Mr. Ransom, Steven has a

friend who's dying right now. Over in St. Joseph's. Steven's there almost every evening."

"I see," Ransom said, mentally noting that the director hadn't answered the question. "Can you give us Sheridan's business address?"

When Carnegie didn't answer immediately, Gerald looked up from his notebook, his stub of a pencil held against the page. Carnegie stared at Ransom for a long moment, then pulled open the center drawer of his desk and extracted a business card, which he handed to the detective.

"That's his address. I really do need to reiterate that the Sheridans couldn't have had anything to do with Nuevo's death. Hell, they didn't even know him! And why would they want to do something that would hurt their theater like this?"

"It remains to be seen whether or not the Center will suffer," Ransom replied. "Sometimes this type of thing can have an oddly positive effect."

Carnegie refused to be deflected. "If the media finds out that you're questioning them, they'll be all over them. According to Steven, the media has already been hounding them for statements about the death. If you involve them in your investigation—which is totally unnecessary—you'll just be causing them more grief."

Ransom slipped the card into his pocket without bothering to look at it. "I'll keep that in mind."

The detectives left Carnegie's office. Ransom stopped at Bonnie Payton's desk while Gerald closed the door.

"Ms. Payton, could you show us to the elevator?"

The assistant was so startled by the request that it was a long time before she answered. She broke into a canny grin.

"Certainly," she said, rising from her chair. "This way."

Before following her, Ransom glanced down at the phone on her desk. There was a single red button, then a row of clear ones.

Only the first three were labeled with extension numbers. The second button was lit. He brought it to Gerald's attention, then they joined Ms. Payton, who had already made it to the door.

Once they were out of the offices, she said, "All right, detective, what did you want to ask me?"

"It's been my experience that assistants are very observant—"

He was stopped by the expression on her face. She had lowered her head and her eyes swept up at him from under her long, dark lashes. He got the message.

"Have you worked for Mr. Carnegie since the beginning?"

She nodded, and looked quite amused that she'd been able to abash the detective, however slightly. "One of his first acts was to hire me."

"So you've been working here with him while the plans were made to bring in this opera?"

"Before that."

"Has Steven Sheridan been in to see him very often?"

"I don't know what you mean by often," she replied, her shoulders efficiently rising and falling. "The Sheridan Foundation is financing this opera, for the most part, and Mr. Sheridan is in charge of that. It makes sense that he'd meet with my boss." There was a moment's hesitation on her part, then she continued before he could ask his next question. "But . . . unless I miss my guess, you want to know about their relationship. Is that right?"

"I was wondering about it, yes."

"What could it have to do with your investigation? Or are you just nosy?"

Ransom manufactured a self-deprecating smile. "Occupational hazard."

She pursed her lips. "I'm not sure I like this. If you want to know about the two of them, why don't you ask them?"

"I did. We like to have everything verified."

"Don't you think he told you the truth?"

"Part of it," Ransom replied. "Why don't you tell me the rest?"

162

She made several rapid clicking sounds with her tongue. "Well, I still don't like it, but if you must know, they're lovers."

"Do you know that for a fact?"

She shook her head. "But everybody in the office thinks so."

"Why is that?"

She sighed. "They make such a point of ignoring each other in public—not like people that don't like each other, but like people who're trying to make everyone think there's anything there. If there wasn't anything between them, I think they'd be more at ease."

"You see?" he said after a beat. "I was right about assistants."

"But what does it matter?" Gerald said as they climbed into the car.

"Maybe it doesn't." Ransom pulled out a cigar and pushed in the lighter. "But there's protecting and there's protecting. I don't like the idea of Carnegie lying to us about Sheridan."

"He didn't lie," Gerald said as he turned the key in the ignition. "He just didn't tell us about it. Maybe he didn't think of it."

The lighter popped out. Ransom pressed the glowing coil against the end of his cigar and puffed. "He didn't claim forgetfulness, he claimed to be protecting them. Which I find a bit odd, under the circumstances."

Gerald shook his head. "I think you're making too much of it, Jer. Protecting the Sheridans might be part of his job. Or even . . . if he has the kind of thing going with Steven Sheridan that people think he does, maybe he was doing it out of . . . out of . . ."

Ransom shot him a curious glance. "Love, Gerald."

"Right. Tell me something: How did you know that Sheridan was the guy with him?"

"How else? Emily." He took a drag from the cigar and blew the smoke out the window. "I think it's obvious that he didn't want us to know about his relationship with Sheridan. The question is, why?"

"If we can believe that Payton woman, they were trying to keep it a secret from everyone, not just us."

"But why?" Ransom said irritably. "this is the twenty-first century and we're talking about a theater here. It's not as if anyone around them would be shocked."

"He could've had a lot of reasons for lying that don't have anything to do with this murder."

"Yes," Ransom replied, the right side of his mouth crooking upward. "Like a general fear of the police. Fear that their sexuality would prejudice the police against them."

Gerald didn't respond. He stared out through the windshield and tapped his thumb steadily against the steering wheel. "You want to go to Sheridan's office now?"

"Yes." He took a deep drag from the cigar and sent a cloud of smoke cascading across the inside of the windshield.

They parked directly in front of the entrance to the Wacker Drive office building that housed the Sheridan Foundation. One of the perks of being a cop that Ransom most enjoyed was the ability to illegally park with impunity. They went into the building, checked the directory, and rode a characterless elevator up to the fifteenth floor.

After the elegant Sheridan Center, the drab foundation office came as quite a surprise. A lone secretary sat behind a semicircular desk in the windowless lobby. She was chatting on the phone with the stifled boredom of someone who gets neither enough work nor enough sunlight. When she saw them, she said, "Hold on a minute" into the receiver, then put her hand over the mouthpiece. "Can I help you?"

"Detectives Ransom and White. We're here to see Mr. Sheridan," said Ransom.

"Oh, yes," she said, her face opening with recognition. She

uncovered the mouthpiece. "I'll have to call you back." She replaced the receiver and rose from her chair. "He's expecting you."

"I thought he might be," said Ransom.

The detectives followed as the young woman unceremoniously led them down a hallway that looked as if it had been erected out of cheap drywall and covered with several coats of paint to give the illusion of freshness. She stopped at the first door on the left and knocked, then went in.

Sheridan's office was hardly an improvement over the hallway. Its size and decor could best be described as serviceable: furniture of the rental variety and job-lot watercolors framed on the dull walls. The only plus to this office was a good-sized window, whose advantages were minimized by the fact that it looked directly out onto another building less than fifty feet away.

"The detectives are here to see you," the woman said.

Steven Sheridan came out from behind his desk to greet them. The woman departed, closing the door behind her.

"Hello," he said, shaking Ransom's hand.

"This is quite a change from the offices over at your center, if you don't mind my saying it."

"It's not my center," Sheridan said without emotion. "And there's a difference between administering money and getting to spend it."

"Ah."

"Have a seat. Ed called and told me you might pay me a visit."

He directed them to a grouping of four low chairs, covered in a heavy violet fabric, that were strategically situated by the window.

"I had a feeling Mr. Carnegie might warn you we were coming," Ransom said once they were seated.

Sheridan's features took on a doll-like surprise. "Warn me? He wasn't warning me, he was just . . ." An embarrassed smile spread across his face. "God, it's very disarming to talk to the police! Ed wasn't exactly warning me, but I think he thought he made a bad impression with you when he neglected to tell you I was with him backstage."

"So he told you about that?"

Gerald got out his notebook and pencil. When Sheridan replied, he made a point of not looking at him. To Ransom, it seemed as if the foundation's director was at pains to appear unruffled.

"Yes, he was upset about it. As I said, he was afraid he gave you the wrong impression."

"Which impression was that?"

There was a beat before he answered. "That there was something to hide. I assure you, Ed was only trying to preserve the family name."

Though Sheridan was trying to maintain his sophisticated demeanor, Ransom noticed a bit of coldness in his tone when he mentioned his family.

"I see," Ransom said. "Could you tell us why you went backstage Sunday night?"

"Certainly," Sheridan said, noticeably more at ease. "It was at my mother's insistence. She thought a representative of the family should greet the cast and wish them good luck before the show. She, of course, wouldn't lower herself to do something like that, so I was elected. After I saw her to her seat, I went back out to the lobby and met Ed, and we went backstage."

"How?"

"I . . . I beg your pardon?"

"How did you get backstage? You didn't go through the auditorium."

Sheridan looked surprised that he knew this. "Oh. We went around the outside of the building through the stage door. We didn't want to draw attention to ourselves."

"Hmm," said Ransom. Wiesel hadn't mentioned them, but then, why would he? He wouldn't have thought anything unusual about either Carnegie or Sheridan's presence. "Go on."

"There's really nothing to tell. We went to Maria Cortez's dressing room, and she and Nuevo were having a fight. I was all

166

for forgetting the whole thing, but Ed thought it would be best to break it up. I think . . . he might have thought it would end up disrupting the performance. Like maybe one of them would refuse to go on or something like that. It could've been disastrous."

Ransom smiled. Apparently that had been a very detailed conversation over the phone with Carnegie. "No more disastrous than having one of the leads drop dead."

Sheridan faltered. "No, but . . . well, of course, we didn't know that that was going to happen at the time."

He forgot himself enough to look at Gerald, who had hastily scribbling notes.

"Did you go into Nuevo's dressing room?"

"No. There was no reason to. We saw him in Cortez's room."

"Mm-hmm. Do you know any of the members of the company?"

"No, not really."

"So it would be useless to ask you if you noticed anyone or anything out of the ordinary."

Sheridan thought for a moment, then shook his head. "It was really busy back there with the crew and everything. Well, there was a young lady standing not too far away from Cortez's dressing room. Ed told me that was her maid."

"Her assistant, yes," Ransom said, correcting him on Barbara's behalf. "What did you do once you'd broken up the scene in Maria's dressing room? Greet the rest of the cast?"

"We stopped and spoke to Franco Giannini, and we tried the other woman . . . I can't remember her name . . . the one playing Micaela."

Ransom found it hard not to smile. "Gabrielle Charbonneau."

"Yes. She wasn't in her dressing room. After that it was getting late, so we gave up and went out."

"The same way you came in?"

"Uh-huh."

There was a long pause during which Ransom gazed at Sheridan with a notable lack of expression.

"Well," he said at last, "that all seems straightforward enough. Which makes it all the more curious that Mr. Carnegie felt the need to be . . . well, let's say less than up front."

Sheridan heaved a weary sigh, then folded his arms across his chest. "That's because you don't know my mother."

"Your mother?"

"My mother would do anything to avoid having a scandal attached to our family name."

Ransom glanced at Gerald. "Apparently, I'm missing something. There's been a murder in the Center. Assuming that you had nothing to do with it, I fail to see how your family name would be sullied."

Sheridan's lips flatlined. "Oh, Mr. Ransom, I'm not talking about a little thing like murder. I'm talking about something far worse: homosexuality. Mother would rather have our name attached to murder than have anyone know that her son is gay."

"You mean simply because you were backstage with Carnegie? She knew you were with him."

"Yes, she did. But she wouldn't want the newspapers to know it."

Ransom looked at him for a very long time, unable to hide how perplexed he felt. "I'm missing something, Mr. Sheridan. I don't see what the papers could've made out of it."

"That's because you're not my mother," Sheridan replied, his disdain palpable. "Nothing, of course! But as far as mother is concerned, even if a paper just said that Ed and I had been backstage at the same time, in her mind, she'd imagine everyone reading something into it."

"Then why did she have you do it at all?"

"Because it was the proper thing to do for the occasion, and because we didn't know anything newsworthy was going to happen backstage."

"Your mother is a benefactor of the arts," Ransom said

smoothly after another long pause. "It's hard to imagine her holding that attitude."

"She doesn't dislike other people's homosexuals, only those in her own family."

There was a lengthy pause. "Those?"

Sheridan eyed him shrewdly. "I'm surprised you don't know about this, detective."

Ransom shrugged. "I don't spend a lot of time around the water cooler. Why don't you fill me in?"

He leaned forward. "You think the Sheridan Center was built to benefit the arts, or the city?" He shook his head. "It's not a monument to my father's memory, detective. It's my mother's way of silencing tongues. She has spent a fortune since his death, and even more when he was alive, to cover up the fact that Daddy was fond of the company of men."

"How does throwing money around accomplish that?"

Sheridan laughed at what he took to be Ransom's naïveté. "As long as she's pouring money into projects that benefit the city, nobody is going to openly smear the name of my dear, departed Daddy."

Ransom allowed this time to sink in before continuing. "All that may be true, but it doesn't explain why Mr. Carnegie would keep the fact that you were backstage with him a secret from us."

He sat back in his chair. "Like many people, Ed has learned to be afraid of my mother."

Ransom's right eyebrow immediately went up. "Afraid?"

"She threatened him. That very morning."

"*Threatened* him."

"Over brunch," Sheridan replied with a wry smile. "She's nothing if not civilized."

"How did she threaten him?"

Sheridan sighed. "Not openly. There was no 'you do this and you're dead.' But she made it clear to him that if there was any notoriety about the two of us she would destroy him. It wasn't

169

an idle threat, either. She could do it. If she ousted him from the Center, she could easily see to it that he couldn't find a comparable position anywhere in the country, let alone the city."

"But according to Mr. Carnegie, there isn't really anything between the two of you anymore. All of that was over in college."

Sheridan shifted in his chair. "Maybe she's afraid of guilt by association."

Ransom cocked his head to one side. "Then the more pertinent question is, if your mother felt that way about it, why did she back Carnegie's appointment in the first place?"

"I don't know," he replied, lowering his eyes to the floor.

This was followed by a long silence during which Ransom held the young man in a steady gaze. Sheridan was finding it difficult to remain composed under the forced attention.

"Well, perhaps your mother can clear that point up for us," Ransom said, almost springing to his feet. Gerald was on his feet soon after.

Sheridan rose slowly. The skin seemed to have stretched tightly across his face. "I don't see what my sex life has to do with your investigation."

Ordinarily, Ransom was very adept at holding his reactions in check when questioning anyone, but there were times when an outward display of surprise could be used to his advantage.

"I didn't realize that was what we were discussing, Mr. Sheridan."

"I just . . . Ed and I don't have that kind of relationship . . . anymore."

"I understand that. Mr. Carnegie told us that you currently have a friend, one who's in the hospital." With a show of forgetfulness, he looked to Gerald. "What was his name again?"

Playing along, Gerald began to flip back through his notebook.

"Jerry," Sheridan said, his cheeks flushed with anger. "Jerry Parker. I swear to God, if you bother him, I'll—"

"You'll what?" Ransom said, his right brow arching.

"He's dying! He's been in a coma for days. There's nothing he can do to help you." He looked Ransom in the eye. "This doesn't have anything to do with us! Just leave us alone!"

Ransom was uncharacteristically silent all the way back to the car. Gerald was surprised when his partner didn't pull out a cigar the moment he took his place in the passenger seat.

"What's the matter?" he asked as he started the car.

There was a dreamlike quality to Ransom's voice when he answered. "I don't like what I'm thinking."

"What's that?"

He gave his head a brisk shake to clear it. "Something's really not right here." His voice trailed off for a moment and his eyes narrowed. "Carnegie and Sheridan had to be bullied into the truth, and I still get the feeling they're lying to us, and I don't understand why."

"His mother—" Gerald began, but Ransom cut him off.

"Even if what he said about his mother was true, what of it? Why wouldn't Carnegie just tell us the truth to begin with and ask us to be discreet with the information?"

Gerald thought about this. "Fear?"

"Yes, but fear of what? This is a murder investigation. Could they be so afraid of Mrs. Sheridan that they'd lie to the police? Somehow I don't believe it."

"I don't know a lot about Mrs. Sheridan," Gerald said, "but I've heard she's got a lot of power."

Ransom sighed. "Carnegie lied, and it was a very stupid lie! He knew they'd been seen backstage together." He added almost inaudibly, "Why would he do that?"

Gerald smacked his lips and shrugged. "I still think you're making too much of it. He probably just didn't think of it when we questioned him, and then when you confronted him about Sheridan, he panicked and gave that excuse."

Ransom looked up. "Panic? That's an interesting idea."

"Thanks," Gerald said, rubbing his palms on his pants legs. "I have them now and then."

Ransom pulled out one of his plastic-tipped cigars and unwrapped it. "The trouble is, whatever reason they may have for lying, I don't see how they could be connected with the murder. What would they have to gain from it?" He stopped with his hand poised over the dashboard lighter. Then, without pushing it in, he sat back against the seat. "Jerry Parker is dying."

"Who?" Gerald asked.

"Sheridan's friend, the one in the hospital."

"So? What does he have to do with it?"

"Maybe nothing. But there's one thing we should check on," he said as he reached into his pocket.

"You don't really want to go and see if he's really in a coma, do you? We could do that over the phone. And what the hell difference does it make?"

Ransom pulled the cell phone out of his pocket and flipped it open. "It may make a lot of difference, and there's one thing I don't think they'd tell us over the phone." He quickly dialed a number.

"Then who are you calling?"

With a raised index finger, Ransom signaled him to wait.

"Hello?" said a tentative voice on the other end of the line.

Ransom smiled. Even her voice was wrinkled. "It's Jeremy."

Gerald stifled a grin. Ransom only used his first name when speaking with his surrogate grandmother.

"Hello, Jeremy," she said. "How is the investigation going?" She made it sound quite ordinary.

"That's what I'm calling you about. How would you like to do a bit of sleuthing for me?"

"What do you have in mind?" she asked soberly.

"There is a matter that needs to be handled delicately, so of course, I thought of you. . . ."

10

The afternoon sky was heavily overcast with thick, gray clouds, and the absence of sunlight made the Sheridan's Astor Street home look even less appealing than usual. Ransom clucked his tongue as they went up the short walk to the front door, but he didn't comment. Gerald was relieved, since at times his partner's tirades about the architecture and geography of the city could be rather daunting.

When they reached the front door, Gerald pressed the bell. There was a lengthy wait before the door was opened by the maid.

"Detectives Ransom and White to see Mrs. Sheridan," Ransom said, showing his shield.

Surprise registered on the maid's face, broadly enough to qualify her for a role in a stage farce. Her blank brown eyes widened and her mouth dropped open, then snapped shut like a straight-toothed bear trap.

"You're the police?" she asked.

"Yes."

"Um . . . come in."

She closed the door after them, then led them down the dark corridor to the living room.

"I'll tell Mrs. Sheridan you're here," she said.

As she left the room, she glanced back over her shoulder at them as if she couldn't quite bring herself to believe they were really there.

While they waited, Ransom and Gerald surveyed the room. The carefully scattered chairs and the central loveseat were all covered in brocades in various shades. The wall next to the doorway was lined with glass cabinets whose shelves held expensive china figurines and pieces of crystal. At the far end of the room was a wing chair large enough to be reminiscent of a throne. Behind it was a floor lamp with a faded, white fringed shade, and beside it a piecrust table on which a stack of correspondence lay. The letters were weighed down by a jewel-encrusted cigarette box. Out of curiosity, Ransom lifted the lid. It was empty.

There was a fireplace in the center of the north wall, sandwiched between matching built-in bookshelves that contained an impressive collection of old, leather-bound editions of the classics, from the Greeks to the end of the nineteenth century. Ransom almost salivated when he discovered the worn leather set of the complete works of Dickens on a low shelf.

Mrs. Sheridan arrived in a cloud of heavy perfume. She wore a plain black dress with a gold belt and had a string of pearls around her neck. She looked anything but pleased to see them.

"You are detectives? I am Margaret Sheridan."

From her imperious tone, Ransom wondered if she expected them to bow.

"Why have you come here?"

Ransom produced an impish smile. "You're aware that Riccardo Nuevo was murdered in your theater on Sunday night."

"What does that have to do with me?"

"We were hoping you could clear up a couple of things for us."

She held his gaze, unwavering, as if challenging him to look away. "I was in the audience, Mr . . . ?"

"Ransom."

"Mr. Ransom. I fail to see how I could be of any more help to you than anyone else who was in the audience."

"We're checking on everyone who went backstage before the performance."

There was a slight beat before she replied. "I have never been backstage at the Sheridan Center."

Ransom had to marvel at her wiliness. She had to know what he was talking about, yet she wasn't going to volunteer any information. And she kept them standing to drive home the point that she didn't expect them to stay. Ransom allowed a trace of amusement into his expression, calculated to rankle the iron-willed woman.

"I was referring to your son."

"My son?" she said haughtily, drawing herself up so that she effectively seemed an inch taller than she had a moment before.

"Yes. We understand that he went backstage."

"What could that possibly have to do with anything? Neither my son nor I have anything to do with the operation of the Center, so neither of us know any of the people involved in this incident. It was tragic enough that it had to happen in the Center at all, let alone on opening night. My son went backstage only to—"

"We know why he went backstage," Ransom said, cutting her off abruptly. "We've already spoken with your son, and he told us about it. We are here to verify his story."

"His *story*?" She managed to look even more affronted.

"We were told that he went backstage approximately fifteen minutes before curtain. Can you verify this?"

"I didn't check my watch."

"And that he returned about fifteen minutes later."

"Again, I did not check my watch." A faint smile appeared.

Gerald was finding it difficult to hide his own amusement. He truly enjoyed the occasions when someone made the mistake of matching wills with his partner.

After a short silence, with no change of expression, Ransom said, "What can you tell us about your son's relationship with Edward Carnegie?"

"I beg your pardon?" she demanded.

"I understand that your son had a romantic relationship with Edward Carnegie."

"How dare you suggest such a thing!" she said in a well-modulated, icy blast. "How dare you! Do you realize that I could easily have you fired?"

"Not . . . without a lot of notoriety," Ransom replied cagily.

This clearly took some of the wind out of Mrs. Sheridan's sails. Her jaw was still set firmly, but she appeared to deflate to her original height.

"As for suggesting such a thing, the suggestion didn't come from me. Both Carnegie and your son told us about it."

Her eyes narrowed. "Why would they do that? What could that have to do with your investigation?"

"That's another question that remains to be answered. It may very well have nothing to do with it. But Carnegie lied to us when we first questioned him. He neglected to tell us that your son was backstage with him. And any lie in a murder investigation is going to look very suspicious. He explained that he'd been trying to protect your family name."

"Did he?" She made it sound as if she thought this a not-too-clever bit of subterfuge on Carnegie's part.

"Yes. But your son seems to feel the real reason was that you didn't want anyone to know about their relationship. Is that true?"

"Of course it's true! My family's name means something in this city. Do you think I would want anyone to know about my son?"

After a long pause, Ransom said, "I must say, I'm very confused. If you felt this way about the relationship, I would think that Carnegie would be the last person you would've wanted heading your Center, since it would bring him into constant contact with your son."

"Steven does not have much contact with Mr. Carnegie. He has nothing to do with the day-to-day running of the Center. Our role has been primarily financial."

"Yes, through your foundation," Ransom said without emphasis. "I read that your contribution has been major."

"It has run into several million dollars," she said with indiscreet pride.

Ransom successfully kept himself from looking impressed, even though he was—but not in a way that would have pleased Mrs. Sheridan. If what Steven had told him was true, then Ransom found it impressive that Mrs. Sheridan had spent so much money to still any possible whispering about her late husband.

"I understand you also made it possible to bring in *Carmen*."

"Yes." She clipped the word off as if she were painfully aware that this was her one mistake. "The Sheridan Foundation financed it."

The right corner of Ransom's mouth moved to the side. "A move that also brought your son and Mr. Carnegie in contact."

Mrs. Sheridan raised her chin. "You could hardly expect me to build the Center and then leave it empty. It was incumbent upon me to see to it that at least the opening production was taken care of. After that I had hoped that the Center would become self-sufficient. Of course, were it to run into trouble, I couldn't let it flounder."

Ransom shook his head slowly. "I'm sorry, Mrs. Sheridan. I'm still surprised that, feeling the way you do, you would do something that would keep throwing your son and Carnegie together." Suddenly an idea occurred to him. He couldn't keep his face from lighting up with surprise. "Unless . . ."

"I don't know what you're thinking, Mr. Ransom," Mrs. Sheridan said, noticeably marshaling her fortitude again, "but I deeply resent your prying into our family matters. Neither I nor my son have anything to do with this murder!"

"I'll be the one to decide that, Mrs. Sheridan," Ransom said evenly. "And your family matters only interest me when a potential suspect chooses to lie about them."

For once Mrs. Sheridan looked unsure of herself. "Are you referring to Steven or to Mr. Carnegie?"

"I'm referring to everyone who was backstage on Sunday night."

"If you consider my son a suspect, then you're a fool." She sounded almost sad. "He doesn't have the spine for it. I've given him every opportunity to develop one, but he hasn't. He's nothing like his father."

Or too much like him, thought Ransom.

"One last thing, Mrs. Sheridan. Carnegie told us that you had him thoroughly checked out. Does that mean by a private investigator?"

"Yes."

"Is that how you knew he was still seeing your son?"

She bridled. "He wasn't 'seeing' my son. But they were in contact."

"Oh, that's right, that's right," Ransom said with an apologetic smile. "Steven currently has a friend, doesn't he?"

"Yes," she replied coldly. "He goes to see him every night after dinner." She sounded as if she thought this more disgraceful than anything else, presumably because those visits would be public.

Ransom said, "Steven lives here?"

"Why is that surprising?"

"Your son is an adult," Ransom said matter-of-factly, "with a job."

She almost laughed. "I don't . . . the foundation doesn't pay him all that well, so he still lives here. Where I can keep an eye on him."

"Are you going to fill me in?" said Gerald as they headed back to area headquarters.

"On what?"

"You think you know why Mrs. Sheridan got Carnegie hired, and she didn't like that."

Ransom smiled and smoked his cigar. "Yes . . . that seemed to hit the nail on the head."

Gerald sighed with exasperation. "You didn't say it. You want to let me in on it?"

Ransom turned to him. "I suspect Mrs. Sheridan has been pimping for her son."

"What?" he exclaimed, so shocked he swerved and narrowly missed a blue Volkswagen that was illegally parked at the corner. "You're kidding!"

"Think about it, Gerald. If she objects to her son's lifestyle, and yet believes it to be inevitable and doesn't want it public, what better way to take care of everything than by hiring one of his friends, who he'll then be together with as a matter of course, as part of their jobs? If she was hoping to stem any rumors, she failed. Everyone thinks they're having an affair anyway."

Gerald gave this some thought. "Well, that might all be interesting, but what does it have to do with anything?"

Ransom took another drag from the cigar and blew the smoke out the window. "I'm sure I don't know. Carnegie and Sheridan may very well be up to something, but I don't see why they would kill Nuevo. If for some reason Sheridan wanted to destroy the Center he would've done better to blow it up. The only thing killing Nuevo accomplished is possibly hurting the Santa Marta Opera Company. The Center will go on as long as Margaret Sheridan wants it to, whether or not it's been tainted by this murder."

"If they are up to something, what do you think it is?"

"My guess would be the obvious: money. Mrs. Sheridan may have contempt for her son's lack of a spine, but she can take the credit for it. She's given him a job that pays so little he's forced to stay under her thumb."

"He could just leave if he wanted to." His tone implied little sympathy for Sheridan. "Nobody has to live like that!"

"Not everybody knows that. Growing up in that stifling atmosphere, it might be more difficult to break away than you can imagine. Maybe he's discovered a way to get out from under that thumb."

"But that doesn't may any sense," Gerald protested. "If he

wanted money, couldn't he just bilk the foundation? Hell, he's the head of it."

"What do you want to bet that his mother has him watched?"

Gerald was peering through the windshield, his brow deeply furrowed. "But . . . but . . ."

"I know," said Ransom wearily. "It doesn't explain the murder. If Sheridan and Carnegie are somehow embezzling money, I would think the last thing they'd want is an investigation. It doesn't make sense for them to have killed Nuevo. Why draw attention to themselves?" He was silent for seconds, his mind racing. Then an idea struck him. "Unless they didn't expect to."

"What? What does that mean?"

A satisfied smile spread across his face. He puffed on his cigar. "We'll know that when we see what Emily finds out."

It was after five o'clock before Lynn Francis could make herself available to drive Emily to the hospital. Lynn steered the car through the driveway into the parking lot, and was lucky enough to find a space just being vacated on the first level as they came in.

She turned off the motor and looked at Emily. "Why did Ransom want you to do this?"

Emily smiled coyly. "Jeremy would not like it to be known, but somewhere inside him there is a streak of kindness."

"What does that have to do with it?"

"He needs the information, but he really doesn't want to upset these people. He thought I might be able to do it without being intrusive."

Lynn undid her seatbelt. "I'll go up with you."

"There's no need. I can manage," Emily said, sensitive to the young woman's feelings. This was the hospital where Lynn's partner, Maggie, had died. Although Emily was grateful for Lynn's assistance thus far, she didn't want to cause her any pain by requiring her to accompany her to the ward in which Maggie had spent her last days.

"No," Lynn said, "I'm all right, and I'm coming with you. I'm going to make sure you're safe."

"What could happen to me in a hospital?" Emily asked innocently.

Lynn laughed. "Don't think you're fooling me. Look, Emily, I know what you're thinking, and I really am all right." She glanced out the window at the stone edifice. "I'm not happy to be back here, but I'm dealing with these things as they come up. I'll be fine."

"I know you will," Emily said, gently patting Lynn's hand. "But, you know, this might work better if I'm on my own."

"I'll tell you what, we'll compromise. I'll see you up to the floor and then wait for you in the visitor's lounge."

"That will do very nicely," Emily said gratefully.

Emily took Lynn's arm as they crossed the parking lot and the drive that led to the emergency room. Then they went through the glass doors and straight to the elevators. Being an intrinsically pragmatic person, Lynn had known when Emily asked for her assistance that she would feel an unpleasant sense of déjà vu on coming back to this hospital, but she hadn't been aware of just how strong the feeling would be. A sense of dread came over her as they waited for the elevator. She fought to keep this at bay, but wasn't successful enough to keep Emily from noticing the increased tension throughout her body. After a while she became aware that Emily was scrutinizing her with concern.

"I'm all right," Lynn said confidently. "I knew it wouldn't be easy."

Emily gave Lynn's arm an affectionate squeeze, then the elevator doors opened with a hollow metallic clank. When they reached the eleventh floor, Lynn showed Emily to the nurses' station.

"Lynn! Hi!" said the young woman behind the counter, clearly surprised. "How're you doing?"

"Hi, Rose. I'm okay. My friend Emily is here to see Jerry Parker."

"Ah, Jerry." She turned a sympathetic eye on Emily. "Are you his grandmother?"

"No," she replied with a smile, "just a friend."

"Oh," the nurse replied with a *tsk*. "I was hoping you were family. None of them have been to see him."

"But he does have visitors, doesn't he?"

"Oh, yes. A friend or two here and there. And he has a special friend who comes to see him regular."

"Steven," said Emily.

"Yes! You know him?"

"No, I just know of him."

"Which room is Jerry in?" Lynn asked.

The nurse gave them the room number, and they walked away from the desk.

Lynn whispered, "It's the third room down the hall on the right. The lounge is that area we passed through just off the elevators. I'll be waiting for you there."

She left Emily, who started down the hallway. In between the rooms there were carts loaded with linens, and a little further down the hall a nurse was busy with a trolley full of medications. Beside the third doorway was a small sign with the patient's last name, beneath which hung a clipboard full of medical charts.

Emily went in. The room was dark except for a dim light above the bed. Her heart sank when she saw the occupant of the bed. Jerry Parker was what she would consider a boy, and yet his illness had left him looking ancient. His skull-like face was chalky and lined, and his hair looked as if it were turning gray.

It had been her intention to quickly do what she had come for and then leave, hopefully without being a disturbance. But once she'd seen Parker, she couldn't bring herself to hurry. She pushed a chair up beside the bed, wincing as the chair legs noisily scraped the tile floor, then sat down. She took Parker's desiccated hand and folded her hands around it. She sat quietly with him for several minutes, watching his face and silently willing him to be at peace.

However, she didn't forget her reason for being there. Still holding his hand, she looked up and strained her eyes at the bags hanging from the hooks at the top of the IV pole. Much to her dismay, she found what she was looking for.

"Who are you?" came a voice from the doorway. It wasn't loud, but Emily had become so used to the quiet of the room that the sudden interruption made her heart skip a beat. She turned to look at the doorway and saw Steven Sheridan standing with his hand on the doorknob.

"You startled me," she said, her tone free of accusation.

"Sorry. I was just surprised to find anyone here. Who are you? What are you doing here?"

"I wanted to pay Jerry a visit."

Steven kept his voice low as he stepped into the room. "I . . . haven't seen you before."

"No. No, I only just recently learned that he was sick." She looked back at the bed. "It's a shock to find him this way."

They watched Parker in silence for a while. Then Emily said, "You haven't told me who you are."

"I'm Steven Sheridan. Jerry and I are very close."

"I see."

"Are you his . . . his . . . ?"

"I'm not related, I'm just a friend of the family," Emily said, gently laying Parker's hand at his side.

Steven visibly relaxed. "I'm surprised his family would tell anyone he was here."

"It's disgraceful that they haven't been to see him," Emily said with feeling.

"They disowned him a long time ago. That's why I didn't know whether or not . . . you see, I've never met any of them."

Emily clucked her tongue in disgust. They fell silent again.

"I sit with him, and talk to him as much as I can," Steven said out of the blue. He sounded as if he were hoping for approval.

"That is the best thing you can do for him," Emily replied.

She gazed at the young man in the bed, her mind's eye stripping away the damage that had been done by illness, giving her some idea of how he'd looked when he was well. She knew this was only her fancy, but had a feeling that she wasn't very far off. She said, "He's very handsome, isn't he?"

Steven emitted a guttural, choking sound that he cut off almost before it started. But he couldn't stop the tears from welling in his eyes. "Yes, he is."

Emily placed her fingers lightly on his arm and made comforting noises. It was a while before Sheridan was sufficiently quieted down to speak.

"I'm sorry."

"There's no need to be," Emily said.

"I meant . . . to him. I try not to break down in front of him because . . ." His voice trailed off helplessly, and he choked back a sob.

"I'm sure he understands."

"Because I think—" he began, almost as if he hadn't heard her, but he stopped. He turned to Emily and said quietly, "Do you think he can still hear me?"

"I'm sure of it," Emily replied sincerely.

Sheridan had taken enough control of himself that he no longer had to fight back audible signs of grief, but tears silently streamed down his face.

"We had so many plans. We were going to go away together. Now . . . he's been like this for days, and they tell me he's not going to last much longer." He looked to Emily as if he thought she might be able to verify this. He read the answer in her sympathetic eyes. She had seen enough death to recognize when it is near at hand.

In an effort to draw his mind away from the tragedy at hand, if only for a moment, she said, "Have you given any thought to yourself?"

"What do you mean?"

"To what you're going to do with yourself?"

"You mean after—?" He looked down at the bed, then back at Emily. A fresh stream of tears ran down his cheeks.

Emily nodded.

"I'm going to go away," he said fervently. "I'm going to get as far away from here as possible. And never come back!"

She stayed with him a few minutes longer, her hand still offering a steady touch to his arm. Neither of them spoke. Finally, she said softly, "I think I'll leave the two of you alone now."

She disengaged herself from him and headed for the door. Just before crossing the threshold, she heard Sheridan call a quiet thank-you after her.

Emily was so lost in thought as she went back up the hallway that she found herself in the visitor's lounge without realizing how she'd gotten there. Lynn was watching for her. She rose from an uncomfortable brown plaid couch and crossed the room to meet her.

"You were longer than I thought you'd be." She pressed the button for the elevator. "I almost came looking for you."

"Hmm?" Emily said absently, waking from her reverie.

"You took a long time."

"Yes . . . yes, I was interrupted."

Before Lynn could ask her to explain, the elevator doors opened. Two young men stepped off and paused to hold the door for them as Lynn helped Emily onto the elevator. Emily thanked them, and they released the door.

Once they were alone, Lynn said, "What interrupted you?"

"Not what, who. Steven Sheridan arrived while I was in the room."

"What!" Lynn exclaimed with the dismay of a protective daughter. "You were alone with him?"

"Yes."

Lynn's expression did a quick transformation from shock to anger. "Ransom *never* should've asked you to do this! It was too dangerous!"

"Oh, no, my dear, he was quite right to have me do it. He just didn't realize we would be so late in starting."

"But you ended up alone with someone who might be a murderer!"

"I don't know about that," Emily said doubtfully. "But I know that that young man has enough to carry as it is. Jeremy was right: If Mr. Sheridan thought the police were nosing around his friend, I don't think he could bear it."

"What did he think when he saw you there?"

"He thought I was a little old lady visiting a friend," she replied with a wistful sigh.

Lynn was tempted to question her further, but Emily was once again lost in thought, and Lynn decided it was probably best to leave it for the time being.

"So now we know, as you suspected, that Steven Sheridan has access to morphine," Emily said.

She was sitting across the kitchen table from Ransom. They were having tea while Lynn, who had decided to stay on for the evening, prepared dinner. The room was filled with the pleasing aroma of roasting meat.

"I had Gerald call the lab this afternoon and have them go ahead and test for morphine. If they're testing for a specific poison, they can do it pretty fast. It's when we don't have any idea what was used that it takes so damn long. I take it Sheridan wouldn't have much trouble actually stealing some of it."

"I shouldn't think so. I would think it would be quite simple." Emily paused and gently cleared her throat. "You realize, of course, that even if they find morphine, that doesn't mean that Mr. Sheridan was the one who did it."

Ransom bristled slightly. "Yes, I know that. But it's another piece of circumstantial evidence. Especially without knowing how anyone else would have access to the drug."

"Is it really that hard to come by?" said Lynn as she stirred the contents of a pot on the stove.

"Maybe not. But I think the average person would be stumped if they suddenly decided they wanted to get some."

Emily sighed and took a sip of the hot tea from her blue china cup. "I do hope Mr. Sheridan didn't do it."

"Oh, great," said Ransom with a sly grin. "You don't want it to be Sheridan, and Gerald doesn't want it to be Gabrielle Charbonneau. Maybe I should pick a suspect to root for."

Emily returned a smile. "There are plenty to go around."

Ransom set his mug on a coaster atop the lace tablecloth. "Seriously, Emily, I've never known anyone to get around you. I realize you feel sorry for Sheridan, but does that mean you think he couldn't be the killer?"

"Oh, not at all! I would think anyone as frustrated in his life as Mr. Sheridan appears to be would be capable of murder. I only meant that I would be very sorry to see him come into any more trouble than he's already had."

"Even if he brought it on himself?"

Emily shrugged resignedly.

"Well, if it makes you feel any better, the one big problem with Sheridan as the killer is motive. It's possible—and mind you, it's only a possibility so far, because I have no proof—that Sheridan and Carnegie are embezzling money somehow from the foundation. Sheridan told you he's planning to go away?"

"Yes. And never return."

"He doesn't have the money to do that on his own, if we can go by what his mother said." He paused, then shook his head with disgust. "The problem is, even if they're doing that, I don't see how the murder fits into it. It doesn't make sense."

"No, it doesn't," Emily concurred. "I can tell you something else I learned from Mr. Sheridan. I don't think his relationship with Mr. Carnegie is at all what his mother thinks it is."

"Really?" Ransom said, raising an eyebrow.

"The love he feels for Mr. Parker is obvious. I think his mother is wrong, and as for Carnegie's assistant . . . well, that's just a lot of office tittle-tattle." Emily sounded thoroughly repulsed when she mentioned this last.

"Perhaps Carnegie and Sheridan are just partners in crime," said Ransom.

"Yes . . . Oh dear, I hadn't thought of that. . . ." Emily said vacantly.

"What is it?"

She adjusted herself in her seat. "The timing, Jeremy. We don't know how long Mr. Sheridan's friend, Jerry Parker, has been so ill."

"So?"

"It may have been very recent."

"I'm sorry, Emily, I'm not following you."

"You see, Mr. Sheridan told me that they had planned to go away together. Past tense, you see. Mr. Carnegie came onto the scene a little over six months ago, at Sheridan's suggestion. It may only have been since then that Mr. Parker became so ill."

"Oh, I see," Ransom said after a long pause.

"I don't," said Lynn.

Ransom explained, "Sheridan may have planned to break free of his mother and go off with his partner, Parker, and brought Carnegie, an old friend, into the picture to help them get the money to do that."

"Exactly!" said Emily.

Ransom mulled this over for a moment, then heaved a frustrated sigh. "They only problem is, I still don't see what all that has to do with Nuevo's murder."

"Possibly nothing," said Emily as she took another sip of tea.

They fell silent. Lynn opened the refrigerator and pulled a head of lettuce and a pair of ripe tomatoes out of the crisper.

"Well, Mr. Detective," she said as she righted herself and closed the door, "I'll tell you one thing, I don't think much of you sending Emily in to do your job for you. Don't you have some policewoman or something that can go undercover and do that sort of thing?"

"No one as effective as Emily," Ransom replied. He turned to Emily. "But I never would've asked you to do it if I'd thought there was any chance of you running into Sheridan."

"Nonsense!" Emily exclaimed lightly. "I was never in any danger." There was a long pause, then Emily coughed delicately. "Jeremy, there's something I'd like to ask you about. If it should turn out that you're right about what these men are doing, and it has nothing to do with the murder, what will happen?"

"It wouldn't be the first time that we uncovered one crime while investigating another."

"Yes, but would you feel compelled to do something about it?"

"Emily, what are you saying?"

"Nothing at all," Emily said carelessly. "I was merely curious."

He smiled. "You surprise me! I thought you were straight as an arrow."

Emily raised the cup to her lips. "Sometimes an arrow is meant to miss."

11

The Tuesday-evening performance of *Carmen* could best be described as lackluster. Maria Cortez walked through her role as if determined to convey her contempt for the company for continuing performances, and contempt for the audience for coming to see it. Patrick Laramie, on the other hand, performed the role of Don José not as if he was infatuated with her, but rather as if he were terrified of her—which, if the truth were known, was not far off the mark. Whenever Maria deigned to look at him at all she glared full force, as if she held him personally responsible for her having to perform. Unsure of himself as any underprepared understudy thrust into the leading role would be, he found the diva's added scorn quite unnerving. Although Patrick didn't miss a note throughout the course of the opera, several times he forgot the staging, which meant that more than once while professing his love for Carmen, he turned to embrace her only to find her all the way across the stage from him.

Gabrielle Charbonneau played the role of Micaela with great difficulty, perpetually on the verge of tears. She could hardly bear to look at Patrick during their scenes together. He looked enough like Riccardo to increase her distress. The result was that Gabrielle seemed to be playing as if Micaela knew from the start that her love for Don José was doomed. The audience marveled at her acting.

The only one whose performance was unaffected by current events was Franco Giannini, who attacked the part of Escamillo that evening with a relish that demonstrated bravery in the face of disaster. The audience loved him.

There was a noticeable tension in the auditorium during the final scene. But when Patrick and Maria were able to get through it, albeit halfheartedly, with nobody actually dying, the relief could be felt both in the front of the house and backstage.

Much to Maria's disbelief, the audience also loved Patrick Laramie. With the typical American admiration for someone who fights his way through a disadvantage, they leapt to their feet and cheered when Patrick came out for his curtain call. They might only have given him a C for his performance, but they were more than willing to give him an A+ for effort. He had tried, and they loved it, so much so that the tide of applause had already crested when Maria came out for her bow. For the first time in six months, she did not receive the biggest ovation. And to say that she was displeased would be severely understating the case.

"These people are pigs!" she yelled, throwing her hairbrush at the mirror. "Did you hear how they screamed for that untalented child! And for me what do they do? Nothing!"

Tony Leonard was seated on one of the chairs. "Well, Maria, nobody expected you to be at a hundred percent tonight, after—"

She wheeled around and glared at him.

"It's too soon after Riccardo's death," he concluded meekly.

"That is exactly what I told David Cunningham!" she exclaimed hotly. "He forces me out onto the stage, against my will, and this is what happens! I'm made a fool of! That boy, Patrick, he has performed as if he's in a high school play, and they cheer for him, but not for me!"

Tony held his tongue. It wasn't that he didn't know what to say, but that he was afraid that anything he said would be too much. He knew Maria well enough to know that her skewered performance wasn't due to her distress over Riccardo's death, but her fury that she didn't get her own way. He sat listening to her and watching her as if they were divided by a wall. *The fourth wall*, he thought with an inward smile: the invisible wall that divides the audience from the actors.

She continued her steady stream of vitriol, first directed at the company's founders, then the fellow cast members, and finally back to the audience's response (or lack of it) for her.

As she railed on, Tony became increasingly uneasy at the vehemence with which she continued her monologue. It seemed over the top, even for her. He started to wonder if she was angry about something more than the fact that they'd had to perform again so soon, and the other possible causes made him very uncomfortable.

When Ransom arrived at area headquarters Wednesday morning, he found a note on his desk asking him to call Harris in the lab. He was surprised, because he thought it was a little early to have results. While he was dialing the number, Gerald joined him.

The phone rang twice before being answered by a rather bland, moderately pitched male voice.

"Harris."

"It's Ransom. What do you have for me?"

"Huh? Oh, nothing yet. There was something I wanted to ask you. Detective White called late yesterday and told us you wanted to test everything from the theater, starting with . . ." Ransom heard the sounds of shuffling papers. ". . . Riccardo Nuevo's dressing room for morphine."

"That's correct."

"Okay. I just wanted to make sure you didn't want us to include the stuff from the little brown bottle, right?"

Ransom's ears perked up. "What little brown bottle?"

"Says here it was found in a garbage can by the stage door."

"Of course I want you to test it. Why wouldn't you?"

"Well, it's a bottle of ipecac."

There was a beat, then a broad smile spread across Ransom's face. "Are you sure?"

"That's what the label says. I sniffed the contents. It sure smells like it. Do you know what this stuff does?"

"Yes, I do."

"I mean, there could be poison in it, but I doubt he could've kept it down long enough to digest it."

"No, I think it was meant for something else. Concentrate on the coffee."

"Will do," said Harris.

"What was that all about?" Gerald asked.

"I think we've just cleared up part of the puzzle."

"Yeah?"

"Maria Cortez's mysterious illnesses. Harris just told me they found a small bottle of ipecac in a garbage can."

Gerald wrinkled his nose. "What's that?"

"It's a syrup made from a plant—it induces vomiting."

"I don't get it."

Ransom sighed impatiently. "I suspect that someone was slipping it to Maria Cortez to make her ill, rather than poisoning her. It would explain the effect it had on her. She became ill without warning and then was fine right afterward, remember? It might even have been Nuevo who gave it to her."

"How do you figure that?"

"He was furious with Cortez, and I don't think he was above taking out his aggressions in the form of a childish prank. He might have slipped a little bit of it into her coffee. I don't think she'd be able to taste it, because it takes very little to do the job."

Gerald blinked. "It could've been . . ."

"Yes, Gerald?" said Ransom.

"If someone was just trying to get back at her, it might've been Gabrielle Charbonneau. She didn't like her."

"That's a possibility."

"Well, if this is true, then that means nobody was trying to kill Cortez."

"I wish it did mean that. The only thing it means is that her illness may not have had anything to do with the poisoning. Even that accepted, she still might've been the actual murder target." He stared into space for a moment, his expression so cross he looked almost as if he thought Cortez had done a great disservice by not being the victim, because it would've made things a lot easier. Finally he shook his head. "Let's go."

"Where to?"

"There's a little matter I want to get out of the way before we go back to the theater."

Twenty minutes later they were being shown back into Steven Sheridan's faceless office. Sheridan rose from his chair behind the desk as they entered. Ransom noted that his face was pale and drawn, as if he hadn't slept very well. Then again, it could have been that he had simply suffered the wrath of his mother.

Sheridan waited to speak until the receptionist had left them and closed the door.

"Um . . . gentlemen, I'm . . . I didn't expect to see you again. I thought by now you would've realized I didn't have anything to do with the murder."

"We have a few more questions. May we?" He indicated the chairs facing the desk. Sheridan nodded and the three of them sat down.

Ransom was of two minds about what he was about to do. Any irregularities they run into in the course of an investigation had to be looked into. At the same time, he respected Emily's opinion enough that it was impossible for him to completely set her feelings aside.

"You have more questions for me?" Sheridan said haltingly. "I don't know how else I can help you. I mean, you've already talked to me and to my mother. She verified everything I told you, didn't she?"

"And then some," Ransom replied. "There are still some things that don't seem quite right."

Sheridan glanced at Gerald, who had extracted the pencil from the spiral of his notebook and flipped the notebook open. He looked back at Ransom.

"Oh, for God's sake!" Sheridan exclaimed in a plaintive whine. "We told you, both me and Ed—he just made a mistake when he forgot to tell you I was backstage with him! What more can there be to ask me?"

"Your mother told me that it was quite expensive to bring in the Santa Marta Opera Company."

"Yes, it was." Sheridan grew noticeably paler.

"Can you tell me exactly how much it cost?"

"I don't see what that has to do with anything—"

Ransom raised his palm, signaling for him to stop. "Humor me."

He swallowed. "You mean how much the foundation paid out to the Center?"

"Umm-hmm."

"I . . . I don't know the exact amount."

"Really?" Ransom said with a slight tilt of his head. "Still, I would imagine that it would be easy enough for you to find out, at least a ballpark figure? Are we talking about thousands?"

Sheridan didn't respond.

"Millions?" When he still didn't answer, Ransom added, "Perhaps you have an accountant who could give us some idea?"

Sheridan hesitated, then said, "Well . . . I don't think that'll be necessary, I mean, if you're just looking for a ballpark figure . . . It would be around . . . maybe . . . three million."

There was a muffled snap as this news caused Gerald to temporarily lose control of his pencil, breaking off the tip. He brushed the lead away and reached into his pocket for a pen.

"That's quite a bit of money," Ransom said calmly.

"People don't realize how much it costs to produce an opera," Sheridan said quickly.

"If I seem surprised," said Ransom, fully aware that he didn't seem anything of the sort, "it's because David Cunningham has told us repeatedly that their company is not doing well financially."

"I . . . I don't know anything about that." Sheridan looked as if he were drowning.

"Are you telling me that you don't have an accounting of how the money you've given to the Center has been spent?"

"Not an exact accounting. We've paid out as Edward has made requests. His requests have always come with an explanation. We wouldn't just dole out money for no reason."

"I see," Ransom said slowly. "And Mr. Carnegie could provide an accounting of how the money has been spent?"

Sheridan froze for a second, then said loudly, "What do our financial arrangements have to do with Riccardo Nuevo's murder!"

Under normal circumstances, Ransom would've felt something like a cat toying with a mouse in a situation like this, but he still couldn't shake what Emily has said to him the night before. Mentally he rolled his eyes at himself. He suspected he was beginning to go soft.

"You haven't answered my question, Mr. Sheridan."

He laid his open palms atop the desk, as if he needed to steady himself, and stared vacantly toward the center of the detective's chest. "I think that Ed could . . . I'm sure he's kept detailed records."

"And if we were to look at the books, we wouldn't find any discrepancies?"

"Of course not," Sheridan said with a distinct lack of conviction. His eyes traveled up to Ransom's. "But there may be some surplus. I mean, that wouldn't be that unusual. There wouldn't be anything wrong with that. Ed would just use it for future productions."

"Your mother told us that she expected the Center to be self-sufficient after this opera."

Sheridan's eyes flickered. He flexed his hands. "That's all the more reason to make sure there's a cushion now."

Ransom allowed a long pause. "I see." He rose and started

for the door with Gerald close behind him. "Thank you, Mr. Sheridan."

Sheridan jumped up and stood behind the desk, touching the tips of his fingers to its top. "Mr. Ransom—"

The detectives stopped and faced him. "Yes?"

"If there was an overpayment . . . if we felt it was too much . . . any surplus of money could always be paid back to the foundation."

"That's nice to know."

He started to turn away when Sheridan stopped him again. "You have to believe me! I had nothing to do with Riccardo Nuevo's death! I don't . . . neither of us had any reason to do anything like that!"

Ransom held his gaze for a minute, then sighed. "Right now that's your one saving grace."

Once the detectives were out of his office, Sheridan grabbed for the receiver of his phone. His hands were shaking so badly that he had some difficulty dialing the correct number. The phone was answered on the first ring by Bonnie Payton, who put his call through without question.

"Steven?" Edward Carnegie said when he picked up the phone.

"I have to see you!"

"Today? I don't think that's advisable under the circumstances."

"They were just here again!"

For a few moments Carnegie said nothing. "I don't think we should be seen together."

"You don't understand," Sheridan said pleadingly. "They *know*!"

"They know what?"

"Everything!"

"You need to calm down, Steve," Carnegie said forcefully. "They can't know everything."

"They know about the money!"

There was another silence. "What did you tell them?"

"They told *me*! They asked about how money was paid to the Center. They asked about the books. They said . . . they asked if they would find any discrepancies if they looked at the books."

"They're fishing," Carnegie said, trying to sound less worried than he felt. "What did you tell them?"

"I said I thought the books would be in order."

"They are."

"Not if they compare them to the foundation's books! Don't you see?" Sheridan was beginning to get angry in the face of Carnegie's apparent calm.

"Get hold of yourself!"

"Why would they ask me that if they didn't know?"

Carnegie thought for a minute, then said, "Did you tell them anything else?"

"I didn't know what to say! You know they'll find it if they look! I had to say something!"

This news really did worry the theater manager. "What did you do?"

"I said . . . I said that there might be a surplus."

"You what?!" Carnegie exclaimed. Sheridan would have really panicked if he could've seen how red Carnegie's face was.

"I had to say something," he replied defensively. "They'll find out! I had to explain it somehow!"

"Is that all you said?"

"I told them it was possible there was a surplus, but if there was, it was all right, because it could be used on the next production."

Some of the heat drained from Carnegie's face. This was more than he expected from Sheridan. "Actually, that's pretty good."

"It might not be. They talked to my mother. She said she only intended to finance the first show."

"No, no, that's even better. That gives us more of a reason to have built up a buffer."

For the first time, Sheridan felt a slight sense of relief. "That's what I told them. You think it'll be all right?"

"Sure. Your mother doesn't know anything about managing a theater. That much would be obvious even to these detectives if they spend any time at all talking to her. When they see me—which I'm sure they will—I can say we were just hedging our bets."

Sheridan sighed deeply, his entire body shuddering as the tension dissipated. "I'm really sorry, Ed. I didn't think they would get on to us."

"It's all right. It was really my fault, with my stupid blunder. I should've told them the truth to begin with. They wouldn't have given us a second thought."

This was one thing that had rankled Sheridan ever since the whole thing began, but he'd been afraid to say anything about it. Now that Carnegie had brought it up, he decided to risk it. "Why didn't you?"

"Because I was caught off guard," Carnegie replied, his annoyance obvious. "I didn't think they'd suspect us!"

The detectives got back in their car, but Gerald did not immediately start the engine.

"What do we do now?" he asked.

"I'm damned if I know," Ransom said with a laugh as he pulled out a cigar.

Gerald grimaced. The last three days he'd gone home smelling like he'd spent all day in a jazz club rather than on the job. Just last night his wife, Sherry, had made him shower before coming to the dinner table.

"What happened to your plans to stop smoking?"

Ransom shot him a glance as he lit up. "They're still being worked out."

"So, you want to have a look at the Center's books?"

"No. Not yet," he replied after some thought.

Gerald stared at him. "I don't believe it!"

"What?"

"*You* don't want it to be Sheridan, do you?"

Ransom tried to hide his annoyance. He didn't relish the rare occasions when his partner hit the nail on the head when it came to personal matters. "Emily doesn't want it to be."

"Oh," Gerald said with a knowing smile.

Ransom's lip curled. "I think you know that wouldn't stop me from pursuing him. I think it's pretty clear there's something going on with the finances here—"

"It's not clear to me," said Gerald. "I mean, that's a lot of money for them to have paid out, but it can't have been cheap to bring in this opera, with the cast and crew and hotels and everything. They must've had to pay out a lot of money ahead of time."

"Whether or not that's true, Sheridan's right: I don't see any reason for him to kill Nuevo."

"But the money angle is the only thing we know that isn't right."

"I know that, Gerald," Ransom said irritably. "But what do they have to gain by killing Nuevo? What does *anyone* have to gain, for that matter? All we've been able to get so far is that everyone loved him, and everyone hated Maria Cortez. The only one we know of who might've had a reason to kill him—a pretty slim one, at that—is Gabrielle Charbonneau. And that's only if she heard his rejection of her when he was arguing with Cortez. Everyone seems to have a reason to want to kill Cortez—at least, most of them. Including Nuevo himself. So we're still left not knowing whether or not he was the actual target."

"If you ask me, I don't see how he could've been," Gerald offered. "Killing him doesn't do anything."

Ransom looked up suddenly. "Really?"

"No," Gerald replied uncertainly when he saw the look on

his partner's face. "I think we should focus on who would try to kill Cortez."

"Perhaps you're right," Ransom said with an unreadable smile. "Let's go to the theater."

"You want to rattle Carnegie's cage again?"

"That might be fun," he said in a cloud of smoke. "But I don't think it'll get us anywhere. If Sheridan and Carnegie didn't already have a cover story worked out, they will by the time we get there. I think Cunningham would be a better source if we want to pursue the money matter. He'll probably be at the theater; they must be rehearsing again today. If he's not, we can talk to him later. But we still need to talk to Charbonneau again."

12

The atmosphere at the Sheridan Center for the Performing Arts was going from bad to worse. After Patrick Laramie's inauspicious debut in the role of Don José the previous evening, Daniel Cunningham had held a hasty meeting with John Turner, the assistant director, and it was decided that much more rehearsal was in order if the opera was to continue. The goodwill of the audience, so evident during the curtain calls the night before, could be stretched only so far before they would expect Laramie to give a more polished performance. So once again the principals had been called to the theater to rehearse, as Ransom had surmised.

But there was a pall over the proceedings. With one performance under his belt, Laramie had gained confidence and was improving, but it was evident he wouldn't achieve the level of performance established by Riccardo Nuevo. And once this had been realized by the assistant director, the company manager, and the rest of the principals, what little spirit there was left took a nosedive.

When Ransom and Gerald came into the auditorium, Maria and Laramie were in the middle of their second-act duet. Laramie was giving it his all, while Maria went through the motions with resignation. Turner was seated in the third row with his feet up on the seat in front of him.

The detectives passed through the auditorium and went backstage through the door on the left of the house. They found Franco Giannini standing in the wings, watching the rehearsal.

"Good morning, Mr. Giannini," said Ransom. He looked past the baritone at the stage. "How is it going?"

Franco grimaced. "Pretty much as you'd expect. Patrick just isn't up to the standard of Riccardo. Not that anyone expected him to be."

"He seems to be doing all right."

"Yeah, but I don't think he'll ever be better than all right."

Ransom shrugged. "He's a replacement. Your audience will be pulling for him."

"You think so?" He looked back at the performers who were in a clinch at one of the tables as Don José sang his devotion to Carmen. "Maybe. Don't get me wrong. Patrick's a damn good tenor and a nice guy. This just isn't his part." He turned to Ransom and lowered his voice. "Our diva would never admit it, but Riccardo was just as important to the production as she is." He paused. "Well, maybe not *just* as important, but damn near."

"Don't you think it will survive without him?"

"I don't know," Franco answered doubtfully. "I'm afraid that with a second banana in one of the leads, we'll look like the fluke we really are."

"Really?" Ransom said casually. "You think the success of this company was a fluke?"

"Of course it is," Franco said with a wry smile. "We've been lucky all the way around. Really lucky. We managed to become media darlings. Cunningham and his business partner played themselves up as opera lovers who were doing this because they wanted so badly to give something to the opera world. And that whole bit about taking nobodies and turning them into stars— the press ate it up! They love underdogs-who-succeed-against-all-odds stories. The fortunate thing for us was that we put together a really good production. If we'd flopped right out of the gate, you never would've heard anything about us again. But now everything's different. The media loves to build up and they love to tear down. We're going downhill, detective, and unless I miss my guess, pretty soon the press will be hurrying our demise."

Ransom gave a slight nod. "You sound awfully philosophical about the whole thing."

Franco laughed. "I love the opera and I love to sing, but it's not my life. Right now my lover is upset because I have to rehearse and he's stranded in Chicago with nobody to play with. That's more important to me than anything."

They fell silent and watched Maria and Laramie rehearse for a few minutes. Then Franco turned to Ransom. "When the company is dead, Maria will be the one person to end up smelling like a rose."

"How so?"

He shrugged. "She's already got that thing with the Met. And she'll probably be a hit there. She's a fishwife to work with, but she's nothing if not talented. All the critics will say she was the one person to really survive the death of the Santa Marta Opera Company. They'll probably say she's the one that made the company."

"Hmm," Ransom said thoughtfully. "Is Ms. Charbonneau in the theater?"

Franco nodded. "In her dressing room, I think. If you're going to talk to her, please go easy on the poor thing. I guess in her way she really did love Riccardo, and she's taking this all very, very hard."

They left Franco and headed for the dressing rooms. Ransom sighed and said lightly under his breath: "*Si tu ne m'aimes pas, je t'aime; Mais si je t'aime, prends garde à toi. . . .*"

"What the hell does that mean?" Gerald asked, surprised to have his partner spouting French.

"It's one of the few lines of opera that I know. Roughly translated it means you can love me, but if I love you, watch out."

Before reaching the dressing rooms they saw David Cunningham coming down the hallway from the stage door. He openly rolled his eyes when he saw them.

"Jesus! Aren't we ever going to be rid of you?"

"As soon as we figure out which one of you is a killer," Ransom said with a playful smile meant to knock the manager off balance. It succeeded. From his shocked expression, it looked as if Cunningham hadn't realized until that moment that one of his own company could actually be the murderer, though Ransom had to wonder how the possibility could've escaped him.

"You don't really . . . God, that would be awful!"

"Yes," Ransom said with a smack of his lips. "That would further cripple your company."

"That's not what I was thinking!" Cunningham protested loudly, although the deep crimson that he flushed proved otherwise.

"So sorry," Ransom said with a marked lack of sincerity. "I misunderstood. I'm glad we ran into you, though. There are a couple of questions I wanted to ask you."

"More questions?" He couldn't have sounded more disheartened.

Ransom smiled. "Relatively easy ones. You've mentioned to us that your company is having financial troubles."

"That isn't unusual!"

"I'm not saying that it is—"

Cunningham cut him off. "Nobody understands that! It costs a fortune to put on an opera. Companies that have been in business for years live from one production to the next, and we're new!"

"I'm sure that's true," Ransom said with weary patience, "but that wasn't what I wanted to ask you. Can you tell me about your financial agreement with the Sheridan Center?"

Cunningham stared at him dumbly for a minute. The he said slowly, "Well, I . . . they're paying to put us all up here, which is necessary, because we couldn't have afforded to do it otherwise.

And they're paying a . . . I guess you'd call it a stipend—a small one—over the top."

"The top of what?"

"Salaries. Expenses. Whatever."

Ransom thought for a moment, tapping an index finger against his lips. "How does that relate to ticket sales?"

"What do you mean?"

"How much of the money being paid to your company is coming out of ticket sales?"

"Well . . ." His face pinched as he considered this. "I would think all of it. The run is pretty much sold out now."

"I see," said Ransom. "Weren't there a lot of up-front expenses?"

"What do you mean?"

"We've been told repeatedly that it's expensive to mount an opera. You said so yourself. Aren't there a lot of expenses that have to be paid up front?"

"Oh. Yeah. But you have to remember we actually opened six months ago. The sets, the security bond, rehearsal salaries— all that had to be paid before we opened originally."

"Security bond?" Gerald asked.

Cunningham shook his head. "Yeah. Two weeks' pay put up with the unions against the possibility of us closing unexpectedly."

"Ah," Ransom said with a smile. "One other thing. You have a makeup artist traveling with you, don't you?"

"Sherman? Yeah. Why?"

"He was backstage during the performance. We need to talk to him, and his name wasn't on the company lists. Do you know where he's staying?"

The company manager pursed his lips. "At the same fleabag I'm at. Room five."

Cunningham left them and joined Franco Giannini at the side of the stage. The detectives continued on to Gabrielle Charbonneau's dressing room. They found her seated at the makeup table, her chin propped up on her hands, staring at herself in the mirror. Her face was much paler than it had been when they first spoke with her. She looked as if she hadn't slept since then. She was wearing a plaid skirt and a white blouse, which made her look like a Catholic schoolgirl.

"Ms. Charbonneau?" said Ransom as he and Gerald stopped in the doorway.

Her eyes shifted so that she could see the detectives in the mirror. "Oh. Hello. Were you looking for someone?"

"Actually, we were looking for you. We need to speak to you."

"Oh. Come in."

They stepped into the room. Gerald hesitated, then sat down on one of the twin chairs across from the young woman. Ransom leaned on the counter next to her.

"Ms. Charbonneau, when I spoke with you before, you told me that the argument you overheard between Maria and Nuevo was about her leaving, is that correct?"

"Yes."

"When I asked you if there was any more to it, you said no."

She looked away from him. "I told you the truth about the argument."

"But not all of it, I think."

She didn't answer. Instead she plied at a bit of the lace edging around the collar of her blouse with her index finger, as if she would push the finger through one of the openings.

"Did you hear Nuevo threaten her?"

She stopped prodding the lace and looked at him. "He was angry."

"What did he say?"

She looked back into the mirror. "He said . . . all he said was that he wouldn't let her go."

"Hmm," Ransom said thoughtfully. "Do you know if he had any sort of hold over her? Was there some way he could've prevented her from leaving?"

She sniffed. "No . . . but . . ." Her face lit slightly as she called something to mind. "Once . . . it was during rehearsals when we moved to San Francisco. I wasn't familiar with the backstage there. The space was different. It wasn't as big as the one here, so the scenery and props and everything were harder to get around. During the card-playing scene—you know, when Carmen and her friends are telling her fortune and it keeps coming up with the death card—I tripped over a piece of scenery and it fell. It made a lot of noise. Maria stopped the rehearsal and screamed at me. It was awful! She said I was a clumsy cow and not fit to be a file clerk, let alone in her opera. *Her* opera."

"Yes?" Ransom prompted when she stopped.

"Riccardo took me aside and tried to make me feel better. He told me that Maria could put on airs all she wanted, but she was really just a farm girl."

"A farm girl?"

"Her parents were farmers, dirt poor."

"Farmers?" Ransom asked with interest. "What kind of farm?"

"I don't know. I don't think it was really true. I think he was just saying it to make me feel better. Besides, there's nothing wrong with being a farm girl. I don't think he could hold that over her head."

"Perhaps not. . . ." Having been temporarily diverted from his aim, he returned to the matter at hand. "Now, getting back to the argument, are you sure you didn't hear any more of it?"

He waited for a long time, hoping that she would voluntarily go on. When she didn't, he sighed and said, "Ms. Charbonneau, we've been told that your name came up during the argument."

There was a short pause, then she emitted a heavy gurgling noise. It seemed to bubble up from her chest to throat. She buried her face in her hands and wept.

"Oh, what's the use!" she exclaimed.

Ransom glanced at Gerald, who was watching the young woman with a mixture of compassion and interest, as if he were afraid he was about to hear something that would cast doubts on the innocence of his least-favorite candidate for killer. Ransom looked back to her.

"What do you mean?"

She uncovered her bleary eyes and turned them to him. "What's the use? Everybody knows. *Everybody* knows!"

"Ms. Charbonneau," he said a bit more firmly, "what are you talking about?"

"Maria said it! She told him that instead of bothering her, he should turn his attention to me! Her . . . her exact words were 'that cow who's always mooning over you!' That means that everybody knows that I was . . . that I was . . . interested in him. I can't stand it! I tried to be . . . I didn't realize it was so obvious!"

Ransom pursed his lips, then said kindly, "I don't think it matters whether one is very obvious or very discreet. Other people will usually recognize love when they see it. Unfortunately, there are some who will use that knowledge viciously."

Although this quieted Gabrielle down somewhat, she didn't look appeased. She gazed blankly down at the counter. Then, almost as if in a trance, she said, "He said he didn't want me."

"What did you do?"

She looked up. "What?"

"You were sitting in Nuevo's dressing room when you heard this. What did you do?"

"I . . . nothing. I couldn't move at first. I wanted to get out of there so he wouldn't know I'd heard him, but I felt sick and I just couldn't get my legs to work . . . no, maybe that's not true. Maybe I really wanted him to know I was there, and how much he'd hurt me. But either way, I was still sitting there in his room when he came back."

"What happened then?"

"He knew right away I'd heard him, but he didn't seem to know what to say. I mean, he *did* apologize, but you really can't take something like that back, can you? I somehow got to my feet and I walked past him. I never wanted to see him again."

She suddenly realized with horror what she'd just said. "I mean I just wanted to disappear! I never would've hurt him!"

"What about Maria?"

She turned away, then said sadly, "I could've broken her neck."

When the detectives came out of Gabrielle's dressing room, they could hear Cortez and Laramie going over the same duet again. David Cunningham and Franco Giannini were no longer at the side of the stage.

As they passed by the open door of Maria's dressing room, Ransom spotted Barbara Kean. She was removing the roses from one of the vases and putting them into a large trash bag.

"Good morning, Ms. Kean," Ransom said.

She gave a start, then laughed. "Hi, Mr . . . Ransom, right?"

"Yes. I didn't expect to see you here today."

"I don't see why not. The great woman is here, and I'm paid to be on hand to fetch and carry for her."

Ransom came forward into the room, and Gerald followed.

"Ms. Kean, I was wondering, do you know anything about Maria's background?"

"What, you mean like where she studied singing?"

"I was thinking a little further back than that. Has she ever spoken of her upbringing?"

"To her maid?" she replied with a crooked smile. "Nope. Not a word. I don't know anything about her childhood."

She whisked the roses out of another vase and stuffed them into the trash bag.

"What are you doing?" Ransom asked.

"They're wilting, and her highness doesn't want them around anymore. Of course, I can't just put them in the garbage can! She doesn't want to watch them die there—her words, not mine." She noticed how he was staring at the vases, then added, "I can do this, right? Nobody said anything about leaving everything here. It's all right for me to throw them out?"

"What?" he said, coming back to himself. "Oh, yes, yes. I just realized that there's only five of them."

"Isn't that enough?" she said with a laugh, shoving another handful of flowers into the bag.

Ransom looked at Gerald. "You have it in your notes, don't you? Didn't the guard at the stage door say there were six?"

Gerald started to flip back through his notes, but Barbara answered before he could find it.

"Oh, yeah, there were six. You should've heard the hubbub over *that* one!"

"What?"

She faced him. "It was a bouquet of lilies! You should've heard Maria scream when she saw it! She said it meant death, and someone was trying to scare her."

"I suppose there was no card?" Ransom asked.

"Nope. None."

"What did she do with them?"

"Nothing! She decided to keep them here. She said she wasn't going to let herself be frightened. She's like that, you know. They could've been meant to scare her, but she turned them into a sign of her strength." She sounded as if this was the one point on which she admired her mistress.

"Yes, but they're not here now," said Ransom. "What happened to them?"

"Oh! She told me to throw them out yesterday. After what happened with Riccardo and everything they did seem a bit ghoulish."

"So they were here Monday?"

"Yes," she said, blinking at him. "Why? Are they important?"

"If they were still here on Monday, I doubt it very much."

"What—?"

"Thank you," Ransom said, turning and leaving the room so unexpectedly he was gone before she had a chance to respond.

He strode purposefully to the opening of the hallway to the stage door, with Gerald rushing to keep pace.

"What is it?" Gerald asked.

Ransom turned around and looked at him through narrowed eyes. "I'm tired of running around in circles, but I think I'm starting to see the light."

"Want to shed some of it on me?"

He smiled slyly. "Not yet. I wouldn't want to be wrong. Now, do me a favor and get the list of florists who came here Sunday from the guard, and then see if Carnegie's secretary has pictures of the four principals."

"You think one of them sent the lilies to her?"

"No, I don't," Ransom said cryptically.

"Funny that she didn't mention them, isn't it? I mean, when you told her she might've been the intended victim."

"No, it's not funny at all."

Gerald stared at him. He didn't mind being relegated to the legwork, but he didn't like being kept in the dark, although after all the time he'd spent as Ransom's partner he didn't know why he should except things to be any different.

"Okay," he said with a sigh. "While I'm doing chores, what are you going to be doing?"

"Playing a very wild hunch."

Gerald went down the hall and passed through the stage door. Ransom took out his cell phone, flipped it open, and dialed. It was answered in two rings.

"Harris."

"It's Ransom."

"Oh, I was just about to call you—"

"Let me guess," Ransom interrupted. "No morphine."

"That's right," Harris said with some surprise. "How did you know?"

"Never mind that. There's something I need to know. When they went through the dressing rooms, specifically Maria Cortez's, was there a vase full of lilies there?"

"Just a minute."

He put down the receiver. While Ransom waited, he could hear the sounds of machines wheezing and technicians bantering as they worked. Although he couldn't really fathom the idea of spending one's days with test tubes and specimens, they sounded as if they enjoyed their work as much as he enjoyed detecting.

Harris returned quickly. "Yep. We got a sample of the water from it. Did you want us to test it?"

"No," said Ransom, thinking to himself that Harris could probably throw the sample away. "But there is one other specific thing I want you to test the coffee for right away . . ."

Ransom waited in the lobby for Gerald, who joined him carrying a manila envelope.

"The pictures," he said, handing it to Ransom. The list of florists was clipped to the outside.

As they went to their car, Ransom opened the envelope and pulled out the contents. There were four eight-by-ten glossy head shots, professionally done: Gabrielle Charbonneau, staring at the camera with a wide smile, but still a touch of sadness about the eyes, as if she was happy but knew the feeling would be short-lived; Franco Giannini, the light reflecting off the gray at his temples, making him look slightly angelic and even more suave than in real life; Maria Cortez, her eyes flashing at the camera as if aware of her beauty and defying the photographer to try and capture it; and finally, Riccardo Nuevo. His photo was the darkest, with the left half of his face lit and the right disappearing into shadow.

Ransom slid the photos back into the envelope and folded the flap inside.

"Not exactly mug shots," Gerald said as they got into the car.

"They'll do," Ransom said sardonically.

Gerald started the car and they headed for the Starlight Motel. On the way, Ransom began the task of phoning the florists to see which of the six had delivered the lilies to the theater. He found it on the third try.

"As I thought," he said as he disconnected and snapped the phone shut.

"What?"

He slipped the phone into his pocket. "Huron Floral Shop. They delivered the lilies. That was one of the clerks. He looked up the bill. It was paid in cash, so they don't have the name of the person who sent them."

"Man or woman?" Gerald asked.

"The clerk didn't know. The sale was made by a Mr. Rand, the owner, and he was out. The clerk said he'd be back in half an hour, so we can stop there after we've talked to Mr. Dunston."

Gerald didn't say anything. Ransom looked at him out of the corner of his eye. "You're being uncommonly quiet."

"You've been on the phone."

"Is that why?" Ransom said. "I thought maybe you were worried that Ms. Charbonneau might be our killer."

Gerald sighed. "It doesn't look good that she heard what they said about her."

"On the contrary, I think it's very promising."

"Even though she said she wanted to wring Maria's neck?"

"Good God, Gerald! I wanted to do that much to her, and I only talked to her for ten minutes. I would've thought it much more suspicious if she *didn't* want to wring Maria's neck, especially given the way the great diva treated her."

"But if jealousy or rejection are reasons for murder—"

"And they both are."

"Then she had two good motives."

"Except for one thing," said Ransom. "I believe her."

Gerald screwed up his face. "About what? When she said she didn't kill Riccardo?"

"No, I believe that when she overheard that argument, it was the first time she realized she didn't have a chance with Riccardo, and that everybody knew her feelings. Think about what Giannini had to say about her: Even though he travels with his lover,

Gabrielle thinks she still has a chance with him. I think she's as self-deluded as they come. Which, in this case, is a mark in her favor."

"What do you mean?"

"Just that she couldn't have done it, because for her it would have had to have been on the spur of the moment. I hardly believe she was carrying poison around with her just in case she ever had call to use it. And I don't think she could've run out in the middle of the opera to get it. Especially not if it's what I think it is. This murder was planned. In advance."

"And the wrong person was killed?"

"Oh, no," Ransom said. "Nuevo was the target all along."

When they arrived at the Starlight Motel, there were no cars in the narrow parking lot, so Gerald was able to steer the car into the angled space directly in front of Room 5. He switched off the engine and they climbed out of the car.

When they reached the door, Gerald knocked, then stepped back.

"Just a minute!" called a high-pitched, lilting male voice.

The door was opened by a young man in a white tank top and blue running shorts. His hair was an exotic mixture of dark gray and gold.

"Oh, God!" he exclaimed with obvious shock. "I thought you'd be David! Nobody else knows I'm here. Who are you?"

"Sorry to startle you," said Ransom, pulling out his badge. "I'm Detective Ransom, this is Detective White. You're Sherman Dunston?"

Dunston glanced at the shield with his slightly crossed eyes. "Yes. And I haven't done anything that's illegal in the state of Illinois."

Ransom smiled. "We'd like to talk to you about the death of Riccardo Nuevo."

"Really?" Dunston's face lit up. "Cool! Come on in!" He

flung the door open and admitted the detectives, then shut the door behind them.

This room was much the same as Cunningham's, shop-worn but very clean. However, Dunston had made an attempt to personalize his surroundings. A small china vase of carnations was placed in the center of the dresser, and on the nightstand there was a small picture of a young, round-faced blond man in an expensive gold frame. Beside it was a dog-eared copy of a book by Carolyn Hart, splayed open and lying facedown. An indentation in the bed indicated that Dunston had been sitting there reading when they interrupted him.

"Please, sit, sit!" he said, motioning them to the chairs by the windows. He sat on the edge of the bed. "I've never been questioned by the police before! How exciting! Of course, I've never been around anyone that's been killed before, either, so I guess that's why."

During this Gerald took out his notebook and pencil and laid them on his knee. When Dunston saw this, he exclaimed with delight. "And you're going to take notes! Cool! Anything I say, etcetera, etcetera, I've heard it a hundred times on the TV!"

"Mr. Dunston," Ransom said lightly, "there's no need to be nervous."

"Do I sound nervous?" he said with a laugh. "I'm not! I always sound this way. Except when I'm working. Those stars, you know, when you're making them up, they want to believe there isn't a thought in your head except for their beauty. But usually I'm just like this." He gave another laugh, then his cheeks turned pink. "Well, not exactly like this. I guess I am a little nervous. Not that that's suspicious or anything. You don't have to suspect me!"

"Occupational hazard," said Ransom.

"Suspecting people?"

"No, making people nervous."

Dunston looked at him with wide brown eyes and swallowed. "You don't suspect me, do you? I mean, I wouldn't have done anything to Riccardo. He was nice, if a bit thick."

"No, we don't suspect you of anything. You're the makeup artist, correct?"

"Uh-huh."

"There's only one of you to do the entire cast?"

Dunston laughed less nervously this time. "Oh, no! The chorus do themselves—this outfit isn't exactly rolling in dough. When we started this crazy thing I helped the chorus out, but that was mainly teaching them how to do it if they didn't know. Same with the new supers in each town. But otherwise, I stick to the principals."

"The four of them?"

"No, I'm responsible for the four leads, Carmen's two friends, Frasquita and Mercedes, and a few of the men."

"That's quite a load."

"Not really. Most of the men actually do themselves. It's not hard. The women are a little more involved."

"But you did Nuevo's makeup."

Dunston's eyes widened comically. "Don't tell me! He was murdered by a noxious dose in his foundation!"

Ransom laughed. "Perhaps, but not the way you mean it. How was he Sunday night?"

"Riccardo? You ever see a snare drum? That's how he was. His skin was stretched taut. I asked him if he was nervous, and he said no. He wasn't, you know. He was mad. I found that out later."

"How do you mean?"

"When I was done with him, he went and had quite the little scene with madam."

Ransom's right eyebrow slid up. "You were in his dressing room during the argument?"

He shook his head vigorously. "No, no, I left right on his heels. I only heard the very beginning."

"So you don't know what it was about?"

"I can *guess* that much!" Dunston said broadly. "That article in the Sunday paper!"

"You stay backstage during the whole opera?"

He nodded. "They need a lot of touch-ups. They sweat a lot during the opera." He produced his sly smile. "Pardon me, *Riccardo* sweated. Madam perspires profusely, though she would never admit it. Franco doesn't do either. He's pretty incredible! I once mentioned to him that he doesn't sweat, and he said . . ." Here Dunston drew himself up regally and did an uncanny recreation of Giannini's manner. "Of course not! Escamillo? Sweat? You must be mad!" He laughed. "He was playing, you see. Franco's a real sweetheart."

Gerald looked up at the young man and pursed his lips to one side.

Ransom said, "What do you do while the opera's going on?"

Dunston shrugged. "Sometimes I watch from the wings. Especially during "Habanera." I rarely miss that one. I love the way they do it. Sometimes I stand backstage and talk to Barbara—Maria's assistant. Sometimes we sit in madam's dressing room and play cards. But that's dangerous. Madam wouldn't like it if she saw us doing it."

"And Sunday night, which were you doing?"

"It was opening night, baby!" Dunston said. "I was watching from the wings."

"How about during the intermissions?"

"That's usually when I do the touch-ups."

Ransom crossed his legs. "So you were with them during both intermissions?"

Dunston looked blank for a second, then closed his eyes and wrinkled his nose. "I'm trying to remember. Um . . . I did them both during the first intermission. During the second . . . I did a quick touch-up on Riccardo, and Maria said she didn't need me."

He opened his eyes and looked eagerly at the detective as if longing for approval.

"Very good," Ransom said. "Now, while you were backstage Sunday night, did you see anyone go into Riccardo's dressing room?"

"Not during the opera, no."

"How about before, or during the intermissions?"

"Well . . . Gabrielle went in there before . . . I think it was just when the argument was starting."

"Did you happen to notice when she came out?"

He shook his head. "Sorry, but I had a lot of work to do before the opera."

"Okay. How about during the intermissions?"

"No . . . the only person I remember seeing go in there was . . . Maria, during the second intermission."

This jibed with Maria's story of having gone to his room to apologize.

"How long was she with him?" Ransom asked.

"Huh? Oh, he wasn't there."

Gerald looked up from his notebook. Ransom uncrossed his legs and sat forward. "I beg your pardon?"

"No, I'm pretty sure—I was talking to Barbara—"

"Barbara Kean? She wasn't with Maria during the second intermission?"

"No, madam didn't want her. She was still in a mood! Both she and Riccardo were, after that argument. Didn't say a word to each other offstage. Anyway, me and Barbara were over by the rocks . . . the mountain set. It had been rolled off and set in its place backstage, so it was a safe place to be. I know I saw Riccardo head down the hall toward Gabrielle's dressing room, which is a story unto itself. . . ."

"Let's stick to Maria," Ransom said lightly.

"Madam missed him by a minute. She went in right after he left."

"How long was she in there?"

"Just a second, I'd say."

"Did she have anything with her?"

A row of lines broke out across the young man's forehead. "Huh? Like what?"

"Was she carrying a cup of coffee?"

"Oh! Yeah. Ha! I was hoping it wasn't hot, because I thought it would end up in Riccardo's face. But he wasn't there, so he was safe."

"He was safe. . . ." Ransom said slowly, an idea forming in his mind. "Did you by chance notice if she had it with her when she went back to her own dressing room?"

Dunston closed his eyes for a second. "Yep. Yes, she did."

Gerald looked up with surprise.

Ransom said, "Did she go back to his room?"

"Uh-uh. I didn't see her."

"Would you have?"

"During the intermission? I think so. Me and Barbara stayed where we were until the last act started."

A smile spread across Ransom's face. "Thank you very much, Mr. Dunston," he said as he rose.

"Don't tell me I've helped the police!" Dunston exclaimed with amusement.

"I can't tell you how much you've helped the police, Mr. Dunston."

"But her coffee cup was found in his dressing room," said Gerald as they got back into the car. "The kid must be wrong. She must've gone back."

"I should say that is obvious."

"So he's wrong, right?"

"Whatever you say, Gerald."

His partner sighed with exasperation and put the car in gear. The drive to the Huron Floral Shop was accomplished in a record fifteen minutes due to unaccountably light traffic and Gerald's miraculous good fortune in finding nothing but green lights all the way.

The shop was one door down from a corner store that looked like it had been vacated years before. The floral shop's sign was fern green and encrusted with soot, and the name spelled out in a series of small black holes that had once held individual light bulbs. But if the sign indicated death, the shop itself was full of life. The entryway was a semicircular divot paved with brown and crammed with greenery that lined the

the sides, making it impossible to enter the shop without brushing up against leaves. The plants spilled out onto the sidewalk.

There was a young man behind the counter. He was painfully thin and had greasy, dark brown hair. A small gold ring had been pierced through the skin over the bridge of his nose, and there was a silver stud just below the center of his lower lip. Gerald had to fight a wince.

"Can I help you guys?" he said as they approached.

Ransom recognized his voice as the one he'd spoken to over the phone. "Yes. We're here to see Mr. Rand."

The young man's mouth dropped open. "You're the police, right?"

"That's right."

He rolled his eyes. "Mr. Rand's mad at me for telling you anything on the phone. He says I should have made you come in and show an ID."

"Monty!" bellowed a voice that seemed to emanate from the brightly lit cooler behind the young man.

The young man was so surprised that he leapt off the ground like a startled animal as he wheeled around. The detectives looked in the same direction and saw a stern face framed by grizzled gray hair and beard glaring at the young man from the opposite side of the cooler, looming over the top riser on which buckets of roses were perched.

"Wait there!" he said, then disappeared. He reemerged through a pair of heavy red curtains to the left of the coolers.

"I told you to hold your tongue!"

"Yes, Mr. Rand," Monty replied, thoroughly abashed.

"Now you go on back in the back and get to work! We got a lot of orders to get out!"

"Yes, Mr. Rand," he said.

On his way to the back Monty slued his eyes at the detectives and shot them a half-smile. It was enough to show them that this was a game that owner and employee were used to playing, and that he thought nothing of it.

Ransom turned to Rand. "You didn't want him to talk to us?"

The centers of his cheeks turned red. "That's not it 'tall—"

"Because, you know, we are investigating a murder."

The red intensified. "I'm tryin' to tell you, that's not it 'tall! I just didn't want him handin' out information over the phone. Hell, anybody can call in here and say they're the police and ask about stuff."

"Really?" Ransom said, enjoying discomfiting the shop owner. "Does that often happen?"

"No." He paused and then laughed nervously. "But, 'ya know, say somebody sends flowers to somebody else, and that somebody turns out to have a husband, and that husband tries to find out who that first somebody is . . . can't you see the trouble?"

"Yes, well, your assistant was unable to give us any information other than the fact that the lilies that were delivered to Maria Cortez at the Sheridan Center came from here."

"I delivered 'em myself. They were important, so I didn't trust 'em to nobody else."

"And you were logged in at the theater, so what your assistant told us wasn't exactly a secret."

"I wasn't tryin' to keep secrets," Rand protested, trying not to appear angry. "I just thought he shouldn't have given out anything over the phone."

"Well, we're here now," said Ransom, "and here's my ID. Now, I understand that you don't have the name of who bought the lilies."

"Nope," he said, shaking his head. "Paid cash. I didn't need a name."

"You did the transaction yourself?"

"Uh-huh."

"Was it a man or a woman?"

"Woman."

"Ah!" said Ransom, turning to his partner.

Gerald had been carrying the envelope with the photos. He

opened it, pulled out two photos, and handed them to Ransom, who laid them on the counter in front of the store owner.

"Was it one of these women?"

Rand peered at one picture, then the other, for quite a while before saying anything. Without looking up, he tapped his fingers on the first photo. "I don't think it was her." He stared at it for a time, then shook his head. "Nah. Too fat."

"What about the other one?"

Rand pursed his lips and gazed at the second picture. "More like it. I'd say yes. It's a little hard to tell. When she was here, she was wearing a big floppy hat, bright pink. And these big, round sunglasses. You know, like the movie stars wear."

When they want to go out incognito, Ransom thought. "Are you sure it was her?"

"Pretty sure," Rand said, nodding. "Of the two of 'em, it'd have to be her."

"I'm afraid that's not good enough," said Ransom.

Rand picked up the picture and held it close to his face. "Yep."

"You're sure?"

"Pretty sure," Rand said doubtfully.

"He picked Maria Cortez's picture," Gerald said once they were out on the street and on the way to the car. "That doesn't make sense."

"On the contrary, it makes perfect sense," said Ransom.

Gerald stopped in his tracks. "You *knew*!"

"I suspected." He shoved his hand in his pocket and pulled out the pack of cigars as he stopped. "Damn that pair of idiots, anyway!"

"The florists?"

Ransom stuck a cigar in the corner of his mouth, holding the plastic tip between his lips. "Carnegie and Sheridan. If only they'd been up-front with us to begin with!"

"You mean they *do* have something to do with the murder?"

"No, I mean exactly the opposite." He lit the cigar. "If Carnegie hadn't clutched when we first questioned him and had just told us that Sheridan had been with him backstage, we wouldn't have wasted all that time following their trail."

"Well, wait a minute," said Gerald. "First off, we had to do that. They were lying and they were acting awfully suspicious. And they are up to something, if what you think is true."

"But not murder. That's *why* Carnegie clutched so badly and made the two of them look so suspicious. What they were doing didn't have anything to do with the Santa Marta Opera Company, really. It was a huge monkey wrench in their little scheme when Nuevo was murdered and we showed up on the scene. They're amateurs. They weren't prepared."

"But why would Cortez buy the flowers?" Gerald said as the resumed walking.

"Unless I miss my guess, it was so she could do exactly what she did: make a fuss."

Gerald pondered this. "She was laying a groundwork."

"Exactly," said Ransom.

"But . . ." Gerald hesitated as he sometimes did when about to disagree with one of Ransom's ideas. "Jer, I think she said she went to his dressing room to apologize. She didn't say she actually saw him."

"She did more than imply it," Ransom said, his lips forming a line. "She had to explain the presence of her coffee cup."

"But she didn't leave it there then," Gerald said, growing more perplexed by the minute. "She probably went back later after Nuevo came back."

Ransom shook his head. "No. I think she left the cup there much later."

"You mean purposely? But why leave it there at all? It just placed her there."

"That was the whole idea," Ransom said enigmatically.

"Then why not leave it there the first time?"

"The answer to that should be obvious."

Gerald sighed. He was dying to ask, but for once refused to

play the part of Watson. Instead he said, "You know we don't have any proof of anything."

"I know." Ransom's expression mixed concern with consternation.

Once back in the car, Gerald said, "Where to?"

"I want to talk to Emily."

13

They were seated around the table in Emily's kitchen. The obligatory teakettle sat on a pad in the center of the table. Emily and Gerald had matching blue china cups and saucers. Ransom drummed his fingers lightly atop the table with his left hand; the fingers of his right were wrapped around the handle of the mug that Emily had purchased for his exclusive use.

Emily's hands were folded and resting on the table. Her lips formed a small O, and her brows were knit in so sharp an angle that anyone who didn't know her might have thought she was cross. Ransom had just finished telling her everything he believed to be true about the murder of Riccardo Nuevo.

"Well!" Emily said at last, her face relaxing. "Of course, you understood the significance of the hat."

"The hat?" Gerald said with total surprise. He glanced at Ransom, who was smiling.

"Yes," said Ransom.

"I don't," said Gerald. "Why wear something that would draw attention to her?"

"Oh, but it didn't draw attention to her," said Emily, "it drew attention to itself."

His face brightened. "Oh!"

"I'm positive that was the idea of both the hat and the sunglasses. An exaggerated disguise. So it was the only thing about her your florist really remembered." She turned to Ransom. "You did say that he couldn't really identify her?"

" 'Pretty sure' was the best he could do, and it wouldn't hold up in court."

"Hmm." She paused to take a sip of tea while she considered this. "Well, you've been very busy, I must say!"

"Yes. As the saying goes, we've been led a merry chase. As you thought, Mr. Carnegie and Mr. Sheridan, whatever else they might be up to, aren't involved in the murder." He said this with a tone of finality that caught the old woman's notice. She looked at him over the rim of her cup and smiled affectionately. "I see." She gave a little cough. "I also see, as you did, the possible significance of her having grown up on a farm."

"Why?" Gerald asked.

"What do you think they were growing on that farm, Gerald?"

He stared at his partner for a moment, then slapped his forehead. "Oh, God! But it doesn't have to be that kind of farm! That's just a wild guess!"

"Maybe not so wild. You're quite right, she could've lived on a different kind of farm, but I'll bet she'd still know how to do it. Enough people do."

"Haven't you found out what kind of poison was used yet?" Emily asked.

Ransom shook his head. "No, but I asked them to check for that specifically. We should know soon. The trouble is, it still won't give us any direct evidence."

"I still don't get it," said Gerald. "Why would she leave her own cup there? She had to know it would be checked and we'd find out it wasn't poisoned."

"Oh, no, Detective White," Emily replied. "I'm sure you'll find it was full of poison. If Maria Cortez is the murderess that you believe she is—and I'm sure you're correct—she's a very shrewd and clever woman."

"Perhaps a little too clever," said Ransom. "I believe she's the killer, but we have no direct evidence at all."

"We could confront her with what we do have," said Gerald. "Maybe she'll slip."

"I hardly think Ms. Cortez is the type to break down and confess," Ransom said wryly.

"Maybe not," said Emily, her eyes twinkling at him. "But you never know when she may need to take action again. After all, someone knows what she did, isn't that true? And someone who has killed once won't usually shrink from trying it again, will they?"

Ransom stared at her seriously, a pronounced frown on his face. "I couldn't do that. It would be too dangerous."

"That's one way to look at it." She set her cup back in its saucer and turned her incisive eyes upon him. "But have you considered that I might not be the only one thinking along these lines?"

Maria Cortez was in her suite at the Dover Hotel, looking at herself as she brushed her hair. She liked what she saw: the dark oval face, her large brown eyes, and the full lips she'd painted bright red for her preopera dinner with Tony. She had donned a dark green dress with a dramatically plunging neckline. Tomorrow Tony would be returning to New York; tonight she would make sure she had him in line, first at dinner, and then after the opera when they came back to her suite. The night before Tony had seemed to be wavering. After that disastrous performance with Patrick Laramie, when someone she considered a talentless neophyte had received a warmer ovation than she had, she'd been rightfully incensed, both with the situation and the audience. But she'd played it all wrong with Tony. She should have been angry, but not that angry. She could see the uncertainty in his eyes.

But that would soon pass. Tonight she felt brilliant, and was determined to give an outstanding performance no matter what went on around her, both onstage and off. She had to keep Tony in her court. It was too soon to discard him.

She was just laying the brush on the side of the sink when the phone rang. Her first thought was that it had better not be Tony canceling their date. She crossed the room to the bed on the nightstand and snatched up the receiver.

"Yes?"

"Miss Cortez? This is Sherman. You know, your makeup man?"

"What?" she said in disbelief. "What do you mean, calling me?"

"I know, I'm sorry. I need to talk to you. I'm so confused, I don't know what to do."

"What are you talking about?" she demanded.

"You see, the police were just here. They questioned me all about Sunday night, what went on backstage and everything."

"So? They're asking everyone these things! What of it?"

"Well . . . you see, they were especially interested in who went in and out of Riccardo's dressing room," Dunston said, sounding not at all like he was insinuating anything.

"Yes, yes, I know," Maria said impatiently. "Why are you telling me this?"

"Because . . . of course, I *had* to tell them that I saw you go into his room. . . ."

"I told them this also!"

"Yes, but those detectives, they seemed to think that Riccardo was in there with you."

"So?"

"But he wasn't, you know. I saw Riccardo come back after you left."

"I told the detectives this. . . ."

"I don't think so," Dunston said a little more firmly. "They really seemed to think that Riccardo was there with you."

There was a beat before Maria responded, careful not to

sound as irate as she felt. "I did not tell them I saw him. I told them I went to talk to him. He was not there. There is nothing in this. They've simply jumped to a wrong conclusion."

"Oh, good!" said Dunston with a nervous sigh. "Because I wouldn't want to get you in any trouble when I tell them. Or about the coffee."

"The coffee?" Maria said warily after a pause.

"Yes. It was something I forgot. They asked if you were carrying anything when you left Riccardo's room, and I said no. But later I remembered you were carrying your coffee."

"I think you are mistaken."

"No, no I'm not."

"Of course you are! I left my coffee in Riccardo's room. The police know this. . . ."

"Uh . . . I really don't think so. I think I remember."

"What is this?" Maria bellowed. "Are you taking advantage of Ricky's death to perform a little blackmail?"

"No! No!" Dunston said quickly. "It's . . . I was so confused by what the police said to me. And they seemed to have some wrong impression about things. I wanted to set things right, but . . . like I said, I don't want to get you in trouble. I just wanted to warn you ahead of time."

"If you think you saw something, you should tell them, not me! There is nothing in it! If it eases your mind, tell the police. But don't bother me again!" She slammed down the phone.

In Dunston's motel room, he replaced the receiver on his bedside phone.

"I don't think she fell for it," he said. "She told me to tell you!"

"She is a very smart woman. She would never let you see her take the bait," Ransom explained.

"But to tell me to tell you . . ."

"It's almost six o'clock. She knows you couldn't have time to do that before the opera."

"Uh-huh," Sherman said.

"Now, you understand what we want you to do at the theater?"

"Uh-huh," he said, nodding his head.

Ransom smiled at the young man's eagerness. "You did very well, by the way."

"On the phone? That was nothing!" Dunston said merrily. "It was just like Lunchtime Little Theater!"

At seven-thirty most of the principal players were in their places backstage at the Sheridan Center. Patrick Laramie was using Riccardo's dressing room, although it made him feel like someone who had been left alone in the house of a stranger. Gabrielle Charbonneau was seated at the table in her own dressing room, staring dismally at her reflection. If Ransom had happened to see her, he might've thought she hadn't moved since they'd last questioned her.

Only Franco Giannini remained relatively undisturbed. He and Paul Chamberlain sat in the guest chairs in his dressing room, chatting over glasses of wine.

"We are not much longer for this world," Franco said, taking a sip.

"What do you mean?" Paul replied. He knew full well what his partner meant, but also knew that he wanted to talk about it.

"You can almost hear the wheezing as the Santa Marta Opera Company gasps for its last breaths."

"It's not dead yet," said Paul.

"It won't be long now." Franco shook his head ruefully and took another sip of wine.

"You don't think . . . I mean, it's sold out here, isn't it? It'll have to play out its run."

Franco smiled. "It doesn't have to do anything. Whatever does happen, I think the company is dead. As dead as poor Riccardo."

"Would that be so bad?" Paul asked softly.

Franco laughed. "It's been a much longer run than I thought we'd have!" He paused, then sighed. "Personally, I'll be glad to get back home with you and back to our normal lives!"

Paul smiled and lifted his glass. It was then that they heard raised voices in the hallway.

"Ah!" said Franco wryly. "The diva has arrived."

"You're late!" David Cunningham exclaimed. He'd been pacing outside of her door ever since the stage manager informed him that she'd missed the half-hour call.

"The service in the restaurant was terrible," she said without a hint of apology. "Blame the maître d'."

"Well, at least you're here now," he replied, knowing better than to challenge her further.

"That's right."

Cunningham went away with an ineffectual flea in his ear as Maria swung open the door of her dressing room. She found Barbara Kean laying out the costume Carmen wore in the first act. Maria's usual designer cup of coffee sat in the center of the makeup table.

"Oh! Miss Cortez! I was wondering if something had happened to you."

"Am I a child, that if I'm a few minutes late I have so many mothers worrying after me?"

"I didn't mean anything except concern," Barbara said with a shrug.

"Are you finished here?"

Barbara glanced around the room, doing a mental inventory. "Yes, for now."

"Good! Then you can go until the end of the first act."

"Are you sure?" Barbara asked, somewhat surprised. "You don't want any help with your hair or anything?"

"Of course I'm sure! I'm late and I'm hurried. I don't want

you fluttering around me! Now go! If you want to be of use, find that makeup boy and tell him to get himself in here!"

"Okay," said Barbara. She left, closing the door after her.

It was only a couple of minutes before Sherman Dunston appeared. He greeted her quietly as he placed his coffee mug on the counter near her cup.

"What is the matter with you?" Maria said, her eyes flashing at him.

He almost jumped. "What? There's nothing the matter. I just . . . I was just worried that I might have offended you when I called."

Her lips formed themselves into a hard line. "You should try to sound not so much like a blackmailer."

He managed to look shocked. "I mean . . . that never entered my mind. I was just confused, is all."

"I know that. So, did you tell the police, as I told you to?"

"I didn't have a chance yet. There's no hurry."

Maria picked up her coffee cup and lifted it to her lips, but before she drank any, she grimaced and sat it back on the counter. "The smell turns my stomach tonight. Get me a glass of water, would you?"

"Water?"

"Yes! You know how bad my stomach has been! Be quick about it!"

"Do you want me to put it in here?" he said, reaching for her cup.

"No! There's a glass on the sink."

He went into the bathroom and could be heard running the water. After a moment, he turned off the tap and returned with the glass. She took it from him and drank.

As Dunston picked up a makeup sponge, he glanced down at his own mug. "Okay," he said loudly. "I think we can start now."

Maria sat back in her chair and closed her eyes. But before Dunston began his work, they were interrupted by the arrival of

Ransom and Gerald. Maria opened her eyes and was obviously not pleased to see them, but beyond her displeasure, there was fear behind her eyes.

"Get out!" she yelled. "I have no time for you now! The opera is about to start!"

"No, Miss Cortez, I'm afraid the opera is over for you."

She sat up. For once she looked unsure of herself. "What do you mean?"

"Excuse us, Mr. Dunston," Ransom said to the makeup artist.

Gerald opened the door for him and went so far as to give him a gentle pat on the back as he passed through it. Gerald then closed the door.

"I'm afraid you have a lot of explaining to do," Ransom said, standing over her.

"What is the meaning of this?"

He reached into his pocket and pulled out a small bottle made of dark brown plastic. He put it on the counter in front of her. "Do you know what this is?"

She glared at it with such ferocity that Ransom was surprised it didn't melt. "No!"

"Of course you do. It's a bottle of ipecac. It was found in the garbage can on the way to the stage door."

"What of it? What is it to do with me?"

"You threw it away on Saturday night, didn't you?"

"What?" she exclaimed.

"You must've thought the garbage would be emptied long before anyone looked into Riccardo's death. You had that planned for Sunday night, when it could do the most damage. You threw this away on Saturday night after taking a little bit."

She shook her head, attempting to look puzzled. "Why would I take this? What is it for?"

"To make yourself sick," Ransom replied, leaning toward her. "To make yourself very convincingly sick."

"You're mad! Why would I do such a thing?"

"That's a good question," Ransom said, leaning back against

the counter. "I have a better one. Why would you send yourself lilies?"

"What?" Maria said after a beat.

"The florist recognized you," said Ransom, stretching the florist's tentative identification into a certainty to serve his purpose. "He's a big opera fan. He said he couldn't mistake you."

"That's . . . that's nonsense!" she sputtered. "Why would I do this?"

"To create an impression. The impression that someone was trying to kill you."

"I didn't—"

He cut her off, raising his palm. "I know, you didn't claim anyone was trying to kill you. You're far too clever for that. You let me do it for you. Even before you murdered Nuevo, you didn't say a word about thinking your life was in danger, you simply did your bit with the ipecac so that it would look like earlier attempts had been made on you, and sent the flowers as a bogus warning. You even played down the meaning when the lilies were delivered."

"I didn't !" she exclaimed angrily.

"But the business of the coffee, that was *too* clever! That's where you tripped yourself up."

She glanced in the direction of the door. "So that's it! That grotesque little boy has been telling his stories to you! He's barely even a halfwit!"

"He saw you go into Riccardo's dressing room when Riccardo wasn't there. You came back out without seeing him."

"I never said that I saw him!" she proclaimed, glancing at the mug that still sat next to her cup. "I told you that I went there to apologize. He was not there." She paused and contrived to look unhappy. "It is sad, is it not, that the last words between us were hot ones, and that I never got the chance to apologize?"

"You never got the chance," said Ransom, "because you poisoned him."

"You're mad!" she shot back.

"Mr. Dunston also saw you take your coffee with you when you went back to your dressing room."

"Have you seen the eyes of that creature? They are crossed! He cannot tell what he is seeing! He's mistaken!"

"I don't think so," Ransom said calmly.

"Then you're a fool!"

"That's perfectly true. Your motive was in front of me all the time and I didn't see it. I'll tell you what you did. You sat in your dressing room and listened for Riccardo to leave his. As we've been told repeatedly, these walls are thin as paper. You could easily hear his door open and close. You went in there— your apology story all ready just in case anybody saw you, or in case you were wrong and Riccardo was still there. You poisoned his coffee and went back to your room."

"I have explained why I went to see him, and you have no proof of anything else! The whole idea is absurd!" Her eyes involuntary shot to the mug again, though only for a second.

"But you didn't accidentally leave your coffee in his room, as you told us."

"I tell you I did! I was not thinking! I just left it there."

"Why?"

"What?" she said, completely confused.

"What was there to distract you?" Ransom pressed. "Especially since Riccardo wasn't there for you to talk to. There was no reason for you to set your cup down at all. You didn't wait for Riccardo to return. Mr. Dunston told us you were in and out in a very short time."

"That boy is an idiot! He doesn't know what he's talking about!"

"And then there's the fact that you took your coffee back with you."

"I did not do that!" she exclaimed. "I have told you, the boy is cross-eyed! He's blind! He's mistaken! There's no proof!"

"But there is proof," said Ransom.

For once, behind Maria's defiance the detective sensed fear. "What proof?"

"The coffee, Ms. Cortez, the coffee. I talked to the lab a little while ago, and they have found that your coffee was loaded with nicotine."

"You see!" she exclaimed triumphantly. "Someone *was* trying to kill me!"

He shook his head. "The trouble is, so was Riccardo's."

"What?"

"They tested the dregs in his mug. It was poisoned as well. If someone was trying to kill you, why was there also poison in his coffee?"

There was a long pause during which Maria stared up at him unblinkingly. Then with a wave of her hand she said, "I know nothing of this! How should I know how it got into his mug? You say my coffee was poisoned, and that should tell you that I am in danger. Everything else I have explained."

"Everything except this," Ransom said, reaching out for Dunston's coffee mug.

Maria let out a cry and lunged for it, but Ransom was too quick for her. He had it out of her reach before she got near it.

Gerald caught her arm. "None of that, now," he said.

She looked up at him for a moment; then, all of the anger seemed to drain out of her. She shook her arm free of him.

"Unless I miss my guess," said Ransom, "this is full of nicotine. It doesn't take much to be very, very deadly. Then again, neither do you."

She looked at him for a full minute before responding, then laughed with resignation.

"This damned company! I was always too good for them! But David . . . he would hold me to my contract. He knew they couldn't survive without me."

Ransom raised his right eyebrow. "I'm surprised you thought it couldn't survive without Riccardo."

She cocked her head. "Without him, I thought maybe the death would be a little slower, but just as sure." Without warning, she snatched up her cup and started to drain the contents.

Ransom was caught by surprise for a split second, then

yelled, "No!" and grabbed at her arm, but although some of the coffee sloshed onto her face, she managed to down most of it, holding her arm so rigid that Ransom couldn't get the cup away from her.

Once she had swallowed she let go of the cup and collapsed wearily back in her chair.

Ransom looked at Gerald and said, "Call an ambulance!"

By the time the paramedics rushed Maria off to the hospital, the audience had been told that the performance had been canceled and that refunds could be had at the box office. Their disappointment was audible even to those who hovered around the periphery of the action backstage.

Franco and Paul had come running from Franco's dressing room when they heard the shouts. Both looked thoroughly flabbergasted by what they found. Gabrielle arrived a few seconds later. Surprisingly, she seemed neither shocked nor happy, as Ransom thought she well might have been at the knowledge that her nemesis had not only killed the object of her affection, but had tried to kill herself. Instead, Gabrielle looked relieved, as if now that the solution was in hand, the world could right itself. Even if the world was, for her, a lonely one.

The announcement to the audience was made by Edward Carnegie, who had been summoned from his office the minute the newest tragedy had struck. He stood at the edge of the stage door entrance, propping it open as the paramedics wheeled Maria out to the ambulance.

When he saw Ransom and Gerald, he rather reluctantly went down the hallway to them.

"Is it true?" he asked Ransom. "She murdered Nuevo?"

"Yes." Ransom kept his eyes leveled at the Center's manager. "Will she make it?"

"We don't know how much poison she drank, but frankly, I doubt it."

"Hmm," Carnegie said thoughtfully. "It . . . it might be better that way."

"Yes."

Carnegie looked down at the floor. "I think I should explain something. You know, Steven has been a friend for a very long time, and I know his situation, and—"

"Mr. Carnegie," Ransom cut him off. "there is no need for an explanation."

He looked up apprehensively. "Really?"

"I understand. You were shocked by the murder. That's why you forgot to tell us about Mr. Sheridan."

Carnegie swallowed. "That's not—" He broke off when he noticed the expression on Ransom's face. He lowered his eyes. "Are you . . . are you saying that your investigation is over?"

"Yes," the detective replied emotionlessly after a long pause. "You're free to go."

14

Emily and Ransom were seated on a pair of metal lawn chairs just beyond the back steps of Emily's home. It was the only place that she would allow him to smoke in her presence. She still didn't approve of the habit, but had come to accept it as a part of his life. They were lit only by a dim porch light over the stairs behind them. It was late Wednesday evening, and warmer than it had been.

"I should've known," Ransom said after a long silence. "I should've moved it out of her reach the minute I came into the room."

"How could you have known?" Emily said, not for the first time. "You barely allowed her enough time to poison that young man's coffee, let alone her own. If she intended to try to make you think it was another failed attempt on her life by adding poison to her own cup as well, she could've more easily done that later."

He peered at her through the darkness. "You understood that business about the coffee cups right away, didn't you?"

"No," she said, "not until you learned that she hadn't left her cup there the first time . . . and that she, herself, might've been the murderer. I've been a bit of a Johnnie-come-lately on this case myself."

She was trying to make him feel better, but it wasn't working. "But you saw it when I didn't."

"I thought it made sense. She simply put the poison in her own coffee—she was going to put some there later, so it really didn't matter. She listened for Riccardo to leave his dressing room, then went there and poured some of the contents of her cup into his. If for some reason she was caught in his room, she could just use her apology excuse and no one would think any more of it."

"Except how out of character that would be for her."

"Granted."

Ransom took a puff of his cigar, then laughed. "Gerald is still trying to figure out why she didn't leave the cup there then."

"Mr. White is a very able detective," Emily said on Gerald's behalf, "but Maria Cortez's plan was quite intricate, in its way. Of course, she couldn't leave her cup the first time because Riccardo would've seen it. She used it to poison his coffee, took it away, then I suppose in the confusion afterward, she put it back in his room."

"That would be my guess," said Ransom. "I would also guess that she dumped out the remainder of his coffee, if he left any."

"That's one thing that puzzles me," said Emily. "Why didn't she wash out the mug?"

"Probably because she thought it would look suspicious, and she didn't know we'd be able to test the dregs." Ransom's lips curled in the darkness. "Either that or she thought it was beneath her. What I don't understand is why she bothered with the business with the cups at all. She should've just poisoned him and left herself out of it."

Emily sighed. "It was, I think, as you said to her: She was being too clever. I'd be willing to wager that she thought it might not look like murder at all. After all, Mr. Nuevo's death was from respiratory failure, and though that might be unusual for a man of his youth and state of health, it's not unheard of. I don't think she knew the autopsy would show anything unusual. I believe she set up her elaborate plan as nothing more than . . . well, a safety net, if you will. If the police did come looking for a murderer, she felt she was safe if they thought they were looking for *her* murderer." Emily paused for a moment. "By the way, did you find the poison?"

He nodded. "In her purse, of all places. Small bottle. Concentrated nicotine. She could easily have extracted it from a can of chewing tobacco. There's a kitchen in her hotel suite. Pretty much all she had to do was boil it down and strain it."

"And did you find out if she grew up on a tobacco farm?" Emily asked with interest.

For the first time that evening, Ransom laughed. "As a matter of fact, her family raised sugar cane. So Gerald is one up on us!" His laughter died away, and he took another drag from his cigar, blowing the smoke away from Emily. "I was a fool, though. Her motive was right in front of me. She wanted to get free of that company. She knew Cunningham would fight her, even before he told her he would. She knew what kind of shape they were in, and for better or for worse they were banking on her."

"But why kill Riccardo Nuevo?" Emily asked.

"Because it threw the company into chaos. Franco Giannini pointed it out to me: With a second string in one of the leads, they would look like the fluke they were. Cortez was furious that they didn't close down for a while because of the death—I'm sure she expected that would happen, and that they'd be in even worse financial shape than they already were. But they were going downhill, even without having to shut down. Killing Nuevo also ridded Maria of a lover who was becoming bothersome. Tony Leonard should consider himself fortunate that she died when she did. He could've been next, when she was done with him." He emitted a sharp breath. "It was right there in front of me. The opera company was falling apart right before my eyes."

"You had a lot of distractions," said Emily. She cleared her throat. "If I may ask, what is to become of Messrs. Sheridan and Carnegie?"

"What do you mean?" he asked. He was glad that she couldn't clearly see his face in the darkness. He could fairly feel her eyes sparkling at him.

"I believe you know what I'm referring to," she said.

"I don't know that they're involved in any wrongdoing. No crime has been reported."

"I was only wondering," Emily said nonchalantly, "why any-one would have tried to embezzle money in such a grand way. It seems to me it would've been much safer to pad the accounts while the Center was being built."

Ransom sighed. "Carnegie wasn't brought on board until after the Center was almost complete. All of the budgeting before that was handled by the Center's board of directors. Carnegie and Sheridan's plan—and I'm not saying there was one—prob-ably wasn't as bold as it seems. If there hadn't been a murder, any . . . potential loss of money would've been discovered pretty quickly, I think. But they would've been out of the country before that happened."

"And now?"

"As I said, I don't know of any plan . . . or crime . . . but I would think they'd be gone very soon, if they haven't gone al-ready." He added under his breath, "At least, they'd better be."

"What was that?" Emily asked with amusement.

"Nothing." He tapped his cigar on the arm of his chair, send-ing the ashes cascading onto the grass. He sighed heavily. "I still blame myself for Cortez's death, you know."

"I know," she said kindly. "But you shouldn't."

"*Why* did she poison her own coffee right away the second time?" he said to the air.

Emily eyed him for a moment, then said, "Perhaps she could see her plan falling apart, and wanted to have a handy way out. She might have tried to convince herself that she could kill Mr.

Dunston and get away with it, but I think inside she knew it was over."

"It was the last thing I expected her to do."

"Ah, but you didn't see her Carmen," said Emily. "If you had, you would've expected a dramatic gesture!"